# STAKEOUTS
### and
# STROLLERS

# STAKEOUTS and STROLLERS

A MYSTERY

# ROB PHILLIPS

MINOTAUR BOOKS
NEW YORK

This is a work of fiction. All of the names, characters, organizations, places, and events portrayed in this work are either products of the author's imagination or used fictitiously.

First published in the United States by Minotaur Books, an imprint of St. Martin's Publishing Group

*EU Representative:* Macmillan Publishers Ireland Ltd, 1st Floor, The Liffey Trust Centre, 117–126 Sheriff Street Upper, Dublin 1, D01 YC43

STAKEOUTS AND STROLLERS. Copyright © 2026 by Rob Phillips. All rights reserved. Printed in the United States of America. For information, address St. Martin's Publishing Group, 120 Broadway, New York, NY 10271.

www.minotaurbooks.com

The Library of Congress Cataloging-in-Publication Data is available upon request.

ISBN 978-1-250-38587-1 (hardcover)
ISBN 978-1-250-38588-8 (ebook)

The publisher of this book does not authorize the use or reproduction of any part of this book in any manner for the purpose of training artificial intelligence technologies or systems. The publisher of this book expressly reserves this book from the Text and Data Mining exception in accordance with Article 4(3) of the European Union Digital Single Market Directive 2019/790.

Our books may be purchased in bulk for specialty retail/wholesale, literacy, corporate/premium, educational, and subscription box use. Please contact MacmillanSpecialMarkets@macmillan.com.

First Edition: 2026

10  9  8  7  6  5  4  3  2  1

*For Emmy:*
*I love you bigger than the whole world.*

# STAKEOUTS
### and
# STROLLERS

# PROLOGUE

Usually, the booze made him angry.

Tonight, Shawn Finley felt introspective.

*What kind of father ghosts his teenage daughter when she needs him most?*

*What kind of man are you?*

"Probably a dead man," he said aloud to his shrink, Dr. Jim Beam.

He wasn't sure he could outrun them. He had ghosted them too. That was a foolish decision.

Worse, he'd made things personal. He had embarrassed them.

They wouldn't let it go. They had money and resources and severe attitudes about loyalty. He was certain they would hunt him. He was certain who they'd send for him.

The room he was holed up in was an appropriate refuge for a man of deficient character: cheap, shabby, filthy. Mystery stains splotched the tawny shag carpet and the tropical-patterned bedspread. The outmoded TV set displayed scratchy static. The water in the shower was ice-cold. The glass by the sink was spotty. He drank from it anyway.

He finished his session with Dr. Beam and tossed the glass on the bed. Then he consulted with his friend Mary Jane.

He drew in a pull of smoke and set the roach in the ashtray. He exhaled slowly and felt his trap muscles uncurl. He thought the smoke improved the room's smell considerably.

The view outside was no Amalfi Coast. A truck stop. A crude diner. An adult video store. He heard indiscriminate traffic sounds from the big rigs and occasional shouts from his transitory neighbors. He saw nothing. The curtains had been drawn for days.

He took out his phone and swiped through the album again. He'd saved pictures of his daughter, starting at birth and stopping at age ten. The last picture was from their road trip six years ago, when he gave her driving lessons in the family 4Runner. *Ten wasn't too early to learn*, he thought. Plus, she might need to drive young. He and the girl's mother had not been reliable guardians.

Another text message came in.

Please tell me where you are?

He typed in a response and stared at it for a time. Slowly, he deleted it.

*What kind of man are you?* he asked himself.

He believed he'd done the right thing, leaving her alone like this for now. She wasn't safe with him. And his mind wasn't right, even on the rare occasions when he was sober. He always felt scattered, distracted. He could never concentrate on anything: a task, a conversation, his own child.

Smoking calmed him, narrowed his focus. It also clouded his thinking. Leaving the Bay, he'd convinced himself he was being followed. He'd driven north, then south, then north again, U-turn after U-turn to expose the tail. There was none. He had ended up here, at the Roach Inn.

If he could hold himself together long enough, he could go see her. Oregon was a long way. It might be out of their reach. They both might be safe there.

First, he'd have to turn back and grab everything he'd left behind. He must retrieve her sixteenth birthday gift. Better late than never, though "never" was a distinct possibility.

Maybe he could wean himself off his various dependencies on the drive north. Oregon hadn't been his home for a long time. Maybe he could finally settle down there, just him and her.

He coughed out some smoke.

*Who the hell are you kidding?*

He went to the bathroom and splashed cold water on his face. He looked at his reflection in the mirror. His eyes drooped. His jowls sagged. His cheeks had drug-induced spots. His hair and stubble looked grayer than yesterday. He didn't recognize himself anymore. She wouldn't either.

*What kind of father are you?*

He heard three light knocks at the door. Gentle, from a woman's hand. Maybe the woman he met in the lobby. She'd asked if he was holding. He said he had a few things for sale in his room.

He couldn't be too careful. He opened the bedside drawer and retrieved his gun, a Glock 19 semiautomatic pistol. He held the gun down at his side and walked softly on his tiptoes toward the door.

He stood silently for a moment and listened. The knocking ceased. He checked the peephole. Empty. He cracked the door open and peered outside.

Something heavy slammed into his forehead, a crack of thunder on his pale skin.

The gun flew from his hand and he landed hard on his back inside the room. The warm feelings from Mary Jane and Dr. Beam dissolved.

Instantly he knew he was bleeding. He could feel blood trickle onto his cheek. Then the pain started—raw, stifling, like a heat dome shoved tight over his head.

His assumption was correct. They'd sent their fixer to fix him.

He stared up at the hollow mouth of a gun. It gazed at him callously, just like its handler, the man he'd once called a colleague.

The man's massive frame swallowed the doorway. The snake tattoo bulged from his thick neck. A Celtic carnyx should have preceded his arrival. He was the physical representation of malice.

"Shawny Boy," the man said. "I've got a little message from the fellas."

# CHAPTER 1

"You took our baby girl on a stakeout this afternoon?"

"Yep," I said. "Slept the whole time. She's a natural."

"A stakeout," Ryan repeated.

"Yeah."

"Spying on people," she said.

"Ryan, we spy on Callie while she sleeps."

"Callie's our daughter and she's six months old," Ryan said. "Isn't it dangerous to bring her with you?"

"No more dangerous than changing a diaper."

Ryan sighed through the phone. I heard her yawn. I yawned back.

"I dropped her off at home with no issues," I said. "She's in mint condition."

"And thankfully fast asleep," Ryan said. "So you're back on 'stakeout' tonight?"

"Yep."

"Where are you?"

"About five minutes from the house."

"I'm gonna lie down."

"I'm gonna sit in the car."

"Charlie," Ryan said, "please do not bring our precious child on some creepy case."

"It's called surveillance."

"Surveil this."

"Love you."

"Love you too."

I hung up and checked the baby monitor on my phone.

Callie Shaw lay peacefully in her crib muttering soft, sweet gibberish.

*"Heeeooooooow."*

Her tiny head tilted to the right, facing the crib bars. Her right arm lay down at her side and her left arm extended upward with her hand clasped in a fist, as if she were salsa dancing without a partner. Her sleeveless sleep sack looked like a satin slip dress on the night-vision screen.

*"Oooouuuhuhhhhh."*

Callie was born January 5th weighing eight pounds and one ounce. She was now seventeen pounds and three ounces, all Pillsbury rolls and cheeks. She drank Similac like a gremlin. She had her mother's big green eyes, her dad's stubborn curiosity, a smile that would add ten years to your life, and a cry that would shred your brain. She was loud and moody and produced bodily substances requiring hazmat gear. But she was worth every second.

*"Eeeeaaaahhh."*

Callie was six months and four days old with a severe case of FOMO. Ryan and I just couldn't get her to sleep, which meant we didn't sleep either. Ever. We hired a night nurse for the week with money we didn't have.

Sleep training a baby was expensive anywhere. In San Francisco it meant a triple mortgage.

*"Gurrrrble-aloe."*

"Remember the first lesson on a stakeout," I said to Callie's screen. "Park at least two houses down from the target so they don't spot the tail."

I kept the baby monitor on and tucked my phone into a cupholder. My client's wife was headed out for the evening.

The house on Leavenworth looked like a six-million-dollar Lego piece adorned in flamingo-pink stucco. The garage, a smaller pink Lego, sat underneath. The driveway was the size of a sandbox, quickly merging with the residential street.

Deborah Wellington backed her white Range Rover out of the garage and headed north, her headlights shining dimly in the dusk. I started up Mango, my old sunflower-yellow Bronco, waited a beat, and followed.

The tail lasted all of seven blocks. On Beach Street, Mrs. Wellington turned left into a parking garage. I found a spot on the opposite curb facing the entrance.

A minute later she emerged from the garage and began walking east, away from me, a black brushed-leather purse slung over her left shoulder. It looked like Prada. Ryan has taught me all about Prada.

My dash clock read a quarter till nine. Mrs. Wellington had told her husband she was meeting a girlfriend for a late drink.

I cut the engine and crossed the street. I had no idea what to wear for a tail job. It all depended on where Mrs. Wellington was headed, and I had no idea about that either. I settled for what I might've worn to a local tavern in my younger, hipper days: black V-neck shirt, gray chinos, and white Vans. I added a plain black cap for subterfuge.

Hotel Zephyr looked more suited for Miami Beach than Fisherman's Wharf, but it had a nice view of Pier 39 and the waterfront. The lobby was retro industrial chic, featuring exposed pipes and faux shipping containers. A stuffed marlin hung on one wall. A cartoon mural of Popeye splashed another wall.

It was Friday night in mid-July and the place buzzed with tourists. I settled into a *Jetsons*-style chair and watched through a porthole as Mrs. Wellington exchanged pleasantries with a man not named Mr. Wellington.

He was just over six feet tall, handsome, clean shaven, and dark-haired. His flow was terrific. He was trying really hard to look thirty-five instead of twenty-five, with slim-fit jeans choking his calves and brown loafers with no socks and a gray sport coat worn over a white button-down with the tails out.

Mrs. Wellington was forty-eight years old trying really hard to look twenty-five. Her subtle face work helped: no visible wrinkles around the eyes or forehead. Her outfit helped too: a white off-the-shoulder floral top, distressed split-ankle jeans with exposed buttons and design tears at the thigh and kneecap, brown Gucci belt, and brown wedges. Her dark hair was expertly bleached blond. Her skin had a slight tint of tanning-bed brown. She wore no wedding ring. Neither did the young man who was not her husband.

Together they looked rich and quite satisfied with their richness. They smiled at each other. No kiss. No embrace. But there was a glint in Mrs. Wellington's eyes.

*Exploratory adoration.*

Ryan gives me that look all the time. Well, she used to before we started pounding NoDoz.

Mrs. Wellington stood next to the young man while he checked in at the front desk. He had no luggage either. I turned on my phone's camera app, stood, and moved closer to the desk. He and Mrs. Wellington had their backs turned. I held the phone to my right ear and walked past them, nodding my head and mouthing "Yeah" as if the ghost on the other line was making a ton of sense. As I passed, I snapped five pictures by pressing the volume button with my right thumb.

I did a semicircle around the lobby holding the same ridiculous conversation with myself. I took a couple more discreet photos catching the sides of their faces. Then I walked out the front entrance and back to my car.

I didn't drop the fake phone call until I got behind the wheel. I pressed the home button on the phone. Nothing. I plugged it into my portable power bank. A minute later it fired back up. No pictures.

The baby monitor had killed the battery.

"Shit," I told myself.

I could let the phone charge for a few minutes, go back inside, and hope to catch them in the courtyard having a drink. But in all likelihood, they'd gone upstairs to get acquainted.

My phone buzzed.

"How's it going?" Ryan asked.

"Shitty. I hear screaming."

"Callie's awake."

"That was fast."

"Can you pick up some Tylenol on the way home?"

"We have Tylenol," I said.

"Baby Tylenol."

"For what?"

"Grace says it'll help Callie's teeth."

"Callie doesn't have teeth."

"Her gums," Ryan said. "Smart-ass. You know what I mean."

"Wait, who's Grace?"

"Grace Chen, the night nurse?"

"Oh, yes. Thirty-five bucks an hour. How could I forget."

"Forty."

"Terrific."

"She gets here tomorrow night," Ryan said. "Insists she'll sleep on the couch."

"How long is she here?"

"A week."

"Did you offer her our bed?"

"Yes."

"And she refused?"

"Yes."

"Good. If I was getting thirty-five bucks an hour, I'd sleep on the curb."

"Forty. It'll be worth the money."

"Let's hope so."

She yawned. I yawned.

"Who are you following, again?"

"Surveilling. That's confidential, ma'am."

"You've been waiting to say that, haven't you?"

"Yep."

"Shut up and tell me."

"Deborah Wellington," I said.

"Wellington," Ryan repeated. "Wife of Arthur Wellington? 'First family of San Francisco' Wellington?"

"Yep."

"Did you speak with Mr. Wellington?"

"Powell did."

"I read he's become more reclusive as he's gotten older."

"His wife hasn't."

"Why are you spying on her?"

"*Surveilling.*"

"Whatever."

"Arthur Wellington thinks she's cheating on him," I said.

"Is she?"

"Looking that way."

Ryan sighed. Quite dramatically, I thought.

"Can you make a store run?" she asked again.

"I might need to hang here a little longer."

"How much longer?"

"I don't know. Stakeouts aren't exactly timed."

"Please bring it soon. Grace says Callie should take a dose before bed. It'll help her sleep."

"Sweetie, I'm working here. It's my first case. I'm trying not to fuck it up."

"Are you fucking it up?"

"Yeah."

Ryan yawned. I yawned.

"Do you have a gun?" she asked.

"Do we own a gun?"

"No."

"Then no."

"I'd feel better if you had a gun."

"I don't need a gun. I just need a camera that works."

"Use your phone."

"Brilliant, thanks."

My phone was up to 12 percent. I got out and walked back to Zephyr.

Mrs. Wellington and Mr. Handsome weren't in the lobby. Or the lounge. Or the courtyard.

I found the gift shop off the lobby, past a metal hanging mermaid with a green-striped bikini top. The woman behind the counter looked up from her magazine.

"Y'all got any baby Tylenol?" I asked.

# CHAPTER 2

"So she cheats on her husband a half mile from her house," Dwayne Powell said.

"It appears so," I said.

"Why?"

"Convenience," I suggested. "Cheaper than a big getaway."

"Maybe he's married. Or got a girlfriend."

"Maybe it gets her rocks off, cheating on her husband a half mile from her house."

"Why not wait till the old man leaves?"

"Paranoia, maybe. Afraid of cameras. Hidden ones."

"Arthur Wellington's got assets worth protecting."

"More than a few."

It was Saturday. I was having a patio lunch with my new boss at 4505 on Divisadero, the closest thing to Texas barbecue in this town. A sign outside read *Vegetarians converted daily*.

Predictably, the morning began like a hangover. By eleven thirty the fog had burned off into a bright and sunny early-summer day. I'd chosen a traditional lunch: barbecue sandwich with baked beans and potato salad. Powell took a bite of his Frank-aroni. Fried mac and cheese with hot dog slices inside. A 4505 special.

"How's the baby?" he asked.

"Teething like crazy. Could hand her a live grenade and she'd chew it like a Ring Pop."

"Sleeping any?"

"Me or her?"

"Both."

"Neither," I said.

Inspector Dwayne Powell was the proud founder and owner of Powell & Associates, a private investigation firm serving the City and County of San Francisco. He started the company with his two sons, James and Reggie, after retiring from the San Francisco Police Department.

Inspector Powell was a decorated veteran, a world-class investigator, a successful entrepreneur, a community leader, a proud member of the San Francisco African American Chamber of Commerce, and an adjunct instructor on criminal justice at UC Berkeley.

Off the clock, he was a quiet, pleasant man. On the clock, he was an indefatigable hard-ass. He had a stern face and incredulous eyes that questioned every facial tic you made and every word you said. Talking business with him was like boxing a middleweight champ. He'd circle, feint, jab you with a heavy stare, uppercut you with interrogative discourse. I was stepping into the ring again.

"All right," Powell said. "How'd the pictures turn out?"

"You see, that's the thing," I said.

"What thing?"

"Oh, just a little . . . thing."

"You messed this up, didn't you?"

"Well, yeah."

Powell did not believe in curse words. He believed they showed weakness. For fifty-two years he'd learned to suppress them. Occasionally they bubbled up, like lava spurts from a volcanic fissure.

"Explain," he said.

"I miss those old disposable cameras. You know, the ones where you just wind the little knob to the right? Kinda tedious, but without all the extra features you've gotta deal with on your phone, like a call coming in, or a battery . . . dying."

Powell frowned.

"I had them, boss. They were perfect, right inside the lobby. Neither of them noticed me."

"If you drained your battery screwing around on TikTok, I'll fire you right here."

"It was the baby monitor. I was checking on Callie."

Powell wiped his mouth and Hate Smiled at me.

His regular smile was actually quite cheerful. Charming, even. The Hate Smile was something else. The average recipient saw no distinction, but there was something different in the eyes. They narrowed slightly, disdainfully. I'd seen the Hate Smile before. It was like a left hook to the temple.

"So, which is it?" Powell asked.

"Which is what?"

"Are you dumb or lazy?"

"Am I . . . ?"

"Dumb or lazy. There's a big difference between book smart and streetwise, Charlie."

He took another bite of his Frankaroni and deftly prevented the cheese from smudging his neatly trimmed mustache and goatee.

He sat there and chewed silently. I sat there and waited for the big right cross.

"A long time ago," Powell said, "I had a young man in my unit, nineteen years old. Said he got into Princeton. Wanted the army instead, make his granddaddy proud. Kid couldn't tie a knot."

"How long did he last?"

"Back to the Ivy League."

"I can tie a knot."

"How are you with phone chargers?"

I walked right into that one. Standing eight count.

"Seriously," Powell said, "why are you doing this? Not like it pays well. It ain't glamorous."

"I like it," I said.

"Yeah, I get it. You just don't wanna drag your butt back to the newspaper and go back to work. You'd rather do this and give Uber rides."

"This *is* work. You do it."

"This is my career. I've been doing this thirty years. Your first case and you've got no pictures, no idea who this guy is. How long did you stay on them after the lobby?"

"I left to charge my phone for a few minutes. When I went back inside, they were gone. I figured they'd gone upstairs for a while, so I bought baby Tylenol and dropped it off at the house."

"Baby Tylenol," Powell said.

"Yeah. For Callie's gums. Supposed to help her sleep."

"That's sweet," Powell said.

"Then I went back to the lobby and waited for two hours. They didn't show. I got tired of waiting so I walked to the parking garage. Mrs. Wellington's car was already gone."

"Then what?"

"I went home and got spit up on."

Powell sighed. He tossed his napkin onto his empty plate.

"Wellington won't like this," he said.

"Because his wife presumably booked a hotel room with another man, or because I missed the pictures?"

"Both."

"I imagine Wellington's used to getting what he wants."

"He's used to being in control. Only gets worse for men like him the older they get. I know the feeling."

"I'm sorry, boss. Won't happen again."

Powell reached into the pocket of his pressed slacks and took out his phone. He studied it fiercely, as he did everything. After a few taps he set his phone on the table.

"Wellington wants us to follow his wife again."

"I'll take care of it."

"In your Bronco?"

"Yeah."

"How old is that thing? Can you even charge a phone in it?"

"It's an eighty-five. The cigarette lighter doesn't work. But I've got a portable charger."

"Next time, use it," Powell said. "And find another car. It's too bright for surveillance. I could spot it from space. And it's gonna break down on the job one of these days."

"Ryan's home with Callie, so she has the Highlander. Mango doesn't have room for a baby car seat."

"Mango?"

"Yeah. One of my Uber rides named it. Cute little kid."

Hate Smile.

"I'm not gonna tell Wellington about the pictures," Powell said. "Next time you gotta get it right. Our client expects, and I quote, 'incontrovertible evidence of infidelity.'"

"He sounds like a prick."

"He's paying for your diapers."

"Thanks for lunch."

"You're welcome."

Powell stood.

"Charlie, what are the requirements to be a licensed private investigator in the state of California?"

"Nope," I said. "Not this shit again."

"Remind me."

I sighed.

"Must be eighteen or older, go through a background check, pass a multiple-choice test."

"And?"

"And have at least three years of compensated experience in investigative work totaling six thousand hours."

"Or?"

"Two and a half years, totaling five thousand hours, plus an associate degree in police science, criminal law, or justice."

"Which you don't have."

"Which I don't have."

"How many years did it take you to earn a private investigator's license here in California?"

"Six weeks."

"And why is that?"

"You fudged the numbers because you think I have great potential, Inspector Powell."

"And stop doing stakeouts in that bright-ass yellow car."

"You think the Safeway on Market has gas drops?" I asked.

"How the fuck should I know?" Powell said.

# CHAPTER 3

"No sex," Ryan said, and tossed me a paper bag and a bottle of water through the passenger-side window.

"What?"

"For thirty days. Better enjoy that burger."

"Why?"

"You woke me up, you bastard," she said. "The first day in six months I haven't had to wake up for anything, except maybe to pee. And I probably would've just gone in my pajamas."

"Wonderful imagery."

"Here's some Pretzel Goldfish for a snack later. You're welcome, by the way."

"Thank you, sweetie. I really had no other choice."

"You could've starved."

"Can't focus without food."

"You could've called DoorDash."

"Requires an address. I can't type in 'Mango.'"

"You could've ordered a pizza and asked them to drop it here."

"And tell them I'm sitting across the street in a parked car? I'd look like a creep."

"You *do* look like a creep."

Ryan hopped inside Mango. She'd parked her Highlander behind me, three houses down from the Wellingtons' across Leavenworth.

At Powell's request, I'd spent Sunday following Deborah Wellington. All her errand running made me hungry. I called Ryan for delivery. Even in her weekend garb—Stanford hoodie, hair up, minimal makeup—Ryan was stunning.

"I want some of these fries as a service charge," she said.

"I can think of another way to tip you."

"Uh-uh. Nope. Thirty days, remember?"

"You won't stick to that."

"I know."

"Although we do have a houseguest for... how many more nights?"

"Six."

"Six," I repeated.

We locked eyes. I smiled. She smiled. We laughed.

"Who are we kidding," Ryan said. "We can't stay awake long enough to talk dirty to each other. And when we're awake, we're getting screamed at."

Ryan nibbled on her fry. I bit off half the burger. Three tourists passed us on foot, probably on their way back from Lombard Street. The sun was out. Mango's dashboard didn't have an outside temperature reading, but my phone said it was seventy-three degrees. I had the front windows cracked. Birds chirped pleasantly at each other.

"This whole thing is my fault," Ryan said.

"Why?"

"I told you once, just once, that you looked *sort of*, not totally, but *sort of* like a young Harrison Ford, and instead of going back to reporting, now you think you can jet off on all these little adventures like you're Indiana fucking Jones."

"We're sitting in a car," I said.

"Best date we've had in a while."

"Only date we've had in a while."

"I'm gonna check on Callie," Ryan said.

"Good. Stay any longer and you would've blown my cover."

"You are one romantic son of a bitch."

She kissed me on the cheek.

"Please be careful," she said. "And tell Mr. Powell I said hello."

She got out of the car, got back in the Highlander, and drove away. She looked impossibly good for someone who birthed a human just a few months ago and, as half-Supermom, half–Badass Exec, didn't have time for gyms or Pelotons or personal trainers. This was gonna be the longest month of my life.

Forty-five minutes later, just after I'd polished off my celibacy burger, the garage door on Leavenworth opened and Deborah Wellington clip-clopped into the driveway wearing gold low-heeled sandals and a turquoise dress. She had the waggish walk of a college cheerleader. Her left hand sported a wedding ring the size of a space rock. I spotted it twenty feet away. I could've spotted it two hundred feet away.

Mango followed the Rover out of North Beach and onto the 101 and through the ensuing fog on the Golden Gate Bridge. I'd always felt uneasy crossing the bridge. There was something about the spectral nature of the fog poking through the cables and suspender ropes, enveloping every inch of the foot, car, and bike traffic. It seemed the colossal towers marked entry to a new, uncharted dimension. Except I knew Sausalito quite well. The most intimidating part about Sausalito was its lunch prices.

After ten more minutes on the 101, flanked by high brushy hills, the Rover pulled into a parking space near the covered entrance to Herring Harbor. I backed into a space near the rear with a complete view of the entrance and cut the engine. The parking lot was mostly full, with only a few empty spots.

As Mrs. Wellington got out of the Rover, Mr. Handsome opened the wrought iron security gate and greeted her outside. He wore a navy blazer over a pink button-down and tan slacks. His hair looked even more awesome than it had Friday night.

He drew her close to him. They kissed passionately. He dipped her shoulder down slightly and leaned into her, reminiscent of the famous photo of the returning soldier and the nurse in Times Square. I snapped some pics with Powell's Canon Rebel camera.

Mr. Handsome entered a code on the security keypad and escorted his mistress through the gate. I called Powell.

"She's in Sausalito with the same guy."

"Where?"

"Houseboat. Gate's locked. Couldn't make out the code through the camera."

"They started putting those in to keep tourists out."

"Yeah."

"Pictures this time?"

"Yeah. Arthur Wellington was right to suspect his wife. I've got 'em kissing outside the gate. Wasn't a friendly peck on the cheek either."

"Good work."

"Can I go home?"

"No."

"What else does Wellington need to see?"

"See if you can find out which boat it is," Powell said. "Or his car. Something. I want to know who this guy is."

"Yes, sir."

I plugged the phone back into the charger and sighed. The burger was gone. The Pretzel Goldfish were gone. Ryan wasn't gonna drive fifteen miles for another delivery. Powell wasn't gonna let me drive home. I checked on Callie. She wasn't in her crib. Probably getting her late-afternoon bottle. At least someone was well-fed.

Sunlight glistened on the dark blue water. I could see a line of houseboats behind the main entrance. The residents in Sausalito insisted they should be called "floating homes." If I paid close to a million bucks to live on a boat, I'd brush up the name too. Many were painted in bright blues and pinks and yellows. They sat unfazed by a slight breeze stirring the waves, carefree, staring out at the idyllic seascape.

My phone buzzed. It was Ryan.

Where are you?

                                                          Sausalito.

Is it pretty?

                                                             Always.

Callie pooped on the floor again.

                                                           Beautiful.

For the next two hours I tried to keep myself entertained.

At seven thirty, I made a mental list of Callie's best moments to date. Among them: the big smile she gave me around four weeks, when she put my voice with my face for the first time; the day she started on solid foods and sucked her thumb after each bite to savor the flavor; the first time she noticed her feet when she lifted her legs back and touched her toes.

I checked the baby monitor again. Callie was splayed out on her back like an uprooted turtle. I checked the phone's battery: 57 percent. The portable charger had stopped working. Wonderful.

I turned off the Spotify app and fumbled through the center console. I found two CDs for the player: *How I Got Over* by The Roots and *Led Zeppelin IV*. My eyes had gotten heavy. I went with the hard rock track.

At 8:57, the sun had fully retreated, but the parking lot lamps provided decent light.

At 9:00, a black Escalade SUV entered the lot. It parked somewhere closer to the entrance, concealed by a cluster of cars.

A moment later, a silver Toyota 4Runner entered the lot and backed into a space two spots to my right. Rearview cameras were something these days.

At 9:02, it occurred to me that I hadn't seen or heard anyone get out of the Escalade or the 4Runner.

At 9:07, a guy got into the car parked next to me on the right and drove off. I could now see inside the 4Runner. Mango's windows were tinted. The 4Runner's driver-side window was down.

A girl sat behind the wheel. She looked quite young, as if driving was a relatively new experience. She wore a hooded denim jacket. Her dark hair was in a ponytail. She appeared to be making good progress on a box of Raisinets. She snacked like a PI, even if she didn't meet the age requirement.

More minutes passed. I thought about Goldfish and Raisinets and a mix of Goldfish and Raisinets and some Gardetto's rye chips. I glanced at the young girl again. I had a brief vision of Callie, semi-grown, sitting alone somewhere in the dark. I felt a sudden rush of Dadness.

I got out, walked around Mango to her door, smiled brightly, and waved.

The girl's mouth dropped mid-chew. Her eyes widened and she blushed a little, as if she'd been pulled over at a traffic stop. I felt like Erik Estrada.

"Howdy," I said.

She stared at me as if I were standing in one of those inflatable T-Rex suits. I did a quick scan of the car's interior. A pair of binoculars lay on the front dash beneath the windshield.

"My name's Charlie," I said, and pointed to Mango. "I'm a private investigator sitting in that old yellow relic. Just wanted to make sure you're okay out here. It's getting late. Doesn't seem too safe."

The girl wore a Blink-182 shirt underneath her denim jacket. The right side of her face was now visible. I noticed the skin below her right eye was red and puffy, the early stages of a shiner. She spoke in a soft adolescent voice.

"You're, like, a . . . cop?"

"No, no, not a cop. I'm out here trying to bust a lady cheating on her old man. Private detective stuff. Like, uh, *Magnum, P.I.*"

She had no idea what that meant. I showed her my license. She gave it only a cursory glance. Her eyes shifted quickly to the parking lot, then back to me.

"I'm fine," she said.

"That eye looks like it hurts."

"It doesn't."

"Okay. You live here?"

"No."

"Family? Friends?"

"No."

"What's your name?"

"None of your business."

I couldn't argue with that.

"Fair enough. I'll be next door if you need anything."

I started toward Mango.

"Wait."

I stopped and watched her check the parking lot again.

Finally she said, "You're really a private detective?"

"Yep."

"You get paid to find people?"

"Yep."

"Are you any good?"

"Not really."

She frowned.

I pointed at the binoculars on the dash. "Are you looking for someone?"

She blushed a little more deeply this time, her cheeks matching the bruise on her eye.

"Yeah," she said.

"Who?"

Just then, the security gate creaked open and Mrs. Wellington walked outside with Mr. Handsome.

"Shit," I said. "I mean, shoot. Hang on."

I hustled back to Mango.

Mrs. Wellington's wedding ring was gone. So was Mr. Handsome's navy jacket. His pink shirt was untucked. They held hands. They stared into each other's eyes.

Robert Plant wailed through the car speakers. I picked up the camera.

The lovebirds embraced. I snapped more pictures. I glanced at the girl in the 4Runner. I hadn't spooked her. She popped some more Raisinets as she watched the PDA. I felt like I was at a drive-in movie theater.

Finally, the kissing stopped. I put the camera down. Mrs. Wellington walked—somewhat unsteadily, I thought—to her white Range Rover and opened the driver-side door. She glanced back at him before hopping inside. He watched her start the Rover and drive away.

Just as Mr. Handsome turned to head back inside, the brights of the black Escalade blinded him. The car's tires screeched. It shot forward out of its parking space and slammed to a stop in front of him. I couldn't see inside the Escalade's windows. They were as dark as mine.

Mr. Handsome squinted. He held up his left hand in a futile attempt to shield his eyes from the headlights' glare.

A guy who looked like Thor's ex-convict cousin got out of the driver's seat and rumbled toward him. The guy's dark hair was in a man bun. He wore a black chin strap beard below a prominent hook nose. He looked at least six foot three and 230 pounds. Muscles puffed underneath a tight white tank top and hooded leather jacket, complemented by torn jeans and black combat boots. A tattoo of what looked like a snake curled down his neck below his right jawline. I felt grateful not to be in his line of sight.

I glanced at the 4Runner. The young girl had set down her Raisinets. She had her binoculars trained on the two men.

I'd reached the last track on the Zeppelin album: "When the Levee Breaks," with its ambulatory riff. I turned off the music and cracked the windows.

Snake Tat cocked a meat-cleaver right hand and slugged Mr. Handsome viciously in the gut. He crumpled to the pavement like a stale biscuit. He made a whimpery groan that sounded like "Awwwfff."

The girl in the 4Runner was still holding her binoculars.

Snake Tat lifted up Mr. Handsome and hit him in the stomach

again and shoved him back to the ground and kicked him hard in the ribs. I thought about flipping on my headlights to break it up. Then Snake Tat stood over Mr. Handsome's chest and pulled a pistol from his leather jacket.

"Whoa," I said to Mango.

My stomach stopped growling. I felt the same sinking sensation I had the first time I stepped on a roller coaster. I'd never seen a gun in action except at a Texas shooting range or deer stand, and I wasn't a huge fan of either place.

The man pointed the gun down as if he were staring into a urinal. He cocked the hammer and spoke in a low, gravelly voice, spitting words through clenched teeth.

"I know who you are, Scottie," he said. "I know who you are and where you live."

He pointed the gun at Scottie's head.

"Stay the fuck away from her," he said. "This is your only warning."

He bent down and tore open Scottie's pink shirt. He slapped Scottie hard three times across the face. Scottie yelped.

Snake Tat stood up, uncocked the gun, and tucked it into his waistband.

I'd forgotten about the camera. I snatched it up, slinked lower in my seat, and zoomed in on the neck tattoo. Two interlocked snakes hissing at each other. I snapped a pic.

I looked over at the girl in the 4Runner. She had slinked down in her seat too. Her binoculars were gone. She looked horrified.

Snake Tat threw a quick glance around the parking lot. *No witnesses.* He checked the knuckles on his right hand. He smiled to himself. Then he sauntered back toward the Escalade and climbed inside.

The Escalade had some sort of cover on its license plates. It sped off into the night.

I set the camera down and realized my hands were trembling. I placed them both on the steering wheel. I could hear my heart beating to the edge of my skin. Maybe Ryan was right about me needing a gun.

A moment later, more headlights burst on. Tires squealed. The 4Runner barreled toward the exit and disappeared. It had Oregon plates. I only caught the first two letters through the lamplight: *CY*.

# CHAPTER 4

"Hey, buddy," I said. "You okay?"

"Oh fuck," Scottie said, clutching his exposed abdomen.

"I wanted to help, but the guy had a gun. That was terrifying."

"Fuck," Scottie said again. "I think he cracked a rib."

He turned his head and spit blood onto the pavement. Snake Tat must have nicked his lip while slapping the shit out of him.

"Who was that guy?"

Scottie groaned.

"Can I do anything to help?"

Scottie grunted.

"Should I call the police?"

"No," Scottie said sharply. It made him wince. "No. I'm good, man. I'm good."

"An ambulance?"

"Please, no. I'm fine."

He tried to sit up. That was too painful. He rolled to his stomach and put his hands on the ground to prop himself up, first to his knees and then onto his feet. He threw in a few "fucks" and "shits" along the way. Scottie didn't look like a guy who'd gotten in many fights. He'd lost this one badly. His kinetic smile was gone. He grimaced at me.

"Who are you?"

I smiled pleasantly.

"Oh, I'm your neighbor. Lanny Poffo."

"Lenny?"

"Sure. You're Scottie?"

He looked puzzled.

"Heard him say your name," I said. "Here, I'll help you inside. I'm on my way home too."

"Thanks, but I can make it."

He took one step and shouted another expletive.

"Let me help. My wife's a nurse. She's taught me a few things."

I steered him around toward the entrance with his right arm draped over my shoulder. His acrid cologne drowned out the faint smell of salt in the air. Three steps in, I blocked his right foot with my left and he stumbled to his knees.

"Ahhh, fuck!" he shouted.

I crouched and pulled a thin leather billfold from his back right pocket, snapped a pic of his driver's license with my phone, and dropped the billfold to the ground.

"Oh man, I'm sorry," I said. "It was this damn rock."

I pretended to pick one up and chuck it over the houseboats toward the water.

"You okay?"

"I guess so," he muttered.

"Let's try this again."

"Nah. I can walk."

At the security gate I glanced back at the parking lot and said, "Looks like your wallet fell out. I'll get it."

Scottie had already punched in the security code and opened the gate. I handed him the billfold. An older woman passed us on her way outside. Her jaw dropped at Scottie's beaten face and torn shirt. She stared at him as if he were Freddy Krueger.

"Bachelor party," I said. "You know how those can get."

Without assistance, Scottie hobbled alongside me down a wood-paneled corridor lined with potted plants. We turned left at the corner and stopped three houses down.

"Where did you say you lived?" Scottie asked.

"Oh, I'm down that way," I said.

"Want a beer?"

"Sure."

Scottie's three-story wooden houseboat was an idyllic seaside bachelor pad shaped like a skinny square, painted eggshell blue and topped by a railed deck overlooking the bay. He'd left the lights on. The place had the faint scent of perfume. It was small but stylishly furnished and contemporary, with a living room just off the main entrance and a staircase leading to the bedroom.

In better light, I could see Scottie's right cheek was red and swollen. The corner of his lip had puffed up. There were rips in his pink shirt where the buttons had torn off.

"I'm gonna change," Scottie said. "Make yourself at home, Lenny. I've got beer in the fridge."

He limped upstairs, steadying himself on the railing with one hand and holding his side with the other.

Two pizza boxes and an unopened bottle of Pinot Grigio lay on the kitchen counter. I opened the boxes. All slices were intact. Scottie and Mrs. Wellington had gotten right to business.

Since I hadn't eaten much in six hours, I helped myself to three slices. I found some ice in the freezer and a dishcloth in a drawer by the sink. I put four cubes in the dishcloth and tied it up like a bandana. I took two Bud Lights from the fridge and plopped down in a vegan leather lounge chair by a sliding glass door to the patio. I flipped on Scottie's sixty-inch TV and checked the Giants score. 10–3 Rockies in the eighth.

I glanced at my phone. There were motion and sound notifications from Callie's room. Grace Chen was fishing Callie out of the crib. Callie did not appreciate the gesture.

Ryan texted me.

Callie won't sleep. Grace is taking over. I'm gonna try to sleep a couple hours. Doing okay?

I thought about texting back, The guy I'm following just got his ass kicked by some meathead. Told him I'm his neighbor. And that you're a nurse.

I settled for, Doing fine. Won't be too much longer. Get some rest. Love y'all.

I texted Powell. In Sausalito. I've got what I need.

Powell texted back, Head home and call me in the morning.

I heard a shower running. Good, Scottie was hosing off that cologne. I took the opportunity to study my picture of his driver's license.

Scott Alexander Coburn. *Turned twenty-seven three days ago. Happy birthday, Scottie.* Height: 6'-1". Eyes: Hazel. Address: 2907 Mesa Street, Phoenix, Arizona.

I had the info I needed. But I could impress Powell with a little more. Besides, I was hungry, I was bored, and I was curious. Put that on my headstone.

The fear in the young girl's face stuck with me too. What the hell had she been doing in that parking lot tonight?

Ten minutes later Scottie reappeared, moving gingerly down the steps in gray joggers and no shirt. He had a black hoodie draped over his shoulder. His bare chest looked unnaturally tan and smooth. His stomach had the makings of an eight-pack. He was in good shape. It didn't help him tonight.

Scottie groaned as he lifted his arms to put on the hoodie. His splendid hair, unstyled and unmoussed, was wet and messy. I tossed him a Bud Light. He winced as he caught it.

"Ice for your face," I said. "Beer for your ribs."

"Thanks."

He pressed the ice to his cheek and dabbed at his lip.

"You're gonna need some pain meds too."

"I got something," he said. He tossed the ice on the coffee table. "Let's go outside."

I followed him out the patio door and held his beer as he grunted his way up a short ladder to the top deck. He held both our beers as I climbed up to join him.

We sat in matching teak-framed deck chairs. Moonlight bathed the placid water. Hills sat quietly in the far distance, dimly illuminated by artificial light from neighboring homes.

Scottie downed half his beer in one pull. He reached into the front pocket of his hoodie and took out a lighter, ashtray, papers, and a clear baggie containing maybe an ounce of weed. He set the materials on a glass table between us and began to roll a joint.

"I'm out of Tylenol," he said, and tried to smile.

"Whatever works," I said.

"Want one?"

"No, thanks."

"What did you say you do?"

"I said my wife's a nurse."

"What about you?"

"Doctor."

Scottie nodded as he assembled his herbal medication. He wasn't paying me much attention. Talking probably took his mind off the pain.

"Well," he said, "next time I might need you to stitch me up, Doc."

"Sounded like there might not be a next time," I said.

Scottie stopped rolling and looked up at me. I could see his Adam's apple move.

"Yeah," he said, and lit the thing.

He took a deeper pull on the joint than he had with the beer. He exhaled slowly through his mouth and nose. Satisfied, he lay back in the chair, stretched out his legs, and closed his eyes.

"Sure you don't want a hit? Pretty good shit."

Six months ago, I probably would've taken him up on it.

"Nah," I said. "Got a surgery in the morning."

I drank some beer and looked out at the water. Sausalito always reminded me of *Sesame Street* with its perfect little downtown brick buildings and pristine streets. The angelic cousin to discordant San Francisco. Everything was clean and neat and in its little place. Everybody seemed rich and fulfilled. What had happened to Scottie Coburn didn't happen often.

"What do you do, Scottie?"

"I work in tech."

"In San Francisco?"

"Yeah."

"Must be successful."

Scottie took another puff. The ember from the joint glowed cheerfully in the darkness.

"I'm doing pretty good," he said.

"You buy this place?"

"Nah, Airbnb deal. The owners are in Europe for the summer. My lease was up, so I gave them a call."

"Not a bad rental."

"It ain't cheap, but look at this view, bro. I grew up in the desert. Never seen nothin' like this."

He smiled painfully. He took another hit from his joint.

"You're in tech, huh?"

"Yeah."

"Was your friend out there a client?"

Scottie's eyes opened. His smile disappeared with the smoke.

"No," he said.

"Who was he? He looked like a *Mad Max* character."

"I've never seen him before in my life."

"Never?"

"You saw him. Think you'd remember if you saw a guy like that?"

"Absolutely."

"I'll be seeing that motherfucker in my nightmares," he said, and winced and touched his ribs again.

"You have no idea why he jumped you?"

"Not a clue."

"I heard him say, 'Stay the fuck away from her.' Was he talking about the woman you were with?"

Scottie turned his head to face me. His eyes narrowed.

"You ask a lot of questions," he said.

"Doctors are thorough."

He took another hit and watched more smoke die in the air.

"You saw me with her?" he asked.

"Yeah."

"You recognize her?"

"No."

"Good."

"Should I know her?"

"She's rich," Scottie said. "And she's married."

I feigned surprise. "Oh?"

"And we've been keeping it a secret," he said.

"So why would some dude attack you, threaten you, tell you to stay away, if the whole thing's on the DL?"

"No clue."

"You gonna keep seeing her?"

He sat up and crushed the joint in the ashtray. He downed the rest of his beer. He was nice and faded now. His night was improving. He was no longer getting his ass kicked. He'd made a new pal. He grinned at me.

"My head says no," he said. "My johnson says absolutely."

"That's the most romantic thing I've ever heard."

"She's a smoke show, bro. And she wants it all the time. The other night she messaged me, told me to get my ass to the city because she wanted to smash. I said, 'Your husband's home. He's always home.' She said, 'Then let's get a room.' We found a place like down the street from her house, banged it out real quick."

"Terrific," I said.

"I like married women," he said. "They don't expect anything. They don't need commitment. Most of them just wanna get off."

"Don't we all."

"Right? No harm in that."

Scottie's eyes were getting heavy. They looked half-closed.

"Her husband must not be getting the job done," I said.

"Her husband's like seventy, man."

"But he's got money."

"She and her husband own half the city. She's bored. It's fucking perfect. She's not gonna leave him. She just wants some fun. She's older, but Doc, I'm telling you, she takes care of herself. She's got a tight little ass. And implants."

"I specialize in those, actually."

"Cheers to that," Scottie said.

We clinked bottles. I'd had enough of this guy.

"How'd you meet her?"

"Some work thing. She was there with her husband, wearing this tight cocktail dress. We were alone for a few minutes, got to talking. I scooped her digits."

"What a stud," I said.

Scottie got out of the chair and stretched his arms. The wind picked up. He threw the hood over his head and rubbed his battered side.

"You sure you don't need a doctor?" I asked.

"Nah," Scottie said. "I've been in fights before. A little kush always helps."

"I think you should call the police."

"No," he said sharply. "I can't let them find out she was here."

"Because she and her husband are well-known?"

"Yeah."

"What if this guy comes back?"

"I've got my own guns," Scottie said. "If I ever see that motherfucker again, I'll show him."

He peered out over the deck. "Sometimes I wonder how many fish are in there, you know?"

"Kinda like guessing how many stars are up there."

"Gotta be trillions."

"Of stars?"

"Fish."

"Doubtful," I said.

"We live our lives on a speck of dust suspended on a sunbeam," Scottie said.

"What?"

"The sky. Stars. Space. We're just a speck. A grain of sand. The pale blue dot."

"Who said that?"

"Carl Sagan."

"That's right."

"Don't sweat shit, Doc. Nothing really matters in the end."

I didn't much disagree.

"You know what the biggest fish in the bay is?" Scottie asked.

"Nope."

"Sturgeon. Fuckers are massive, man. Bigger than some sharks. Over twenty feet."

"Fascinating."

"Been swimming these waters for millions of years, Doc. They're sneaky little bastards too. Bottom-feeders. They stay in the shadows. Hard to catch."

"I've heard that."

"I used to fish. Been a long time."

"You've been too busy having fun."

Scottie laugh-coughed. "Guess so."

He sat back down in his chair.

"There was another car," I said.

"Huh?"

"Besides the Escalade. A young girl in a silver 4Runner."

"Really?"

"She sat there and watched you guys with a pair of binoculars. Then she sped off right behind the Escalade."

"Weird."

"Seen her or that car before?"
"Don't think so."
Scottie closed his eyes again. This was going nowhere.
"Well, I better call it a night," I said. "Thanks for the drink."
Scottie held up his empty beer bottle.
"Thanks for the company, Doc," he said.

# CHAPTER 5

"A private investigator?" Grace Chen said.

Callie sat in her lap with a pro wrestler's grip on her morning bottle.

"Yes, ma'am," I said. "Just started."

"Oh my, how interesting."

Ryan looked up from her Mac and rolled her eyes. I decided this wasn't the best time to share last night's events in Sausalito.

"May I ask how you got into this line of work?" Grace said.

"Guess I like to keep people at arm's length," I said.

We were all in the living room trying not to trip over each other. Ryan liked to call our place "diminutive-chic." I stuck with just "diminutive." It was a thousand-square-foot house on Stockton a few blocks from Coit Tower, with a little stairway walk-up from the street. For a baby and two adults—now three—it felt like a two-bedroom bathroom.

Grace smiled at Ryan and looked down at Callie.

"What about these two?"

"They're exceptions," I said.

Ryan was slumped in the media lounger that took up half the room, sipping coffee in one hand, surfing email in the other. Grace and I sat with Callie on the living room couch, her guest bed for the week.

"I've never met a private investigator before," Grace said.

"You thought I'd be taller," I said.

"No, you're plenty tall. Ryan only told me you were, um, between careers."

"He is," Ryan said, staring at her Mac.

Ryan still had on her UGGs and pink pajamas. Her brunette hair was in pigtails. Soon she'd shower and transform into Corporate Boss in a two-piece blazer set. She could out-glam Gal Gadot when she put her mind to it. Sadly, those days had grown sporadic in the Callie Era. There was a time when early mornings together meant clothing-optional around the house, preferably none. Now foreplay meant yawning at each other before a nap.

Grace Chen was attractive and chatty, probably around sixty, with streaks of gray in her shoulder-length dark hair. She wore pink-framed eyeglasses and a swaggy night nurse uniform: navy scrubs and white Jordan 3s with pink trim.

"I like your shoe game," I said to Grace.

"Why, thank you. I was a nurse for twenty-eight years in Oakland. I've learned the value of comfortable feet."

Callie choked the bottle with both hands and scowled at Grace. I knew that look. It was a "Where the fuck has this been?" look.

"I couldn't pry this away from her with a crowbar," Grace said.

Brown follicles had begun to sprout near the front of Callie's adorable little head like a receding hairline on a middle-aged dude. She had fledgling hair everywhere except for a big bald spot in the back. I asked the pediatrician why it looked like grass died under a flowerpot. She assured me it was the result of being on her back so much. Ryan had told me to shut up and insisted that Callie wouldn't have a hollow square back there forever.

"A private investigator," Grace said again. "That is just so interesting. Were you a police officer?"

"No, ma'am."

"Oh. I kind of figured that's the logical stepping stone for that kind of work."

"It is."

"So what did you do before?"

"I was a reporter for the *Chronicle*."

"I see. Did you cover crime?"

"Yes, and some courts, and the Giants for a day."

"One day?"

"Four hours, to be exact."

"What happened?"

"Guy threatened to chuck a baseball at my head."

"Why?"

"He gave up six runs in the first inning. After the game I asked him if he'd ever considered retirement."

"I see," Grace said. "Well, that is quite the résumé."

"Thank you."

"I'm sorry to pry. I'm here on baby business, aren't I? We're giving her those gas drops after every bottle. And we'll work her legs after she sits up for a while."

"Work her legs?"

"Stretch them out a little."

"And that does what, exactly?"

"Helps digestion," Grace said. "My guess is she's had too much milk sloshing around that little belly. That's why she can't sleep."

"We're feeding her too much," Ryan said without looking up.

I glanced at Callie in Grace's lap. Her face did look a little puffy.

"We mostly give her a bottle every three hours," I said.

Grace smiled. "Mostly?"

"Well, sometimes she goes Norma Bates on us and we'll give her a little snack."

"Norma Bates?"

"Shower scene in *Psycho*."

"Interesting comparison."

"That's what I told him," Ryan said without looking up.

"How much is a 'little' snack?" Grace asked.

"Maybe half a bottle," I said.

"Too much. We need to stick to three and a half hours. Three at the very minimum."

"That all makes sense. But here's the thing: I don't like seeing her cry."

"Classic girl dad," Grace said. "She wiggled around your finger the moment you held her, didn't she?"

"Guilty," I said.

The bottle was empty. Callie had inhaled every drop. She took a deep breath and stared off into the deep recesses of the wall, her eyes glassy.

*Milk drunk.*

Ryan closed her laptop and smiled warmly at Grace.

"She's got some Michelin Man arms, doesn't she? We don't want her floating away, Charlie. May I have our little peanut?"

Grace carefully handed Callie to Ryan. Callie didn't complain. Mom and a full belly were the perfect combo.

Ryan kissed Callie's nose and whispered, slowly, her favorite word of the week: "Soft."

Callie giggled.

"*Sawwwft,*" Ryan said, slower this time.

Callie giggled again. I did too, before catching myself and clearing my throat.

"Makes your heart lift, doesn't it?" Grace said.

"Works every time," Ryan said.

Ryan held Callie against her chest for a burpfest. Grace was studying the circles under Ryan's green eyes.

"You guys look tired," she said.

Ryan yawned. I yawned.

"Maybe a little," I said.

"Why don't you take a nap?"

"Unfortunately, work calls for me," Ryan said. "And Charlie may have to fetch a cat from a tree."

"Well, I'm here so you guys can keep your same routine," Grace said. "And *sleep*! Callie needs all your neurons and transmitters firing."

"Neurons?" I said.

"Oh, just nurse-speak. I tend to babble. All these years of night-owling, coffee-slurping, what have you, I'm afraid it's left me a little birdbrained. I'll just talk and talk, stream of consciousness. My husband calls it 'perpetually punch-drunk.'"

"I think I have that too," Ryan said. "Are you sure the couch foldout is okay?"

"Oh, yes. I'm used to sleeping anywhere. My last job was in the North Bay. The family was repainting the house in the middle of bringing their little girl home for the first time. Can you imagine? The place stank. I slept on the floor of the nursery."

Ryan raised her eyebrows at me, which was code for, "Get off your ass and do something."

"Let me grab some fresh blankets and pillowcases," I said.

I lumbered across the butterscotch hardwood floors to the hallway closet. Every inch of the place was hardwood. Most spots creaked. Not ideal for parental stealth.

"Your home is just delightful," I heard Grace say.

"Thank you," Ryan said. "A little small. Correction: it's a *lot* small. But it was paid for. My aunt left this to me when she died."

"I see. Well, the smaller the home, the closer the family, I always say."

"I wish we could be close with just a wee bit of personal space," Ryan said. "So, you mentioned you were a nurse for thirty years?"

"Twenty-eight years and six months," Grace said. "UCSF Children's."

"What drew you to agency work?"

"COVID, unfortunately. Wasn't comfortable in hospitals anymore. One of my three grandchildren is diabetic. Couldn't risk it. Broke my heart. Those were my other grandkids, you know?"

"I know exactly what you mean," Ryan said. "I'd run barefoot on broken glass to keep Callie safe."

I came back with the bedding and set it on one of the couch arms.

"All clean, at your service. Better than the Ritz."

"Thank you," Grace said. "Now, after work I want to hear how you two met. And your adventures as a gumshoe."

"First part's a long story."

"I see. Were you at Stanford too?"

"Not exactly."

Ryan laughed. I ignored her.

"And the second part would put you to sleep."

"I don't believe that in the slightest. The whole thing sounds quite exciting. Don't you think, Ryan?"

"I'm still trying to understand it," Ryan said. "Following people, snooping around, getting into their personal business. Seems like you're asking to get punched or shot."

"We've been over this. One, I'm helping with the bills. Two—present company excluded, Grace—people are bad. People are selfish. They do bad things—to themselves, to each other. I kind of enjoy making sure there's some consequence for it."

"Oh, I get it," Ryan said. "You're Batman."

"No, I think I understand," Grace said. "You've come across a lot of bad people during your time as a journalist."

"I have."

"And instead of simply writing about them, this job allows you to take some measure of action."

"It does."

"I hear Ryan is a marketing expert," Grace said. "Perhaps she could help promote your business."

"Ryan could market a door hinge. But I'm not self-employed. I work for a man named Powell. He was an inspector with the city police."

"Powell," Grace repeated. "He sounds familiar."

"He's had some high-profile cases."

"Oh, I do know him. He won the Medal of Valor, didn't he? For catching that serial killer in Pac Heights?"

"That's how we met."

"You covered that in the paper?"

"Yes, ma'am."

"I'm sure I saw your byline. It was all over the TV for weeks. My goodness."

"Glad it's over," I said.

Callie was zonked out, her mouth wide open. She was too small to snore, but her body gave its best effort by inhaling audible little puffs of air.

"Well, do what you love. That's also what I always say," Grace said. "If COVID taught us anything, it's not to waste time on things that make you miserable."

We all got quiet again, watching Callie sleep.

Then Grace said, "I've watched thousands of babies join this world. I've been serving parents of this community for thirty years. Some are rich. Some are poor. Some are kind. Some are not. Some are self-absorbed. Most all of them are just plain scared."

"Glad to know we're not alone," I said.

"The three of you are going to be just fine. And I assure you, Charlie: Nobody's perfect, but not everyone in this world is evil."

"I don't have any scientific evidence to support this," I said, "but I imagine that parents of daughters are the best of us."

"Daughters are good influences," Grace said. "I raised two."

"I knew I liked you," I said.

# CHAPTER 6

Callie and I had the house to ourselves. Ryan had driven Mango to the office. Grace Chen had gone home to grab another change of clothes and to the grocery store for "diaper cream and some dinner ingredients," she said. Thankfully, those items were mutually exclusive.

Callie was sitting in her *Finding Nemo* baby jumper. Retail: 130 bucks. For a sleepy, slightly hungover dad: priceless. It was a 360-degree distraction machine with characters on all sides: Dory, Crush the sea turtle, Bruce the great white shark, Mr. Ray affixed overhead like a heat lamp, and of course, Nemo floating in a plastic case. You could spin Nemo like the wheel on *The Price Is Right* and the case would light up and make bubbling underwater sounds. Callie wasn't ready for that part yet. She mostly just stared holes in Sheldon the seahorse. Seemed personal.

I called Powell.

"Just downloaded some photos from the camera and sent them to you," I said.

I'd caught him in mid-chew.

"Hang on a sec," he said.

Callie had turned her attention to *Mickey Mouse Clubhouse* on TV. Mickey, Minnie, Donald, and Daisy were scaling a mountain-sized piece of candy corn. No Pluto in this one. Over Christmas, Callie and I watched a Mickey special where the gang went on a holiday cruise. There was no Pluto in that one either. It ruined my viewing experience. Did they forget him? Decide to leave him at home? Was he sad? Who let him out and fed him? I needed my social life back.

Powell looked over the pictures. Finally he said, "Mrs. Wellington, you got some explaining to do."

"Yep."

"Good work."

"Good enough for Arthur Wellington?"

"Let's hope so. Did you get a license plate number on lover boy?"

"I never saw his car. But I'll do you one better. His name's Scottie Coburn. He's renting that houseboat in Sausalito. He's twenty-seven years old. Wears toxic cologne. I think I can still smell it from here. He's an executive at Rivet Security, some tech company. They've got office space in the 5M district."

"Scottie Coburn?"

"Yes. C-o-b-u-r-n. You gonna tell Wellington?"

"Yes."

"You should probably tell him his wife is screwing a guy who might wind up dead. I'm sending one more picture your way."

I texted Powell the pic of Snake Tat standing over Scottie in the parking lot.

"Who the hell is this?" Powell asked.

"Was hoping maybe you'd recognize him. Looks like a professional goon."

"I can't really tell. The picture's blurry."

"I was in a hurry trying to take it. He's got a neck tattoo of two interlocking snakes."

"When was this taken?"

"Right after Mrs. Wellington left. This guy showed up a couple hours after me. Must've been waiting for them to come out. When Mrs. Wellington drove away, he got out and beat Scottie to a pulp. Said to Scottie, quote, 'Stay the fuck away from her.'"

"What was he driving?"

"Black Escalade."

"Plates?"

"Nope, he had some sort of cover on them. You think Mrs. Wellington could be having an affair with this guy too? Maybe he caught her with Scottie and snapped."

"A guy with a giant snake tattoo on his neck seems like an odd choice for a woman like Mrs. Wellington," Powell said.

"So is a twentysomething bro like Scottie," I said. "Maybe Mr. Wellington already knew about Scottie and sent this guy to tune him up."

"If Wellington already knew about Scottie, there'd be no reason for him to hire us."

"True."

"Maybe Scottie has more than one married lover, which would mean more than one jealous husband," Powell said.

"I don't think so," I said. "When we chatted, he only mentioned Mrs. Wellington. I think he's smitten."

"You talked to Scottie?"

"I helped him up and got him inside. He was in rough shape. Maybe a cracked rib."

"You can't talk to the person you're tailing," Powell said. "That's Gumshoe 101 stuff."

"I told Scottie I'm his neighbor. He thinks I do boob jobs for a living. He probably won't remember much, anyway. When I left, he was finishing off a bag of purple kush."

"You smoked weed with him?"

"Just a beer. And three slices of pizza. Took a picture of his driver's license."

Powell chewed on that for a moment.

"Pretty slick," he said. "Any idea where they met?"

"He said it was some cocktail party, a work function. They met at the Zephyr hotel a couple nights ago because she wanted a quickie."

"I need to talk to Mr. Wellington," Powell said.

"That won't be an easy conversation."

"It never is. But he hired us to provide information. He understands it may not be pleasant."

"There's something else," I said. "Another car appeared to be following the Escalade. Couple spaces down from me."

"Another car?"

"Young girl, probably just passed her driver's test. Sat in her car a long time. Seemed odd, so I got out and talked with her just before the fight. She had a black eye. I asked if she needed any help."

"Did you get a name?"

"No. She said she was looking for someone. I didn't find out who. But get this: She pulled out a pair of binoculars to watch the whole fight. The Escalade left, then she left. If she wasn't slightly older than Callie, I'd swear it was a tail job."

"Description of her car?"

"Silver 4Runner. Oregon plates. *CY-something.* You know any teenage PIs?"

"No," Powell said. "I'm gonna talk to Wellington and show him your pictures. See if SFPD can identify the man who assaulted Scottie. He might have a record. Wellington might like to know that violent people are aware of, and perhaps involved in, his wife's affairs. Best case, it's a potential PR problem for a very prominent family. Worst case, she might be in danger hanging around this guy."

"What about Nancy Drew?"

"Track down her plates. Maybe she knows who this guy is."

"Sure, boss."

"And after that, get some sleep."

"I can't sleep till Callie does."

"Guess you're screwed, then."

I peeled myself off the couch and stretched. Every ligament in my body cracked and said, "What the fuck, Charlie?" After twelve hours in the car yesterday, I felt like somebody had removed me from a carry-on and unfolded me.

Sheldon the seahorse must've mouthed off to Callie. She turned to him, slowly—as she did everything at this point—and eyeballed him. She reached out with a closed fist and cracked him on his three-inch nose.

I was watching the most wholesome fight of all time. Better than the mess I'd seen last night.

# CHAPTER 7

I called Inspector Joseph Whitmore with the San Francisco Police Department. Instead of "Joseph" or "Joe" or "Inspector Whitmore," I mostly called him "Tex." Tex was from Sacramento, not Texas, but he was the only person I'd met in California with an accent anywhere close to mine. He was two inches taller than me, long-limbed and lumbering like Big Tex at the State Fair, with an easy smile and a sharper mind.

"Charlie Shaw," he said. "Piss anyone off yet today?"

"Still early," I said. "Remember the two favors you owe me?"

"For what?"

"For the two dates Ryan and I set you up on."

"The first girl hated me. The second one never stopped talking. What do you want?"

"Last night I tailed a guy who got jumped outside his house. Some goon beat him up."

"Robbery?"

"Only thing he stole was my guy's teeth."

"Be careful with this private dick stuff," Tex said. "You really wanna get shot for a few bucks?"

"Not especially," I said. "If I text you a picture, can you ask around the station, see if anyone recognizes him? Guy's got a neck tattoo of two snakes."

"Send me the picture. What's the second favor?"

"Help me run a partial plate on a car."

"What's in it for me?"

"I'll set you up with the girl of your dreams."

"Only if Ryan picks her," Tex said. "And you don't get a say."

"Done."

"Give me the car info."

"Silver 4Runner, older model, maybe late aughts. Oregon plates. Starts with *CY*."

"Give me the rest."

"That's all I got. Curious if it's ever been flagged in your system."

"Okay," Tex said. "But the computer's gonna spit out a haystack. This your first case with Inspector Powell?"

"Yep."

"How do you like detecting so far?"

"I have no idea what I'm doing," I said. "Can you get back to me today?"

"I'll see what I can do," Tex said. "I'm a homicide detective, remember? We're not exactly sitting around eating Cheetos up here."

I went to the kitchen and poured another cup of tea. I didn't like coffee. Tea got the job done and tasted better. I sat on the floor in front of Callie. Grace had dressed her in a sleeveless denim onesie with a pink headband. Her giant, curious green eyes bugged out at me. They were less crossed than last week. Her arms still had what I called "baby muscles"—rolls that made her arms look like baguettes.

She put her hand on my nose and felt around. No fist. She liked me, I guess.

"You're kinda cute," I said. "Wanna go on another stakeout?"

Twenty minutes later, after I'd fumbled around and packed the essentials—diapers, diaper cream, baby wipes, burp cloths, a fresh change of clothes, and freshly made formula from the Baby Brezza—we were on the road back to Sausalito, this time in Ryan's Highlander.

Turns out I didn't need any of that stuff. Callie had fallen asleep before we'd gotten out of North Beach. A while back, I'd read an article about Ford Motor Company designing a bassinet that mimics a car's movements. Sounded pretty cool. But nothing worked faster or better than driving Callie around the block myself.

When we reached Herring Harbor, I backed into a different space facing the entrance. I kept the engine running and the AC on for Callie. The parking lot was practically empty on a weekday morning. Fifteen minutes passed. Thirty. An hour. I didn't see Mrs. Wellington or Scottie Coburn. I didn't see Snake Tat or his black Escalade. I didn't see the mystery girl or her silver 4Runner.

I was getting hungry again. I'd forgotten to pack something for myself again. Callie's formula did not sound appealing. Seagulls loitered on a houseboat roof. Probably discussing lunch too.

*"Gugblueeeeeeeeee."*

Callie was up. An impressive pool of drool had accumulated on the chest of her onesie. I got out the burp cloth and dabbed at it.

*"Arrrrrrrrrrrgh!"* Callie said, as if she were charging a bunker.

"Hi there, sweetheart," I said.

*"Oh-wah! Oh-wah! Oh-wah!"*

She'd turned her siren on. I put the car in drive and headed back home. The "*Oh-wahs*" lasted in perfect succession for the full twenty-five minutes. I offered her a fresh formula bottle. She smacked it onto the floor. I texted Ryan.

**She won't stop crying.**

> You gotta hold her.

**I'm driving.**

> Guess you're screwed then.

Tex called as I parked the car downhill in front of our house on Stockton.

"No one here recognizes the guy with the snake tattoo," he said.

Callie had cranked up the volume again.

"Tex, you'll have to speak up, please," I shouted.

"What's that in the background?"

"Callie."

"She's adorable."

"I know. Let me call you back."

I unbuckled Callie and grabbed her diaper bag and all her travel items—enough for a weeklong vacation—and we climbed the steps inside. Thankfully, Grace was back.

"There's our little angel," she said. "You guys go for a drive?"

"As long as Callie could stand it. I'm so sorry, but I've gotta hand her off."

"Still on the case?"

"Yeah. She just had a nap, but we need a new onesie. And I'm pretty sure a diaper change too."

"Can do," Grace said. "Good luck out there."

I kissed Callie's forehead as she screamed in my face. I went back outside and called Tex.

"Girl's got some pipes," he said. "Like I was saying, nobody recognizes the guy with the snake tat."

"Damn."

"And there's too many plate results on the silver 4Runner you're looking for."

"Damn."

"But a patrol officer found an abandoned silver 4Runner on Watercrest Boulevard around nine this morning. Both tires on the left side were popped."

"Boom," I said. "Where?"

"At 857 Watercrest. House around the corner from the harbor. Lady in the house called and complained. Had never seen that car before. Thought it looked suspicious. Said it was blocking her driveway this morning."

"Was it?"

"Not enough to keep her from getting out."

"Towed?"

"Nah. If it's still there tomorrow, they'll slap one of those orange stickers on it."

"License plate?"

"CYM8530. Car belongs to a Patricia Jiang, 3401 Fishpond in Salem, Oregon."

"Spell her last name, please?"

"J-i-a-n-g."

"Thank you, Tex."

"Now I've got a question for you, Charlie. Why did you want to find this Patricia Jiang?"

"She was parked next to me last night. Appeared to be staking out the same people."

"Very interesting," Tex said.

"Why?"

"Patricia Jiang has been dead for over a week."

# CHAPTER 8

Patricia Jiang had lived in a modest ranch-style home in Salem, Oregon—a one-story, two-bedroom house with vinyl siding and a crooked walkway to the front door shielded by a ratty-looking screen. I entered "3401 Fishpond" into Zillow's search engine and found a picture of the house. The front yard lacked any sign of landscaping. The grass looked spotty and sick. Zillow valued the house at over half a million bucks. Life on the West Coast.

Tex and I found an obituary online that said Patricia Jiang died of complications from COVID at age forty-one. The obit said Patricia Jiang was survived by only three people: a married sister, Alice Jones; a brother-in-law, Michael Jones; and a daughter named Friday. No mention of a husband or life partner.

With no foul play involved, Tex lost interest pretty quickly.

"If her daughter's old enough, she's probably the one driving the car now," he said.

An online search for "Alice and Michael Jones" yielded far too many results. I expected better luck with the daughter, "Friday Jiang," but found nothing. I searched "Friday Jiang" on social media and found nothing. I found the phone number for 3401 Fishpond in Salem, Oregon, and dialed Patricia Jiang's home. No answer.

I went back to Google Maps and clicked on its street-view function. I zoomed in on the house next door to Patricia Jiang's and wrote down its address. I found that phone number online and dialed. A woman answered.

"Hello?"

"Hi. Is Friday home, please?"

"Friday?"

"Yes. She lives at 3401 Fishpond. This is her friend Johnny."

I did my best to sound Friday's age, whatever that was.

"Hi, Johnny," the woman said. "You're looking for the house next door. Would you like the number?"

"Oh, I'm terribly sorry. Sure."

She gave it to me.

"Thank you," I said. "Have you seen Friday recently?"

"Uh, no. Not for a couple days, at least."

"I heard her mom passed. I'm trying to send my condolences."

"Oh, yes. Just awful. I'm afraid we haven't seen Friday much since her mother got very sick."

"Were you close to them, ma'am?"

"I'm afraid not. Patricia . . . Well, she kept to herself. And we don't have any children Friday's age."

"I see."

"I'm worried what's going to happen to her. To lose your mother at sixteen? They were all each other had, as far as I knew."

"Sixteen?" I said.

"Yes. My heart breaks for her."

"Has there been a funeral or a service yet?"

"I'm not aware of a service. Are you a school friend?"

"A, uh, long-distance friend."

The silver 4Runner was still parked in front of 857 Watercrest. Indeed, both left tires were blown out. The SUV leaned slightly into the street like a tree pushed by wind. The left bumper had damage too. I got out and peered inside the windows. A half-empty water bottle and a fresh box of Raisinets sat on the front dash. A pink hair tie lay on the center console. A blanket covered the back seat and a pillow was propped against the right-side door. A large roller bag lay in the back trunk space.

"What are you doing?" a voice shouted.

A gray-haired woman in a lemon sweater and floral capris stood in the doorway with her hands on her hips.

"I'm from the tow company," I said.

"You're not wearing a uniform."

"It's my day off. But we're shorthanded today so I thought I'd have a look."

"Where's your truck?"

"Like I said, it's my day off."

"Oh," the woman said. "Well, I'd like it towed today. It's leaning into the street and it's blocking my driveway. Now your car is too."

"I'm very sorry."

"It doesn't have any right to park here. And I think a homeless person is squatting in there."

"Have you seen someone in the car?"

"No. It was empty when I got up this morning and no one has been back."

"I see."

"But you see the blankets and pillows."

"Yes, ma'am."

"I would appreciate it if someone at your company removed this vehicle from my property as soon as possible."

"Well, technically it's in the street, ma'am . . ."

"As soon as possible."

She turned and slammed the door.

Undeterred, I went back to my car, took out the picnic blanket Ryan and I brought to Alamo Square a couple of weeks ago, and crossed the street to the big grassy field. I was tired of sitting in my car, and if I was going to wait, I preferred to keep my jeans clean. I sat on the blanket and watched the road with my back to the water. Seagulls squawked. Cyclists passed, some with helmets, some without, some dressed like Lance Armstrong, some not, all probably thankful for a flat patch of land. To my left, yacht masts poked skyward in the harbor like giant TV antennas.

I checked my phone. No messages. I checked Callie's crib. She'd gone back to sleep. I yawned.

Some time went by. The garage door at 857 Watercrest opened. Out came a white Cadillac. The old lady had decided to risk leaving home even with the mysterious car out front. Cats were less skittish after a thunderstorm. I yawned again. Maybe I could get away with a quick catnap. Maybe I was wasting my time here.

I decided to give it fifteen more minutes. I was setting my phone alarm when the girl came into view, approaching the 4Runner from the direction of the yacht club, wearing a backpack. She was tall and slender, at least five foot seven, with lanky arms and long legs and big feet that she hadn't quite grown into yet. She wore gray joggers over white Chucks and a gray denim jacket over a Nirvana smile T-shirt. Her stride was unconfident, indecisive, the way freshmen kids shuffle around college campuses. It was not the composed walk of a self-assured young woman, not the bouncy strut of Deborah Wellington. It was the lonely walk of a girl far from home.

I stood, grabbed the blanket, and headed for the street.

The girl was carrying a CVS bag in one hand and a fast-food paper cup in the other. She sipped from the straw. When I reached the curb, I called out to her.

# CHAPTER 9

"Friday?"

She almost dropped the cup. She froze and stared at me.

"Friday Jiang?"

She darted toward the car. She set the bag and cup on the hood, popped the backpack off her shoulder, and rummaged through it. She took out her keys. Thankfully not Mace or a gun.

Ryan's words echoed in my head. *Please be careful.*

The girl reached for the car door.

"Please, one moment," I said. "I'm a friend."

She stopped. I let another cyclist go by and crossed the street.

"Well, I'm not a friend yet. I mean, I'm friendly. Jesus, that sounded weird. I'm trying to say that I just want to help you."

"Help me?"

"Yes."

I stopped at the car. She had turned to fully face me. Her right eye now had a full-on shiner. The puffy red skin below it was turning dark purple.

"You're that guy," she said. "The guy who came up to my window last night."

"The private investigator. Yes. My name is Charlie Shaw."

"What do you want from me, man?"

"I was following the guy who got beat up by that big goon in the parking lot. You saw it happen too."

"I didn't see anything."

"You had binoculars. First you told me you were looking for

someone. Then you watched the fight. I think you were following the goon in the Escalade, except you're a little young for private detective work."

"Leave me alone."

She opened the car door.

"You're not gonna get far in that thing," I said. "Just saying."

I noticed her back muscles move a little. I heard her sniff. She faced me again. A tear rolled past the purple swollen part below her eye and down her cheek. She brushed it away angrily like a horse swatting a fly.

"I know," she said. "Car's in worse shape than it looks."

"More than just the tires?"

"I think the axle's busted too."

"How'd it happen?"

"I hit a pothole somewhere back there. Lost control and hit a guardrail."

"You left that parking lot in a hurry."

She nodded.

"Driving too fast?"

"Yeah. I wanted to get away from there."

"You were scared?"

She nodded again.

I rechecked the bumper again. There was a huge dent on the left side. Some of the silver paint had been scraped off on impact.

"Were you hurt at all?"

"I'm fine," she said.

"Oregon plates. You drive down here from Oregon?"

"Wow. You're some detective, man."

"Not really. You think the axle's busted?"

"Yeah. The car started making this grinding noise. I could barely get it up the street to here."

"We can get this taken care of."

"We?"

"Yeah."

"I don't have any . . ."

"Money? I know. You hungry? My favorite diner's a couple miles that way, the direction you came from. You won't have to walk this time."

"I just ate."

"When's the next time you'll eat?"

She looked at the ground.

"I'm not homeless," she said. "I'm just . . . stuck here."

"I know. We can talk about that too."

She studied her left hand. She picked at her middle cuticle, checking for a broken nail.

"I don't know," she said. "This is how girls end up on *Dateline*."

"I showed you my PI license. Wanna see it again?"

I offered it to her. This time she took it.

"Could be a fake," she said, and handed it back to me.

I pulled out my phone and opened my camera roll.

"I live in North Beach," I said. "Direction of my favorite diner. This is my wife, Ryan. She's a marketing executive. She's a lot smarter than me. This is my daughter, Callie. She's a lot smarter than me too."

She studied the picture. It was taken three months ago at Cupid's Span. Ryan and I stood on either side of Callie's stroller. Callie was asleep, of course.

"Your daughter's adorable."

"I know."

"Your wife is pretty too."

"I know."

"Doesn't mean anything, though. You could still be a creep."

"All right, fine."

I took out my phone and ran a Google Images search for my old staff photo at the *Chronicle*.

"I used to work at the paper," I said, and showed her the picture. "Crime reporter."

Then I pulled up the SFPD website.

"I got to know some people at the police department. Contacts for stories, that sort of thing. Here's the number for the SFPD. See? I'm calling it now."

I put the phone on speaker mode. When prompted by the automated answering service, I pressed the buttons for Tex's extension.

"Inspector Whitmore."

"Tex, Charlie Shaw again."

"Jesus. Am I getting paid overtime for all this?"

"No more favors needed. Listen, I'm at 857 Watercrest. I'm here with a girl by the name of Friday Jiang . . ."

"Finley," Friday said. "Friday Finley."

"Your last name is Finley?"

She nodded.

"Okay, I'm here with Friday Finley. The silver 4Runner belongs to her. The car is still broken down on Watercrest and I'm trying to assist her. She is reticent. Thinks I might have ulterior motives. She's seen too many *Dateline* episodes."

"Me too," Tex said. "Am I on speaker?"

"Yes."

"Miss . . . Finley, is it? Friday Finley?"

"Yes?"

"This is Inspector Joseph Whitmore with the SFPD. We need you to please move your car from the area as soon as possible. Hopefully this is a minor inconvenience for you with minimal damage."

Friday rolled her eyes.

"You can trust Mr. Shaw to help you secure towing service. From what I understand, Mr. Shaw may have some questions about some case that I have zero interest in myself. Just don't laugh at his bad jokes. It only encourages him."

"I save the best ones for Ryan," I said.

"Oh, and Miss Finley—are you there?"

"Yes."

"Mr. Shaw and I ran your license plate and found your name

online. We, uh, read that your mother passed away about a week ago?"

Friday's jaw dropped. She gaped at me.

"Yes," she whispered.

"My condolences. If you need further assistance, this is my direct line at the department. Charlie, you still there?"

"Still here," I said.

"Can I go back to work now?"

"Absolutely. Thank you, Inspector."

I put the phone back in my pocket.

"I'm sorry about your mom too," I said. "Inspector Whitmore and I saw her obituary online. I was waiting for the right time to mention it."

Friday had kind, thoughtful eyes, but now there was a glint of intensity in them, like a flame crackling underneath a stove. Her voice rose. It stopped just below a shout.

"The right time? How do you know all this stuff about me? You called the fucking cops on me?"

"I didn't call the cops *on* you. I'm investigating the man we saw get beat up. In my business, any information is good information. I wanna know why you were there too."

"Yeah? And who the hell are *you*, man?"

"Charlie Shaw. I'm a private investigator . . ."

Friday held up a hand at me as if to say, "Yeah, you told me already. Shut the fuck up." So I did.

A stiff wind gust hit us both. She put her hands in her pockets and looked at the ground.

"Free tow. Free meal. Your choice," I said. "If not, best of luck. Hope whatever's in that bag lasts you awhile."

Friday snapped her head up. There were tears in her eyes again.

"I didn't do anything wrong," she said. "I don't know anything about what happened last night. I don't know who that big guy was. I'm just trying to find my dad, okay?"

"Your dad?"

"Yeah."
"Maybe I can help."
"Why would you bother?"
I shrugged.
"Because I'm a dad too," I said.

# CHAPTER 10

The Fog City restaurant was on the Embarcadero directly across from the string of piers that famously poke out onto the Bay. It looked like a forties diner with its long rectangular architecture and exposed pipes and beams and wood bar countertops around an open kitchen.

Friday Finley and I sat in a leather-coated booth with a view of the waterfront. She hadn't said a word since we'd left Watercrest Boulevard. I'd made a couple of menu suggestions, specifically the salmon sandwich on toast and lime pie for dessert. She ignored me and ordered a cheeseburger and fries and a Diet Coke. I took my own advice on the sandwich and ordered unsweet iced tea. The waitress noticed Friday's black eye and shot me a suspicious look before leaving the table.

Friday continued to say nothing. Normally, I didn't mind silence. It's probably why I liked working for Dwayne Powell. Subconsciously, even though I loved Callie more than life itself, I probably enjoyed some time away from the screaming and the pooping and the spitting up. Occasional dad silence was welcome. Friday's silence bothered me. I felt like I'd betrayed her trust even though I'd only known her thirty minutes.

"What's your favorite Nirvana song?" I asked Friday.

"What?"

"Your T-shirt."

"Oh. I just liked the logo."

"I guess you were like minus-fifteen years old when they broke up."

"'Minus-fifteen'?"

"Never mind."

It was just after five p.m. and young professionals were filling up the place. Across the way, a set of parents and their two children, a boy and a girl, strolled west down the Embarcadero. The boy had an orange Giants foam finger on his left hand. I forgot the Giants had a getaway game against Colorado. I checked the score. Lost again, 6–4. At least they kept it under ten runs.

The food arrived. Friday Finley was hungrier than she'd let on. The burger was half-gone by the time I'd nibbled two bites of the salmon.

"Good?" I asked.

She nodded.

"Friday Finley," I said. "You go by Finley. Not Jiang."

She swallowed and frowned and looked down at her plate.

"It's my dad's name," she said. "My mom went back to her maiden name, Jiang, after they got divorced."

"What's your dad's first name?"

"Shawn."

"Shawn Finley?"

"Yes."

"Have you seen him since your mother died?"

"I haven't seen him since I was ten."

"He lives here?"

"Yes."

"Did you arrange to meet him here? Stay with him?"

"No. I don't know exactly where he lives. I tried to look it up. He hasn't been answering his phone for a week."

"You drove six hundred miles without knowing how to find him?"

"Yeah," she said sheepishly.

"Is there anyone else in your family who could confirm that he's here? Find an address?"

"No," she said flatly.

I decided to stop pressing. I had a bite of my sandwich. Friday noticed. Sensing a break in the conversation, she took another big bite of her burger. She glanced out the window at the Embarcadero, lined with more tourists and residents enjoying the late-afternoon sunshine.

"I take Callie on walks there," I said. "It's kind of a tourist trap, but not if you go early enough in the morning."

"My father's a loser," she said, still staring out the window.

"I'm sorry to hear that."

She turned her head back to me.

"He's had a drinking problem since I was little. He's had a gambling problem. He's been in jail."

"For what?"

"Little stuff, I think."

"Little stuff?"

"He'd get into fights when he lived with us. Drunk fights."

"Did he ever hit your mom?"

"No."

"Did he ever hit you?"

"No."

"When did he leave you and your mom?"

"When I was ten. First he moved to Portland to find work, and I guess that didn't work, so he tried California."

"What does he do for a living?"

"He works on cars. Or he used to, anyway."

"Mechanic?"

"Yeah."

"He taught you about cars?"

"Yeah."

"Good profession."

"If you can stay sober enough to keep it," Friday said. "He never could."

"When was the last time he was in jail?"

"I dunno. He could be there right now for all I know."

"You lost touch with him?"

"My mom did. I talk to him every now and then."

"When did you last speak with him?"

"I called him the day my mom died. She'd been in the hospital a couple days. Pneumonia. I told him that my aunt from New Jersey paid for her to be cremated. I asked if he could help me plan a service. He said he'd send money and come home soon. Said he had something very important lined up and would be out of pocket for a little while. He was very cryptic about it. Sounded like he was in a hurry."

"Was there a service for your mom?"

"Not yet. Couple days went by and I called him again. He didn't answer. I've been trying him for a week."

"Did he send you any money?"

"No."

"When your mom passed, did anybody from the city arrange for possible foster care?"

She huffed at "foster care."

"No. The hospital said they would contact CPS or something, but I haven't heard from them. I can take care of myself."

Something in her face and tone made me believe her. The waitress came by and handed Friday a reusable ice pack.

"It looks like it hurts," she said.

"It doesn't," Friday muttered.

The waitress looked at me. "How'd it happen?"

"She's not telling."

"He didn't hit me," Friday said, "if that's what you're getting at."

The waitress looked at her and then at me.

"All right, then," she said. "You guys need anything?"

"We're fine. Thank you," I said.

She shot me one more look before moving to the next table.

"Okay," I said to Friday. "I get it. You can take care of yourself. You gotta eat, though. That requires dough."

"I had my mom's credit card, but it got declined on the way down here. I had a little cash that my aunt sent. It wasn't much. They weren't close and she's not rich. She has four kids of her own."

"They didn't offer for you to stay with them?"

"No. I've stayed with friends some nights, or at least had dinner with them or taken something back to the house."

"Got any brothers, sisters, anybody else who could help?"

"No."

"How much money you got left?"

"I was broke until this afternoon. Now, maybe fifteen bucks and some change."

"From Pier Thirty-nine?"

"Yeah. How'd you know?"

"Good place to ask for cash. Tourists everywhere."

"I read about it before driving down here," she said. "I sat on a bench by the main entrance. Most people probably thought I was a junkie. Some were nice, though."

I pictured sixteen-year-old Friday Finley, gaunt, gawky, carrying around a swollen eye, begging strangers for lunch money.

"What's your plan now?"

"I don't know. Collect enough to buy a bus ticket home, maybe."

"No," I said.

"No?"

"I'm gonna call a tow service to get your car examined and fixed up. And I'm gonna do my best to find your father. Have you thought about filing a police report?"

"No," she said quickly. "No cops."

"Why not?"

"Because my dad's already got a record," she said. "God knows what he's been up to."

"All right," I said.

"You know I can't pay for the car," she said. "I don't know if I can ever pay you back for any of this."

"Ever babysat before?"

"No."

"It's easy. They're like grumpy cats. They sleep most of the day, anyway. Your burger's getting cold."

She looked down at her plate.

"You still haven't answered my original question," I said. "If you don't have an address for your dad, why were you in a random parking lot in Sausalito last night?"

Friday picked up the ice pack and pressed it against her eye.

"You were right. I was following that car," she said. "The black Escalade."

"Where'd you follow it from?"

"A bar my dad worked at," she said. "Called Cashel Rock."

"Castle Rock?"

"Cashel. C-a-s-h-e-l. Like the place in Ireland."

"Ireland, it is," I said. "Got a passport?"

# CHAPTER 11

Derryville was a fifteen-minute drive across the Bay Bridge from San Francisco, five miles north of Oakland. It was a small town of just over fifteen thousand, nestled against the East Bay with a direct sight line to the Golden Gate Bridge. I didn't know much about it other than the views were spectacular and the place had a reputation as a dump. Worse, the people in charge seemed to embrace its reputation as a dump.

Derryville historically had one of California's highest violent crime rates. Over the years investors saw the town's potential as a pleasant little seaside alcove and made some tepid attempts at renovation. A few tech start-ups set up shop. Most left. The downtown, once a modest collection of Victorian storefronts, got a facelift with a decent-looking promenade of shops and restaurants and a new ten-story hotel. But Derryville wasn't a tourist attraction. It never wanted to be. Mayors and council members and city managers changed but the town's complexion did not. It leaned into its scars. It wasn't a place for a sixteen-year-old girl to be staking out goons. It wasn't a place for me either.

Cashel Rock was a couple of blocks from the made-over downtown on a shabby corner next to a liquor store and a cell phone repair shop. The bar was a decent-sized rectangular establishment with a patio in front and Christmas lights strewn overhead. A bright red door offset the building's dark olive exterior. It had no discernable signage from the street, but a small red neon sign glowed *Cashel Rock* in the front window.

The parking lot was mostly empty when we pulled in just before seven. I parked the Highlander up front with a full view of the lot. A few cars were there. The black Escalade was not among them. Friday Finley didn't know what car Shawn Finley drove or if he had a car at all.

"Let's go over this again," I said. "Your dad specifically said he worked here?"

"Yes."

"When did he tell you that?"

"Last summer sometime. Said he was in between repair jobs but had found this bartending gig through somebody he knew and said he was doing okay. A couple months ago he called me on my birthday and said he was still here."

"When's your birthday?"

"March. He said he would send me a gift."

"Did he?"

"No."

I hadn't met this guy and I couldn't stand him.

"Did you call the bar to check on him before you left Oregon?"

"Yeah. Bunch of times. It just rang off the hook. No answering machine."

"So you drove down here and went inside and asked if your dad was around?"

"Yes. There were two guys in a booth doing paperwork or something."

"The guy with the snake tattoo?"

"No. These two guys had, like, reddish hair. They said my dad worked there but they didn't know where he went. Said they had to ask me to leave because I was underage. So I went back to my car and waited to see if my dad would show up."

"And he didn't."

"No."

"But you saw the guys in the booth get into the Escalade and go to Sausalito, so you followed."

"Yeah. The tattooed guy picked them up in front of the bar. If I'd seen his face, I don't think I would've followed him. He scared the hell out of me."

"Me too," I said. "I'd like a picture of your dad in case I need to show it around the bar. Do you have one on your phone?"

"Sure."

I told her my phone number. Her text popped up a few seconds later.

"Where was this taken?"

"Rockaway Beach in Pacifica," Friday said. "I was ten."

"Six years ago. Picture's recent enough."

"What are you gonna say in there?"

"Won't know till I say it," I said. "Keep the doors locked."

I tucked my sunglasses into my shirt collar and walked inside. The place was dark and cleaner and neater than I expected. The black walls looked like they'd received a coat of fresh paint. The walls were mostly spartan, but the bar was well-stocked with a florid arrangement of liquor bottles backlit behind the shelves. Over the bar hung the Irish flag, a large neon-green shamrock and a sign that read:

*Surely some revelation is at hand;*
*Surely the Second Coming is at hand.*

Four patrons were scattered along the bar on high-back wood chairs. A couple sat at a table near the bathroom. The bar had two TVs. One showed the World Series of Poker. The Giants game was on the other. "Cissy Strut" floated pleasantly through the speakers. A few feet away, two men with reddish-looking hair sat in a leather booth. The taller guy was working on a Mac computer. The shorter, stockier guy played on his phone.

I took a seat at the bar and glanced at the sticky laminated plastic menu. Google had given the food 4.3 stars. One review advised that I stay away from the corned beef. My stomach growled and took over my senses. I thought about ordering the fish-and-chips. Then I remembered I had a guest waiting in the car.

The bartender was dirty blond, slender, and attractive in an earthy way, with a stud in her nose and a stud in her belly button. She had big blue eyes and wore a low-cut white top and cut-off jean shorts that stopped just below her crotch. Her hair was up and dark at the roots. She was working on a tattoo sleeve on the inside of her right arm. It looked halfway finished. A silver cross hung from her neck.

"What can I get you?" she asked.

"Pacifico."

"You got it."

"Is your manager here?"

She pointed to the two guys in the booth.

"Thanks."

I left my beer on the bar and walked over to them. The tall guy on the computer looked like he was trying to solve a logarithm. He wore jeans and a white button-down shirt open at the chest with the sleeves rolled up. He had clear blue eyes and curly strawberry-blond hair cropped close with stubble over a strong chin. He wore a large gold watch on his right wrist and a gold cross around his neck.

The short guy next to him had the same strawberry-blond hair, but that's where the resemblance stopped. The tall guy was nice-looking. The short guy fell off the ugly tree and every branch got their licks in. He had a caveman forehead that sloped like Mount Davidson and a huge flat nose that seemed to cover half his face. His hair was shaved into a buzz cut. His hollow, beady eyes flashed no emotion or discernible intelligence. He wore a black track jacket zipped up only three-fourths of the way, exposing some unsightly chest hair.

"Hi there," I said.

They both ignored me. The tall guy stared at his computer. The short ugly guy stared at his phone.

"My name's Charlie Shaw. I'm a private investigator. I'm looking for one of your employees. Shawn Finley."

The short ugly guy said, "So?" without looking up. He had a high-pitched voice that didn't match his portly appearance.

"Shawn Finley's been out of pocket for about a week," I said. "His daughter can't reach him. She asked me to look for him. She was in here yesterday. Said you guys asked her to leave."

"I can't have minors in my bar," the tall guy said.

"And you are . . ."

"The owner."

"What about you?"

"The co-owner," the short ugly guy said.

"How about actual names?"

They ignored me. The tall guy made a couple of taps on his calculator and typed something on his Mac.

"Guess I need to file a missing person's report with my friends at the San Francisco Police Department."

The tall guy raised his eyes from the computer screen. He gave me a hard stare.

"Dunne," he said. "Colin Dunne."

He pointed to the short ugly guy. "This is my brother Ross."

"Pleased to meet you both. Now, about Shawn Finley. Is he a bartender here?"

"Yeah," Colin Dunne said.

"Does he still work here?"

"Yep."

"Is he here?"

"Nope."

"Got an address for him?"

"Nope."

"Nothing on file?"

Colin smiled patronizingly.

"No," he said. "Nothing on file."

"Shawn's daughter hasn't seen him in six years. Her mother just died. She needs her dad. I'd like to give her some sort of a lead. Any idea when he'll be back?"

"Nope," Colin said.

"A shift schedule for him? Something?"

Ross Dunne finished staring at his phone. He set it on the table.

"You're like a fucking fly buzzing around here," he said. "We must've left a window open."

"You know what they say about flies and horseshit," I said.

Ross's huge face scrunched. He started to get up from his seat. Colin put a hand on his arm.

"Easy," he said to his brother. Then he looked at me.

"Look, Shawn's not the most reliable guy in the world," he said.

"So I've heard."

"He's been sloppy lately, late to work. Almost got in a fight with a customer. He said his ex-wife died. We gave him a few days off, let him clear his head."

"Do you expect him to come back?"

"Look around, man. It's a bar, not a law firm. Staff turns over. If he comes back, he comes back. If he doesn't, he doesn't."

"Fair enough. Y'all have a wonderful day."

Colin Dunne went back to his Mac. Ross Dunne dialed a number on his phone.

I wanted to ask about their friend Snake Tat or their interest in Deborah Wellington, but my gut said that might lead to a confrontation, and I had Friday in the car. I walked back to my chair.

The bartender had overheard some of the conversation. She looked a little rattled. She mouthed, "Shawn?" to me.

I nodded.

She peered over at the booth to confirm that Ross and Colin weren't looking our way. She nodded back to me. I took one sip of beer, opened my wallet, and set a twenty and my business card on the bar.

"No change needed. Thanks."

The girl picked up both items, glanced at the booth one more time, and nodded at me again, her eyes a little wider than before.

I stood and walked outside into the retreating sunlight. I took out my phone and looked again at the photo of Shawn and Friday Finley. Behind them was the beach at sunset. Shawn didn't appear drunk in this one. He was a good-looking guy when clean and sober, barrel-chested and square-jawed with dark, trimmed hair. He and Friday had the same dark, piercing eyes. He looked happy. Friday was elementary-school age in the picture, wearing pigtails and a Mickey Mouse shirt, one arm around her dad's waist. Friday looked happy too. It was the first time I'd seen her smile.

"Any luck?" Friday asked when I got back inside.

"Not yet," I said.

It felt like punching a hole in an inflatable front-lawn Santa. Her eyes dropped and her shoulders sagged a little.

"Those two red-haired guys are brothers. Ross and Colin Dunne," I said. "They own the bar. They pretty much told me what they told you. Your dad's not working there right now. They gave him a few days off after your mom died. Sounds like he's been having a rough go of it."

"You think he drove up to Oregon?"

"I doubt it. It's been over a week. Why would he go now and not tell you he's coming?"

"These guys don't know where to find him?"

"No."

"Do you believe them?"

"I don't know," I said. "Don't have much reason not to."

Friday frowned.

"But they didn't offer their names until I pressed the issue. That's odd," I said. "And last night they were in a car with an armed thug who assaulted and threatened to kill somebody. That's odd too."

Friday stared straight ahead at the bar's entrance.

"My dad's probably dead," she said.

"You don't know that."

"I've tried him over and over. He won't answer his own daughter. His teenage daughter who just lost her mom. Who has absolutely nothing."

She spoke as calmly as if she'd ordered the corned beef at Cashel Rock.

"Nothing," she repeated.

"Maybe he lost his phone. Maybe he broke it. Don't make guesses or assumptions till we know. We could ask my friend Tex with the police."

"No cops," she said. "Please."

She continued to stare at the bar.

"Interesting sign inside," I said. "I wouldn't expect poetry in a place like that."

"Yeats," Friday said. "'The Second Coming.'"

"Never heard of it."

"'The centre cannot hold.'"

"What does that mean?"

"Means the world's a dump," Friday said.

"So you know cars, Irish poetry, and Nirvana."

"I told you, I just like the shirt," she said.

I started the engine.

"Let's sleep on all this," I said. "It's been a long day and we've gotta get your car looked at tomorrow."

"Sleep where?"

"Somewhere in our house. Might be on top of the dryer, but we'll find a spot."

"No," she said. "I can't let you do that for me."

"Got a better idea?"

She shrugged.

"I'm already outnumbered in that house," I said. "Three ladies to one. What's one more?"

"Who's the third?"

"Night nurse. Her name's Grace Chen. You'll like her."

As I put the Highlander in drive, a middle-aged Derryville patrol cop pulled into the space to my left, his siren lights off. He had a blond buzz cut, a matching blond mustache, and an inhospitable stare. He looked at me through dark shades. I smiled and rolled down the window.

"Can I help you, Officer?"

His window stayed up. He stared at me some more.

I shrugged and waved and hit the accelerator. After a beat, the cop followed us out of the lot and stayed fifty feet behind, no sirens, until we reached the 580 loop back to San Francisco.

We passed Treasure Island on the Bay Bridge with the setting sun in our faces.

"What was that about?" Friday asked.

"Wish I knew," I said.

# CHAPTER 12

"What the hell are you doing?"

In the living room, Ryan had yawned, smiled, and introduced herself to Friday Finley. In our bedroom, where she'd asked to speak with me in private, Ryan yawned, snarled, and pushed me so hard I thought my chest might cave.

"Ow," I said.

"We are not running an Airbnb, Charlie. Jesus. Where's she gonna sleep?"

"I was thinking our bed."

"What?"

"Grace can stay on the couch. You and I can snuggle in the sleeping bag on the floor. Maybe make s'mores."

"Charlie . . ."

"I'll run to the store and get them. We need anything else for Callie?"

"Charlie, stop. Now. Please."

That sounded like a good idea, so I did.

"What happened to her eye?" Ryan said.

"I don't know."

"She won't say?"

"Nope."

Ryan's phone lit up. She glanced at it and sighed.

"I love you, Charlie," she said.

"I love you more."

"And one of the things I love most about you is your heart. I'm sure you're just trying to help someone in need."

"I am."

"But we are squeezed in this house like . . ."

"Sardines."

"What?"

"Sardines. That's the expression. We're squeezed in this house like sardines."

"Who says 'sardines' anymore?"

"I thought you were about to."

"Can I finish, please?"

"Yes, dear."

"I'm stressed to hell," Ryan said. "I've got a presentation to leadership in the morning. The new agency we're using didn't send their deliverables on time. When they finally did, I couldn't open them. When I opened them, they weren't what I asked for."

Ryan held up her phone. "And my mother won't stop texting me about the weather. She's afraid we're gonna get swallowed up by wildfires this summer."

"Mute her. That's what I do to my mom."

"And now we've got a second stranger in the house who we know absolutely nothing about. Please, explain to me why you brought home a homeless girl?"

I retold the events of last night and today, withholding the part about Scottie getting jumped outside his house. I explained how I found Friday in the street with no functional car, no money, and nowhere to stay.

"Why can't you call Tex and ask the police to conduct a missing person's search?" Ryan asked.

"Friday doesn't want the cops involved. Her father has a bit of a record."

"Maybe she does too."

"There's nothing about her that suggests she's any danger to us," I said.

"What if she's a thief?"

"I could balance this house on my palm. What's she gonna steal?"

"What if she takes our car keys in the middle of the night?"

"I called her school principal. In Oregon."

"You did what?"

"I told her I was considering Friday's application at a frozen yogurt shop in her hometown."

"Frozen yogurt?"

"Yeah. There's a shop there. I looked it up. Anyway, she said Friday is a straight-A student, National Honor Society, peer mediation team, never in trouble . . ."

"You have seriously gone off the rails," Ryan said.

She stomped over to the tufted chaise longue by the bedroom window and put her head in her hands. She yawned. I yawned.

"I'm going to ask you a question, Charlie. Please don't get angry."

"Never, dear."

"I want to know if this could be, in any way, about your sister."

"About Sophie?"

"You lost Sophie when you were young. This girl is about the age Sophie was, right?"

"It's not about my sister. This girl needs help. Plus, you already invited someone to stay with us, so we're even."

"Yes, I did invite someone, Charlie. I invited Grace. Grace is training our daughter to sleep so *we* can get some sleep ourselves sometime in the next three fucking years."

"This girl's smart. She can pitch in."

"For how long?"

"Till we fix her car."

"What?"

"Whoops, I think I hear Callie crying."

"Charlie Shaw . . ."

Ryan followed me into the living room. Grace was making Callie's bedtime bottle. Friday was in the media lounger, holding Callie. Her backpack and roller bag lay on the floor fully zipped, its contents still intact.

"See," I said to Friday, "you're a natural. Grace, how's our little peanut?"

"She napped two hours straight this afternoon, zero interruptions," Grace said. "We'll push for three tonight. Her thumb is becoming quite the companion."

"Progress," Ryan said. "Grace, meet, uh, Friday Finley. She'll be staying with us for . . ."

"Just for tonight," Friday said.

"We'll see about that," I said.

"We've just met," Grace said. "Miss Finley says she's working a case with you, Charlie?"

I raised my eyebrows at Friday. She looked down at Callie.

"Yes, ma'am," I said. "We're looking for her father."

Friday's head stayed down.

"I see," Grace said. "Say no more. You hired the right man, Miss Finley. Please, take the couch. You look exhausted. Do you guys have any more clean bedsheets for her? I'll take the recliner in the nursery. I like being closer to Callie, anyway. She's not a snorer just yet."

"No, please," Friday said. "I don't want to intrude."

"Don't even think of it."

"Thank you, Grace," Ryan said. "Do both of you mind sharing the guest bathroom? I wish we had more space to offer."

"Not at all," Grace said. "Charlie, want to see what our choices are for dinner once we get Callie to bed?"

"Sure," I said.

I followed her to the kitchen counter packed with brown paper bags. When we heard Ryan and Friday begin to make chitchat, Grace whispered to me.

"That child's spirit is broken," she said.

"I know."

"Mentally and physically. I've seen it too often in hospitals over the years."

"Her mom just died. She's all alone."

Grace nodded slowly.

"Where's she from?"

"Oregon."

"Is she paying you?"

"No. I told her she could work it off helping you babysit."

Grace nodded again. "She reminds me a little of my youngest. Beautiful child."

"Sorry to spring this on you," I said. "You didn't ask to be this cramped. If you'd like to cancel our arrangement, I totally understand."

Grace shook her head and smiled. She held out her right hand for a fist bump. I obliged.

"You're a good man, Charlie Shaw. And don't worry. When you're not on the clock, I'll keep Miss Finley busy."

# CHAPTER 13

A tow truck came for Friday's car at nine the next morning. She and I arrived at 857 Watercrest just in time to see it loaded up. The old lady in the house eyeballed us through her front window. I smiled and gave her a thumbs-up.

Friday and I followed the truck to a repair shop on Lombard. The guy inside confirmed the busted axle. He said they'd have to search for parts on an older model like hers. Might take a little time, but he'd call with a report and an estimate as soon as possible.

I drove Friday, under protest, back to the house.

"You can help Grace with Callie," I said. "And unpack your things. I've got to follow up on that divorce case and do some work in the office."

"Where's your office?"

"Right here."

"I want to help," Friday said.

"You will. Put Callie in her *Finding Nemo* chair. You'll have the time of your life."

It was another brisk and sunny morning. I rolled down the windows and drove to Cavalli Cafe for coffee and free Wi-Fi. No local jails were holding anyone named Shawn Finley. I tried his phone number and got no answer. Friday was right about her father. Shawn Finley didn't have the world's longest rap sheet, but it wasn't something you'd share on a Christmas card. He was forty years old and Salem-bred: born there, started a family there, started a bunch of trouble there. Had a few offenses as a minor: criminal trespass, theft, possession of marijuana. More misdemeanors into adulthood: first-offense DWI, public intoxication twice. Did overnight stays in county jail for the DWI and the public intoxication. First-degree assault ten years ago. Pled out, did twenty days, then probation. The judge had probably had enough of his shit. No mention of family violence, though.

Shawn Finley's last and most recent offense was another public intoxication, this time in Oakland, seventeen months ago. His last known address was an apartment in Eastmont. I called the office. They evicted him fourteen months ago, didn't know where he went and didn't seem to care.

Colin Dunne, the disobliging co-owner of Cashel Rock, was thirty-four years old. His record was pretty clean other than a couple of misdemeanor assaults as a minor in Derryville. The Cashel Rock bar used to be an abandoned vape shop. Colin bought it two years ago and restored it. The local kid had become a local entrepreneur. His home address was 3332 Garden Grove, located in Derryville's more affluent district. It was a mid-century modern two-story covering over 3,200 square feet. The estimated value was just over a million bucks.

Ross Dunne was two years younger than Colin. His name didn't officially appear on the Cashel Rock lease. I was pretty sure I knew why. Ross's rap sheet was considerably longer than his brother's: assault, disturbing the peace, witness intimidation. When he was twenty-one, he did a year in San Quentin for attempted robbery. He probably couldn't get a loan for a bicycle.

Powell called.

"Spoke with Arthur Wellington," he said.

"How'd he take the news?"

"Not well. He's been afraid that his reclusive nature, and the age gap between himself and his wife, would eventually cause strain in their marriage. He was angry when I told him about the affair. He got furious when I told him who Scottie works for."

"Rivet Security?"

"Yes. Wellington has money invested in the company. It's a successful cybersecurity start-up owned by a guy named Dalton Crawford, a transplant from Boston. I got the impression that Mr. Wellington will be having a stern conversation with Mr. Crawford about this affair."

"Did you tell him about Scottie getting jumped in the parking lot after Mrs. Wellington left?"

"Yes."

"Did he have any idea why three punks from Derryville would do that?"

"Three?"

"I haven't identified the one with the snake tattoo, but apparently there were two other guys in the Escalade," I said. "Their names are Ross and Colin Dunne, owners of the Cashel Rock bar. They both have rap sheets. I want to look into them further."

"Wellington said he's not interested in what happened to Scottie," Powell said. "Or anything his wife has gotten involved in. I sent him a final bill."

"Good," I said. "Because I sort of have a . . . client."

"A client?"

"Yes. The girl in the silver 4Runner next to me watching all this happen."

"You found her?"

"Yes. She's not a junior PI. She does need help."

"What kind of help?"

I told him about Friday Finley's trip from Oregon in search of her father, and her unsuccessful visit to Cashel Rock, and her decision to follow her father's employers, Ross and Colin Dunne, to Sausalito that night.

"She hoped the Dunne brothers might lead her to her dad," I said.

"Instead, they led her to Scottie's place," Powell said.

"She sat there in her car, parked next to mine, and watched Scottie get beat up. It scared her. She got the hell outta there. Tex helped me track down her plate. Turns out she wrecked her car on Watercrest. When I found her, she'd been panhandling at Pier Thirty-nine. She's broke."

"And she told you her sob story, and now you've offered to help," Powell said. "Missing person cases don't usually end well."

"I know."

"And these Dunne brothers don't sound like Christmas carolers."

"Aren't you the least bit curious what they might be up to?"

"Got a business to run," Powell said. "And I can't hire a minor as a client."

"I'm not doing this through Powell and Associates."

"She can't pay you?"

"Nope. Her car's in rough shape. She's gonna need help with repairs if she ever wants to go home, dad or no dad."

"What does Ryan think about all this?"

"She's pissed that I'm letting her stay with us."

"In that tiny house?"

"Yeah."

Powell laughed.

"Regardless," I said, "I promised to help."

"Look, I need your help with cases I choose to take," Powell said. "That's why I hired you."

"I know."

"But now you've convinced yourself you've gotta rescue this young lady in distress."

"I'm surrounded by women at home. What can I say? It's softened me up."

"I had another case I wanted to put you on," Powell said. "Older woman in Hunters Point says somebody keeps ringing her doorbell at night, harassing her. Wants somebody to check it out."

"Ding-dong ditchers? You serious?"

"Not every job is *The Maltese Falcon*," Powell said. "Pays the bills."

"I'm afraid I'm committed on this."

"Fine," Powell said. "I'll put one of my sons on the ding-dong ditchers. I'll give you a few days to help Miss Friday Finley."

"Thanks, boss."

"And if you go back to Derryville, watch yourself."

"It doesn't have the best reputation, does it?"

Powell chuckled.

"Ever see those travel stories that say, 'Ten Things to Do in the Bay Area'?"

"Yeah."

"Ever see Derryville on that list?"

"Nope."

"There's a reason for that," Powell said. "It's always been pretty rough. Founded by Irish settlers in the eighteen hundreds, Gold Rush. Industrial town. Lotta good people weighed down by a few bad people in higher places."

"You're talking City Hall?"

"I'm talking organized crime," Powell said. "Ever heard of Jimmy O'Rourke?"

"Yeah. San Francisco mobster."

"Derryville mobster. His parents moved here from Ireland in the late forties when he was a baby. Looking for a better life. Working-class people. Honest wages. Wasn't good enough for Jimmy."

"He was ambitious."

"He was a greedy, nasty crook. While his father poured sweat and blood at the steel mill, Jimmy was out hustling at ten years old. His dad died when he was sixteen. Boiler exploded at the mill. Jimmy went full Corleone after that. Built a small outfit in the late seventies. Wasn't long before he had the town sealed up nice and tight."

"Rackets?"

"You name it."

"Cops?"

"Scared or paid off. He was a bull shark in a pond," Powell said.

"Were you around when he got busted?"

"I'd just started on patrol."

"Ninety-eight?"

"Ninety-eight."

"What happened?"

"He flew too close to the sun."

"Meaning?"

"He tried to clip someone in San Francisco. Bad move. SFPD arrested him. Got convicted and sent back to Ireland to serve his sentence. Transfer deal between the two governments."

"Whatever happened to him?"

"Don't know," Powell said. "He got something like fifty years. Probably still in the clink."

"Does Derryville still have a criminal presence?"

"Criminal presence? Absolutely. Organized criminal presence? Not that I'm aware of. Why?"

"Shawn Finley works at Cashel Rock," I said. "It's an Irish bar."

"So? The town's got Irish heritage."

"We already know the bar owners, these Dunne brothers, like to hurt people. For reasons we don't know, they hurt Scottie bad. Yesterday they were very unhelpful when I went to the bar and asked about Shawn Finley. Then a cop outside followed me to the city limits like a dog marking territory."

"Did you make a scene?"

"No, I was a perfect gentleman."

"Maybe they've had problems with security."

"Maybe. Know any cops over there?"

"Met a couple over the years. That's about it. So, because this girl's dad has disappeared, you suspect foul play?"

"I don't know anything," I said. "Friday says her dad's a drunk and completely unreliable."

"Maybe that's your answer."

"Maybe. I just know these guys are shady, and cops acting like their personal security is shady, and Shawn Finley vanishing without a word to his daughter is shady. Shady, shady, shady."

"I got work to do, Charlie."

"Why does everybody tell me that?"

"Look, when Jimmy O'Rourke ran the show in Derryville, he had a lot of people on the take. Cops too. But that was forty years ago."

"What were you like forty years ago?"

"The toughest twelve-year-old you ever met," Powell said.

# CHAPTER 14

As Powell had predicted, Arthur Wellington called Rivet Security to inform them of Scottie Coburn's indecent behavior. The company promptly fired Scottie's ass.

Dalton Crawford, founder and CEO, wanted to thank us for uncovering the scandal. I dropped by his new corporate headquarters on my way back to Derryville.

San Francisco's doom loop had not yet cast icy fingers on Rivet Security. Its corporate offices occupied the second and third floors of a skyscraper in the 5M district. Crawford had a corner office on the third floor overlooking 5th Street. It rivaled my house in square footage. He had two guest chairs in front of his desk and a larger white leather couch on the far wall. I took one of the guest chairs.

Crawford was in his thirties and, in a word, impeccable. His dark hair was styled in one of those European soccer player fades, shaved on one side and neatly moussed on the other. He wore a pressed black suit with a white dress shirt and thin black tie. His leather loafers gleamed. He had high cheekbones and a narrow nose, thin as a faucet sprayer. His skin was a healthy brown bordering on orange, likely aided by artificial means. He wore no wedding ring or jewelry. I got the impression business was his marriage.

"Thanks for coming by on short notice," Crawford said. "I'm still getting settled in here."

Besides the view, the office wasn't much to look at. Crawford's desk had a laptop and a forty-inch curved monitor and a few papers stacked neatly together. A Baby Yoda doll sat next to his laptop. The walls were painted the same beige as the hallways. The only decorations were a framed diploma from MIT and a framed black-and-white panoramic photograph of the Boston skyline at night.

"Where was your old office?" I asked.

"The old, old office was out of my apartment," Crawford said. "I started the company two years ago. Our most recent office was a much smaller space. We moved here to accommodate our growth."

"What does Rivet Security do?"

"In the simplest terms, we're a cybersecurity company. We protect clients from email phishing attacks, malware, things of that nature. Physical crime still exists, obviously. But cybercrime is the new wave. Statistics say it's a ten-trillion-dollar problem per year worldwide and growing. Our technology is proprietary. I spent years developing the platform while I was in Boston working as an engineer."

I pointed to Baby Yoda. "You're the force for good."

"Exactly," Crawford said. "I'd show you around, but it's a bit of a skeleton crew today."

"Just us here?"

"Just about. Our staff is still hybrid remote for now. Some of our executive staff is here."

"But not Scottie Coburn."

"Nope. As I mentioned on the phone, he's been let go."

"What was Scottie's position at Rivet?"

"Ironically," Crawford said, "he was the chief brand officer."

"Responsible for maintaining the company's image."

"Correct."

"And sleeping with Arthur Wellington's wife doesn't exactly portray the image you want at Rivet."

"Arthur Wellington's a powerful name in this city. Rivet is not a powerful name in this city. I hope someday it will be. But we won't get there by alienating people such as Mr. Wellington. He's been very generous to us."

"With his money?"

"Yes. He sees our potential and has committed to investing in our growth."

"Did Rivet throw a party to celebrate this investment?"

"We had a small function recently and welcomed Mr. and Mrs. Wellington to the office. I assume that's where she and Scottie, uh, connected."

"Did Wellington call you personally when he received our report?"

"He did."

"And you fired Scottie immediately?"

"Over the phone, yes. He hasn't come into the office yet, because he says he's been injured. That's why I called Inspector Powell, and he referred me to you. He said you were the principal investigator on this case."

"I was."

"Did you see Scottie get injured during your investigation?"

"Yes."

"What happened?"

"He got jumped by a stranger. Beaten up badly. The stranger told him to stay away from a woman. Wellington's wife, I presume."

"Scottie told me he has two broken ribs."

"I don't doubt it."

"Who was this stranger who attacked him?"

"I'd never seen him before. Scottie said he'd never seen him before."

"When did you speak with Scottie?" Crawford asked.

"After the attack. I helped him up."

"While you were investigating him?"

"He looked like roadkill," I said. "I thought it was the right thing to do."

Crawford smiled.

"And you thought maybe you could get some information out of him given his physical state."

"Maybe that too," I said.

"What did the stranger look like?"

"Huge guy, man bun, snake tattoo on his neck," I said. "Have you ever seen anyone like that hanging around this office or your old office?"

Crawford thought about it.

"Can't say I have," he said. "A neck tattoo of a snake?"

"Two snakes, actually."

"I think I'd remember that," Crawford said. "Did Scottie file a police report?"

"No."

"That's good."

"Good?"

"Well, it will save the Wellingtons from public embarrassment, don't you think?"

"Sure," I said. "May I ask how Scottie got hired here at Rivet?"

"He'd been a successful marketing rep at Radiant. They're another start-up in town. I went to college with the founder. He referred me to Scottie. Said Scottie was a fast riser."

"Was he?"

"Until now, yes."

"He's kind of young."

"We're a young company and we've got a young staff," Crawford said. "Scottie's talented. He's got enthusiasm. But my colleague warned me he was a little immature."

"Did you have any idea Scottie was involved with Mrs. Wellington?"

"No idea," Crawford said. "I'm up to my eyeballs trying to keep this company moving. Got no time for anybody's sex life. Wish I had time for my own."

"Me too. I've got a six-month-old at home."

Crawford smiled. He hunched forward a little in his chair.

"Charlie," he said, "is there anything else you can tell me about Scottie's behavior? Anything you uncovered in the course of your investigation?"

"Dalton," I said, "are you worried about a wrongful termination suit?"

Crawford smiled again. "You never know."

"Don't blame you. If I uncovered anything else about Scottie, that would be confidential. But I didn't. I only tailed him for two nights."

"With Mrs. Wellington?"

"Yes."

"Well," Crawford said, "I appreciate the work you did. Quite frankly, I'm glad we terminated Scottie before he did something even dumber than this. It's a bit of a black eye for our company, but I assured Mr. Wellington that Scottie's behavior doesn't reflect our core values."

"Sorry it stung you," I said.

"Hey," Crawford said, "you're just doing your job. I guess you're off on a new case now?"

"Next stop, Derryville," I said.

His eyebrows raised slightly.

"Derryville," he said. "Across the bridge?"

"Yep."

"Good luck with that," he said.

# CHAPTER 15

Eight years ago, Ryan and I cruised to Key West and Cozumel on our honeymoon. By the first night I was claustrophobic. The stateroom felt like a Cracker Jack box. The tight quarters were magnified by the waves oscillating under my feet, the kind of sensation you get from a mild California tremor. Ryan said she didn't feel anything and told me to suck it up. That's our marriage in a nutshell.

The house on Stockton felt a little like that, minus the waves. Our bedroom felt like the stateroom. Outside, we had two guests and a six-month-old stacked on top of each other like beach towels.

Callie had just completed a solo act that deserved a standing ovation, a carefully curated set list of howls, shrieks, and blubbering cries. Thank God for Grace. She got Callie back to sleep with a bottle and a back rub. Callie loved back rubs.

Probably half the neighborhood, like myself, couldn't go back to sleep after that fiasco. My alarm clock said 2:28. I went to the fridge for some water.

Friday and Grace were at the kitchen table playing cards. They'd moved the lamp by the living room couch for light. Both had a cup of coffee beside them. The living room TV volume was on low, a tick above mute. A late-night marathon of *House Hunters* was on. Respectfully, I decided I'd been surrounded by estrogen for long enough. I needed a night out with my guy friends—a game, a concert, something. Yeah, that sounded nice. Three years from now I could probably make that work.

"What's the game?" I asked.

"Go Fish," Grace said.

"Mind if I pull up a chair?"

"Of course. Would you like to play?"

"I'll just watch."

"Can't sleep either?"

"Ryan's tossing and turning," I said. "Rough week at work. And Callie did a number on our eardrums."

"Poor girl's a little restless tonight, but she's been kicking butt and taking names," Grace said. "Last night she set a personal record: six straight hours of sleep. We're gonna top it by the time my week's over."

Grace and I fist-bumped.

"Sorry for the rock concert," I said to Friday.

"No worries," she said. "Doubt I could sleep anyway."

"I don't blame you, sweetheart," Grace said. "Me? After thirty years in nursing, I'm like a Navy SEAL. I've learned to sleep when I can. When I've gotta get up, it's go time."

"Tea and coffee help too," I said.

"Want some?"

"Nah. I'm hoping to pass out eventually."

I'd never seen a Go Fish game with only two players. Each started with seven cards instead of five. The game was winding down. The big card pile, known as "the ocean," had been trimmed to two.

"Do you have a three?" Friday asked Grace.

"No, ma'am. Go fish."

Friday did. She drew a three of clubs from the ocean.

"Boom," she said.

She drew again, the reward for manifesting your desired card.

"A three of diamonds," she said. "Game, set, and match."

She gathered the treys together as a set and laid them gracefully on the table. They counted up the number of sets they'd accumulated.

"Well, I'll be," Grace said. "Congratulations, young lady. Excellent performance."

"'Bout time I had some good luck," Friday said.

"Wish we had some on this case," I said.

"No progress?"

"Unfortunately, no. I've been all over Derryville the past two days. Didn't see our cop buddy with the mustache. I showed your dad's picture around town. Restaurants, stores, hotels, motels. Some people recognized him but hadn't seen him lately."

"Where else should we look?"

"Besides Cashel Rock, I have no idea."

"Can we go back?"

"I'm on the fence about 'we,'" I said.

"Why?"

"The Dunne brothers are pretty salty."

"The bar owners?"

"Yeah. They both have records."

"I'm not afraid," Friday said.

"Did you say Derryville?" Grace asked.

"Yeah."

"Oh my," she said.

"Exactly," I said.

"I can help," Friday said. "I hate just sitting around. No offense, Mrs. Chen."

"Please, call me Grace. None taken, sweetie."

"All right," I said. "But you stay in the car. Like last time."

Friday nodded and frowned a little. Grace and I made eye contact. Grace gave me a half smile. We were doing all we could to lift her spirits.

"Friday's been the best assistant I've ever had," Grace said. "Changing diapers, running errands, keeping Callie entertained."

"Callie mostly entertains herself," Friday said. "She's obsessed with the *Finding Nemo* chair."

"That thing was sent from heaven," I said.

"I think she tried to talk yesterday," Friday said. "We sang 'Row, Row, Row Your Boat' to her and she mumbled something like 'Lay,' 'Deh,' and 'Mmmm.'"

"She's in a mimicking stage," Grace said. "Won't be long till she's talking up a storm and you can't get it to stop."

"Long as it replaces the crying," I said.

"Some," Grace said. "Not all."

Friday gathered up the cards and began shuffling them with ease. They collapsed into each other like butter.

"Where'd you learn to do that?" I asked.

"My dad taught me."

Grace and I glanced at each other again.

"No wonder I lost," Grace said. "I got hustled by a pro."

Friday smiled. On these rare occasions, smiling revealed a prominent dimple just below her right cheek.

"Texas Hold'Em, anybody?" she said.

"I think that's my cue," I said. "Grace, I wouldn't play for anything other than coffee beans if I were you. Good night, y'all."

I could hear Friday shuffling the cards as I made my way down the hall and back to bed.

# CHAPTER 16

Our unfriendly Derryville friends hadn't seen Mango yet, so I drove her back to a much busier Cashel Rock. Friday Finley came along as requested. She threatened to walk there herself if I left her in the house again.

"Strictly a surveillance job," I said before we left. "But I wouldn't say it's entirely safe."

"Then let's take this," Friday said, and pulled a Louisville Slugger from her clothes bag. "Brought it for protection driving down from Oregon."

"Easy, McCovey. Don't let Ryan see that."

The Cashel Rock parking lot was full just after ten p.m. I parked on the side of the street adjacent to the bar, where I could still see cars drive up and patrons walk inside.

"What's your plan?" Friday asked.

"I'll know when I see it," I said.

I checked the crib app on my phone. Ryan and Grace were in Callie's nursery spinning a baby mobile of animals and insects. An instrumental version of "Itsy Bitsy Spider" played on the speaker.

"Ooooooooh!" Ryan said, and poked Callie's armpit.

Callie belly-laughed. Best sound in the world.

"Callie really likes you," I said to Friday. "She's only spit up on you once in three days. Twice an hour for me."

"She's adorable," Friday said. "And she looks like both you guys."

"She got all the good parts from Ryan, which is pretty much everything."

"No, she has your eyes. The cheeks and chin and the faces she makes sorta look more like Ryan. Not sure where the little button nose came from, though. That's all hers."

"She's got table manners like me too. I was feeding her this morning and she laughed at one of her sneezes for the first time. Then she spit up on her bib and put all her fingers in her mouth."

"Hope she's not like this on dates one day," Friday said.

"Whoa, stop the presses. That sounded like a joke."

Friday half grinned.

I had the windows cracked. A thin layer of fog had rolled in off the Bay. I could hear rock music bass pounding through the patio speakers. A faint smell of fries and potato skins wafted our way. Luckily we'd eaten first. Friday had brought a fresh box of Raisinets for a snack.

"Want some?" she asked.

"Sure."

Her hair was up again. She wore jeans and her denim jacket over another distressed rock T-shirt, this time the Rolling Stones.

"Are you a Stones fan," I said, "or you just like this shirt too?"

"They're cool," Friday said.

"Bet you like Nirvana too."

"Yeah."

"You just didn't want to bother telling me about yourself when we met."

"Didn't know you yet," Friday said. "And you called the cops on me."

"Fair enough. Want some music? Might pass the time."

"Nah, I'm good right now."

"Got no Stones but I've got a Zeppelin CD. And The Roots. You ever seen a CD?"

"Not in person."

I showed her.

"Cool," she said.

The bruising around her eye had started to lighten and the

swelling had dropped. She'd started wearing light makeup around Grace and Ryan and me, so it was hard to see much in the way of progress except late at night or in the morning before she got dressed.

"At this point, I really think you should consider filing a missing person's report," I said.

Friday shook her head. "No cops if I can help it."

"You heard Tex—Inspector Whitmore—on the phone. He's a good guy."

"Cops only care about missing kids, not adults."

"If something did happen to your dad, every second matters. Tex could come by the bar, maybe lean on these guys more than I can."

Friday shook her head again. "What's the point in the cops finding him if he's just gonna head back to jail?"

"How do you know he'd be heading back to jail?"

"Because I know him."

"And you're afraid the cops would sniff around and find something he's up to."

"Right. But like I said, he's probably dead anyway."

I let her words hang in the salt air. Nothing I could say would reassure her. She also might be right.

A big black bird hopped off the curb in front of us and started pecking at a run-over squirrel. A red eighties-looking Ford Ranger with a smashed fender passed us on its way to the parking lot.

"I've asked a lot about you," I said. "I haven't told you much about me."

"I know about your family," Friday said.

"Not my whole family."

"Like, your parents?"

"Yeah. I'm the son of a roughneck."

"Roughneck?"

"Guys who work the oil rigs."

"Where?"

"Gulf of Mexico. Off the Texas coast."

"You're from Texas?"

"Yeah."

"You don't have much of an accent."

"Got here just in time. My mom and dad were an interesting match. She taught fourth grade. He stood on a platform drilling holes in the Gulf."

"Sounds messy."

"And dangerous. He'd work two weeks on, one week off. When he came home he was either too beat up or too tired to fool with me or my brother and sister. And he liked to drink."

"Did he ever hit you?"

"No. He wasn't a bad guy. He only knew how to work, not raise a family. He wasn't Father of the Year. But we all still got excited when he came home. We still wanted to see him."

Friday turned to look at me for a moment. Something in what I said resonated. She dropped her eyes and turned to face the windshield again.

"Have your parents met Callie?"

"Once back home. My dad's back and knees are shot. Hard to get him on a plane or in a car for any length of time. My brother still lives near them, helps them out."

"What about your sister?"

"She died when she was about your age."

"How?"

"She took her own life."

Friday put down her candy and looked at me.

"God," she said. "I'm so sorry."

"It's been a lot of years now," I said. "You remind me of her, though. Ryan does too, for that matter."

"Really?"

"Smart, funny, headstrong, tough, resourceful. The family was never the same without Sophie. Probably why I came all the way out here after high school."

"For college?"

"Yeah. I was more right-brained, like my mom. Journalism seemed like the furthest thing from pushing drill pipe. I was an okay writer. And I had a big mouth."

"I've noticed," Friday said.

She offered me some more Raisinets. I accepted. In front of us the bird kept pecking at the squirrel's open stomach.

"Great view," she said.

"Derryville," I said.

"How did you and Ryan meet?"

"I'll tell that story if you tell me something."

"I'm not talking about my eye."

"I'm done asking you about that."

"All right. Deal."

"I was a decent high school pitcher," I said. "I got tired of home, small towns. I'd seen people surfing on TV and thought it looked pretty cool. So I applied to a bunch of schools on the West Coast and sent some tape of my games. One only school accepted me."

"Stanford," Friday said.

"Hell no. Stanford probably lit my application on fire."

"Oh. I've just seen Ryan wear the sweatshirt."

"That's where it gets interesting. I got into Santa Clara, 'bout forty-five minutes south of here. The coach asked me to join the team as a walk-on, no scholarship. So I did. I worked my way into the starting rotation by my junior year. We went up to Stanford for a nonconference game that year. I'm pitching. Stanford's good: College World Series team, all that. They light me up for six runs in the first two innings. On my last pitch, I think I've finally got it together. It's 0-and-2, two outs, bases loaded, second inning. I try a slider low and away."

"I don't know what any of that means," Friday said.

"Sorry. So I throw the pitch and this dude sends it on a rocket ship. To Oregon, probably. I'm lucky I even got it over the plate. I've completely blown out my shoulder."

"Oh no."

"Last pitch I ever threw. I walk back to the dugout with the team trainer and I see this girl in the fourth row. It was Ryan in that same Stanford hoodie. I smile at her. Probably more of a wince. My arm is dangling like a wet noodle. I'm in so much pain I feel like someone ripped it off and tried to Scotch tape it back on. Ryan smiles back at me. Well, that was a nice moment after the day I've had, but I figure that's the end of that. I spend the rest of the game back in the training room with the doctor and trainer. They give me a bunch of pain meds, wrap up my shoulder, tell me they'll do tests when we get home. Couple hours later the game ends. We lose 14–2. Our coach is so pissed he doesn't even let us shower before getting on the bus back home. We get on the bus outside the stadium. I see Ryan walking with her friends. I stumble out of my seat and jump off the bus. The engine's running. Coach says, 'What the fuck are you doing, Shaw?' Sorry for the language."

"No worries," Friday said.

"I tell Coach, 'I got one more pitch to try.' I didn't care. I figured my career was over. Turns out it was. I shout to Ryan, 'Hey!' Real smooth, right? I've got morphine or something in me. I feel like I'm floating outside my body. She turns to me. Her hair's longer than it is now. She has it in, like, an updo with curls in the back and a strand on each side of her face curving to her jawline. I'd never seen anybody like her before. She says, 'Are you okay?' I smile and say, 'I'm much better now.' And then she says the most Ryan thing ever: 'You talk better than you pitch.'"

Friday laughed. First time I'd heard that. For three days I'd encountered mostly frowns and one-syllable words. Laughing made her look and sound much younger. Like her actual age.

"Then what happened?" she said.

"Ryan gave me her number. I went back to school, had surgery on my shoulder. I quit the team after the season, worked on the campus paper, drove up to see her every chance I got. Fast-forward a few years, and here we are. Tired and grumpy."

"That's so sweet," Friday said. "The dating part. Not the tired and grumpy part."

In succession, three luxury cars roared past us on the potholed street and into the parking lot: a curaçao blue McLaren 570S, a red Maserati Levante, and a black Ferrari Roma Spider. The trio drove past the bar entrance and around back.

"Well, that's interesting," I said.

# CHAPTER 17

I started up Mango and pulled into the lot, weaving through a line of parked cars past the bar and around back on the cell phone repair shop side. I cut off the headlights and parked next to the shop's dumpster, about fifty yards from the back entrance to Cashel Rock. The dumpster overflowed with trash bags. Food wrappers and plastic cups and cardboard boxes were strewn on the ground. A stiff wind gust blew more garbage around. The whole area stank. Friday rolled up her window.

"You really like to do this?" she asked.

"Sometimes I wonder," I said.

The bar's back-side parking lot ran up against an eight-foot-high concrete wall. A row of ramshackle houses stood on the other side. A streetlamp offered decent lighting.

Friday handed me her binoculars and I squinted at the cars. We'd missed the drivers. They'd parked a few feet from the bar's back door.

"This is, like, an Oscars red carpet from hell," Friday said.

"I can't make out the license plates," I said. "Stay here and lock the doors, please."

I climbed out and looked around. There were no windows on the back side of the bar. No visible cameras. Nothing moved by the back door. Ross and Colin Dunne had installed a steel security door in place of the original. I couldn't see or hear anything inside.

I dropped to a crouch and shuffled car to car, snapping pics of all three license plates with my phone. All three had California plates.

I heard a rattling sound and dropped to my stomach between the McLaren and the Maserati. I felt my entire body tense up. The back door remained closed. A wind gust blew through and I heard the rattling sound again. I glanced up. It was only the dumpster door.

My phone buzzed.

Everything okay? Ryan texted.

She always knew. How did women always know?

Peachy, I texted back.

Friday was slumped in her seat when I got back to Mango.

"Got the plates?" she asked.

"Yep."

"Recognize any of them?"

"Nope. But we'll run all three plates later."

"Just like you ran mine," Friday said.

"Exactly."

"My dad used to work on cars this nice," she said. "He always said cars like that had two things in common: Their drivers were rich and their drivers were assholes."

"I'll bet."

"Such a weird place to park cars that nice. Some scummy dive bar."

"Good observation, Miss Finley."

Mango's windows only slightly suppressed the dumpster stench. Friday shifted in her seat. My shoulder throbbed. Dropping to the cement had fired it up again.

We sat in silence for a minute while I shuffled through my license plate photos.

"What did you want to ask me?" Friday said.

"What?"

"Earlier. When we were parked on the street."

"Oh, nothing. I was just curious how you got your name. Your first name."

"You saying my name's weird?"

"No. I'm saying it's cool and unique."

Friday didn't answer. A couple more minutes passed. The wind picked up. The dumpster rattled some more. I couldn't take the smell much longer.

"My mom fought depression for a long time," Friday said.

"I'm sorry to hear that."

"She had problems. Mental, emotional. She couldn't hold a job either. My dad was a mess too, but I think he got tired of her ups and downs. Probably one reason he left. Both of them had good days. When my dad wasn't drinking he was fun. Sweet. You saw the picture."

"Yeah."

"My mom was the same way. When she was up, she was a good mom. Strong, caring. Funny, even. She was just down way too much. COVID and isolation didn't help. I don't think the virus by itself killed her. I think she just gave up."

"Mental illness is an epidemic in itself."

"My mom named me. I always thought they both did. They were both sort of stoners. A couple years ago she told me why she chose Friday. We were sitting in the backyard. She liked to garden, liked the sunshine. It helped her mood. She told me the average woman lives eighty years. That's just over four thousand weekends. 'You'll see when you get older,' she said. 'Too many of us only live to see the weekend. I want you to live every day like it's Friday.'"

"That's beautiful."

"The irony," Friday said, "is she didn't take her own advice."

# CHAPTER 18

I had the keys in my hand to start up Mango and head home. A big fist rapped on the driver-side window.

Friday screamed.

Ross Dunne had come up behind us. Regrettably, I rolled down my window.

"Oh, hey," I said. "It's Mr. Cashel Rock."

"What the fuck are you doing back here?" Ross said.

I pointed at the cell phone repair shop.

"We're looking for Fraggle Rock," I said. "Is this it? She's always wanted to see Boober."

Ross smiled. His teeth, incredibly, looked straight and clean.

"Fraggle Rock," he said. "That's funny. Maybe I should call the cops. Tell them we've got some creep out back in a car with a teenage girl."

"You know exactly who we are."

"You're right," Ross said. "You're the one who's been snooping around here."

"Asking about Shawn Finley."

"Yeah."

I pointed to Friday.

"Shawn Finley's her father."

"So what?"

"Is he around?"

"No."

"Is he coming back?"

"None of your business."

"It is my business," I said. "She hired me to find him."

"You're trespassing, asshole."

"We're parked next door. You own that too?"

"I'm sick of this shit," Ross said.

He reached into the left pocket of his track jacket. I wasn't interested in discovering its contents. Thankfully my seat belt wasn't buckled yet. I grabbed him by his neck and slammed his head into the steering wheel. I heard something heavy clatter on the concrete.

Ross grunted and stumbled backward. I'd dropped my keys on the floorboard. If he retrieved his gun, time wasn't on my side. I grabbed his neck again and tried to pin his head against the open window. He bit the back of my forearm and wrestled free.

Friday screamed again.

I had a momentary childhood flashback to getting bit by a terrier. This felt about the same: wet, messy, and very unpleasant.

I jumped out as Ross dropped to the ground and searched for a glint of steel in the shadowy lot. I kicked him in the ribs. He yelped. I scanned the ground for any sign of the gun. Ross grabbed my leg and sank his teeth into my thigh. This one wasn't nearly as painful but succeeded in making me jump back. This had to be the ugliest fight of all time. If I survived, I might need a tetanus shot.

Ross stood and charged me like a mama bear. He planted his giant forehead into my stomach and drove me into the driver-side door. He swung a big right fist and missed. It struck the top of the window frame.

It wasn't hard to find scraps in small-town Texas. I'd learned back home that you could stop a train with one good punch to the gut. This punch wasn't as good as the one Snake Tat gave Scottie Coburn the other night. Ross made a nasty dry-heave sound but bounced up quicker than I expected. He rammed me into the car again. The force ripped the wind from my diaphragm.

Ross stood and threw a wild punch at my face. I ducked most of it but caught the edge of his fist on my temple. For a moment everything got blurry, as if my contacts had fallen out. Then I heard him make another unpleasant noise.

I shook my head and rubbed my eyes. Things started to unfog. When my vision cleared, I could see the back of Ross's jeans on the ground. His black jacket was almost imperceptible in the darkness. I squinted closer at the ground. Ross was lying on his stomach.

"Fuck!" he snarled.

Friday was holding the Louisville Slugger. She gripped it in her hands as if she'd stepped into the batter's box. She stared down at Ross.

"Friday," I said. "Drop the bat, please."

She looked at me, her mouth open, eyes wide. Her hands were shaking. Finally, she let go of the bat. It struck the pavement with an unpleasant clunk.

"Are you okay?" I asked.

She nodded her head without speaking. She stared at her shaking hands. My hands started to shake too. I'd made some dumb decisions in my life, but bringing her back around these scumbags should make the Mouth Breather Hall of Fame.

"Where'd you hit him?"

"In his leg and his back," Friday said. "He'd found the gun."

"Where?"

"I kicked it under your car. By the front left tire."

My jaw pounded. My left forearm stung. A hot warm feeling ran from my bad shoulder all the way down my right arm.

I heard Ross groan again as I picked up the gun. It was a Jericho. Looked a lot like the one Snake Tat had pointed at Scottie. I checked the magazine. Loaded. I put the safety on. It was a miracle the damn thing hadn't gone off.

Ross spat at the pavement.

"You're fucking dead for this," he said, his ugly chin hugging the concrete.

"You geniuses might want to install a camera back here," I said. "I'll ask you one more time. Where is Shawn Finley?"

"Both of you," he said. "I'll fucking kill both of you."

"Like my dad?" Friday said.

Ross didn't reply. The faint sound of a siren blared in the distance.

"Shit," I said.

I set the gun on the ground and opened the driver-side door.

"Keys, phone," I said to Friday. "Passcode is 0105. Drive out the cell phone shop side and don't stop till you get past the city limits. Call Dwayne Powell. He's in my list of contacts. Tell him I'm at the Derryville police station and I need help."

"But..."

"Now," I said. "Hurry. Then go home. If you see anyone inside the house, just tell them I dropped you off and I'll be back later."

Friday looked down at the gun and then at Ross. He started to laugh.

"Now," I said.

She took the keys and the phone, hopped inside, started the engine, and backed out. I heard Mango's tires squeal around the corner as the sirens grew louder.

Ross laughed some more. He rolled onto his back to face me.

"You got a long night coming," he said.

Predictably, the patrol car came in through the bar side, its white headlights and red-and-blue flashers flooding the dark lot. The car passed the line of luxury vehicles and stopped ten feet in front of Ross and me. The officer behind the wheel snapped open the door and pulled his pistol from his holster.

I'd been in fights before, but no one had ever pulled a gun on me. This was twice in a span of five minutes.

"Hands up now!" the officer shouted to me.

It was the same cop with the blond buzz cut from my first visit to Derryville.

# CHAPTER 19

I'd never been handcuffed before either. It hurt worse than the movies made it look. The cuffs choked so tight against my skin that I thought the veins inside my wrists might burst. The cop had collected Ross's gun and walked me up against the back wall of the cell phone shop. He put a hand on my right shoulder, and the pissed-off nerve sent hot liquid down my arm again.

"Whose gun was that on the ground?" the cop asked.

"His," I said.

"Are you carrying?"

"No. You already patted me down."

"Where's your car?"

"The little bitch he was with drove away with it," Ross said. He had moved into a sitting position to stretch out his injured right leg. "She clubbed me with a fucking bat."

The cop with the blond buzz cut wore a black Kevlar vest over his Derryville PD uniform. The badge over the vest read *Gramble*.

"Do you have a description of the car?" Gramble asked Ross.

"Bright yellow something," Ross said. "SUV. Bitch color."

"It's mango," I said.

"Who's in it?" Gramble asked.

"My client."

"The girl who assaulted Mr. Dunne?"

"The girl who stopped Mr. Dunne from shooting both of us."

"They were trespassing, scaring the customers," Ross said. "I confronted him and he started the fight. Sucker punched me."

"Bullshit," I said. "I'm a licensed private investigator. My ID is in my wallet in my left back pocket. I was surveilling the area. Legally."

"Why?"

"My client is looking for her father. Shawn Finley. Works or worked here. No one has been very cooperative about his whereabouts. Mr. Dunne pulled a gun on us. That's when things got a little messy. Oh, and he bit me twice."

"We already told him we don't know where the guy went. We're not his fucking babysitter," Ross said. "And I didn't pull a gun. It fell out of my jacket. It's the third time he and that bitch have been sniffing around here. He jumped me and I think she broke my fucking leg. I'm gonna sue both of you."

"Funny," I said. "Five minutes ago you threatened to kill us."

The steel back door to Cashel Rock opened and Colin Dunne stepped outside. He was wearing similar attire from the other day: a black open button-down shirt and designer jeans.

"Ross, you okay?" Colin shouted.

"I'm all right," Ross said. "Go back inside. We got the snoop."

"'We,'" I said.

"Please stay back until I've finished up here, Mr. Dunne," Gramble said. "I've got the suspect."

"'Suspect,'" I said.

Colin surveyed the scene for a moment, then slammed the steel door shut.

"You're under arrest for assault," Gramble said to me.

"And your friend here?"

"Mr. Dunne is not a friend. He is an upstanding member of Derryville."

"How low's the bar for that?"

"Take his fucking ass away," Ross said, still clutching his leg on the ground. "But before you do, give me one more good shot on him."

I thought about saying something else smart but decided not to give either one of them any ideas.

"That's enough," Gramble said. "Mr. Dunne, I'd like you to come down to the station tonight and make a statement. We'll put an APB out on the SUV."

He moved me away from the wall and toward the back seat of the squad car. No mention of any rights.

"Whatever happens next," I said to both of them, "I want you to know that my boss is a former San Francisco cop. He knows what happened and where I am."

"Ain't that special," Gramble said.

# CHAPTER 20

Predictably, a Derryville holding cell smelled like piss and vomit. I spent three hours with the responsible party: a twentysomething groom-to-be who got too hydrated at his bachelor party. He appeared to have started around first light. His cradle-pink button-down shirt was splotched with beer stains. His gelled-up spiky dark hair was tousled. He sat in the back corner doubled over. When he wasn't sleeping, he was groaning and rubbing his forehead.

"When's the wedding?" I said.

"Suptembro," he burbled.

Nobody at Derryville PD had bothered to take my fingerprints or my mug shot. Could have been laziness. Could have been incompetence. Maybe they wanted no record of my visit. I didn't press it. If they decided to rough me up, it would be my word against theirs. Plus, I'd already gotten my ass kicked once tonight.

My bite marks stung. My shoulder/arm had settled into the warm gooey sensation you feel when they inject contrast into your body at a doctor's office. My temple pounded like an Oakenfold song. I didn't have anything to do but try to think.

Was Shawn Finley alive?

Friday Finley believed her father might be dead. Given the cards she'd been dealt in life, I didn't blame her for being pessimistic. So far I'd given her no reason for hope. I couldn't find out where he lived or what car he drove or if he even had a car. All I had was a potential motive for either running away or getting killed. He clearly worked for some bad people. He also had a reputation as a tumbleweed, an indolent lush. He reminded me of Mr. Shiftlet in a short story I'd read as a kid. Both men worked on cars. Both lacked any apparent compass, moral or literal. Both left people behind.

I needed to find something out quickly, one way or the other. Every day Friday was losing more hope and every day was getting more dangerous. I hoped she'd gotten back to the house okay. I hoped she'd gotten the message to Powell. I didn't trust anyone in here.

I'd started to doze off when I heard my name.

"Shaw," the voice said. "Let's go."

I pushed myself off the cold hard concrete.

"Good luck with the wedding," I said to Bachelor Boy.

"Gank you," he muttered.

Cell doors make nasty awful metallic sounds even when they're letting you out. A cop with a double chin walked me out of the holding area and down two hallways into an office that looked more like a deer lodge. Dark wood panels lined the walls. Four stuffed deer heads stared at me in succession on the far wall by the window. Behind the desk were framed pictures of Gramble with a woman and two kids. I sat in a guest chair with cracking pleather.

Gramble was at the desk, still in uniform, now wearing eyeglasses. My wallet was next to him.

"I'm Chief Mike Gramble."

"Gramble on," I said. "Sing my song."

"What?"

"Nothing. I have a Zeppelin CD."

Gramble gave me his hard stare again. It was less intimidating without the aviator shades. Then he smiled pleasantly. His tone was pleasant. A pleasant conversation with a friendly public servant.

"I'd like to chat for a few minutes, Mr. Shaw."

"Am I still under arrest?"

"That's up to you."

I glanced around the room. I'd missed the procession of moose head mounts on the opposite wall.

"You like to hunt?"

"Intensely," Gramble said.

He took off his reading glasses and set them carefully on the desk.

"I know your byline, Mr. Shaw. I've read some of your articles in the *Chronicle*. I've enjoyed them. You won an award for your coverage of the Pac Heights killer, didn't you?"

"Pulitzer nomination."

"My, that's impressive. Now look at you. Peeking behind dumpsters in back alleys. How did an accomplished reporter like yourself transition into this line of work?"

"COVID has led a lot of people down strange paths."

"Meaning?"

"I got fired."

"Why?"

"Layoffs. I was making too much money. At least that's what they told me."

"You think there was another reason?"

"I'm not always the easiest to work with," I said.

"How so?"

"I don't have much of a filter with editors or sources or people in general. And most of the time I probably take too long to file. But I get results."

"I see," Gramble said. "Objectivity and accuracy are very important in any profession. It's hard to find reporters you can trust these days."

"Cops too," I said.

Gramble's pleasant expression disappeared for a moment. Then he found it again, like an actor fumbling for his next line.

"You have a sharp eye for detail when it comes to communicating matters of the law," he said. "At times in your commentary I've also detected a hint of mistrust of the criminal justice system. Would that be correct?"

"We all have our flaws," I said.

"I know about your friend Inspector Powell. I've attended conferences where Inspector Powell has spoken. He's an icon in the Bay Area. I learned a lot from the wisdom he shared with his colleagues in law enforcement. I care about being a good cop, Mr. Shaw. The Derryville Police Department, through my leadership, has become a fine institution."

"I'm sure it's very lucrative."

I wasn't paying much attention to what he said. I was looking at his blond buzz cut. It was perfectly done. He'd probably used a number one on the back and sides and a number two on top. He looked ready for a ride in an army chopper.

"Do you understand why I arrested you?"

"Because Ross Dunne told you to?"

Gramble leaned back in his recliner and cracked his knuckles. He wore a gold wedding ring on his left hand.

"I arrested you," he said, "to keep you from getting hurt, possibly getting killed. You think that fight would've stayed one-on-one for long?"

"Probably not."

"Probably not," Gramble repeated. "Mr. Dunne has informed me that he will not pursue charges against you."

"Well, that's nice to hear."

"You're free to go."

"Thanks."

"On one condition."

I had started to get up. I sat back down.

"I'd like to know why you chose the back alley to observe the Cashel Rock bar."

"The front parking lot was full," I said.

"I see. Did you see anything to help your investigation?"

"Not really."

Gramble studied me for a moment.

"That's too bad," he said.

"Can I ask you a question, Chief?"

"Please," he said.

"What do you know about Shawn Finley?"

"I've never heard of him until now."

"That's too bad," I said.

Gramble slid my wallet to me.

"I'll walk you out."

"Thanks for saving my life."

"Oh, don't mention it, Mr. Shaw. You know, I won't always be there to keep you out of trouble."

"And what does that mean, Chief Gramble?"

"It means Ross and Colin Dunne would like to chalk this whole thing up to a big misunderstanding. They'd like this all to go away. That's a two-way street, of course."

"I thought they were fine, upstanding citizens."

"Oh, they are. And they would like to continue on with their legitimate business. But they need you to allow them to do that. Will you allow them to do that, Mr. Shaw?"

I checked my wallet. My driver's license, investigator's license, credit cards, and cash were all still there. If they didn't already know where I lived, they did now. I thought of Callie asleep in Ryan's arms, skin to skin, the picture of love and comfort. It was time to drop the smart-ass act.

"Derryville's a lovely place," I said, "but I think I've seen enough. Tell the Dunnes no hard feelings."

Gramble smiled again.

"Excellent," he said. "You have a good night, now."

# CHAPTER 21

Dwayne Powell stood from the park bench outside the station and put a finger to his lips.

"Not a word until we're in the car," he said.

Even after midnight, Powell was professionally dressed in loafers and a tan collared shirt tucked in over gray jeans. When we got to his truck he handed me my phone, my keys, four aspirin, a water bottle, and an ice pack.

"You okay?" he asked.

"Yeah. Thanks."

"Anybody put a hand on you?"

"Nah. How's Friday?"

"She's fine. We met up in front of your house. I saw her inside and drove over here."

"She filled you in?"

"All of it."

I downed the aspirin and half the water bottle. I checked my phone. No missed calls or texts.

"Ryan must be asleep," I said.

"Glad somebody is," Powell said.

"Boss, you are the only reason, and I mean *the only* reason, I'm not still in there."

"I know."

We passed through Derryville's attempts at the twenty-first century on our way out of town. Its new shopping district welcomed a steady stream of car and foot traffic. A huge line wrapped around the drive-through at a Carl's Jr. grand opening. My stomach muttered something at me. I didn't feel like eating.

"How long were you at the station?" I asked.

"One hour and thirty-seven minutes," Powell said.

"Did you speak with Chief Mike Gramble?"

"Yes."

"What'd you think of him?"

"I think I'd like to smack the mustache off his face," Powell said.

"Told you he was dirty."

"All I needed was one look at him. One bad cop can ruin the reputation of every good cop."

"He knew all about you. Said he'd heard you speak at events."

"Guess he didn't listen. Did he explain why he arrested you?"

"Assault," I said. "But he didn't process me. Dumps me in a cell, lets me out, and says he was just protecting me from getting jumped by the whole bar. Says Ross Dunne declined to press charges."

"My guess is they want this all to go away," Powell said. "They don't want any trouble with you—or, by proxy, the San Francisco cops."

"Or you."

"Or me," Powell said.

"Did you see Ross or Colin Dunne come by the station?"

"No."

"Guess they didn't need to. Probably have Gramble on speed dial."

I moved the automatic seat back and sank into its leather finish. My adrenaline finally let up and my muscles started to relax. A wave of pain began to coat my entire body. I never wanted to move again. I wanted to stay there forever.

My phone buzzed. It was Friday.

> Mr. Powell said he would get you out. Please tell me you're okay.

I'm fine. On the way home. Get some sleep. We'll talk tomorrow.

"Gramble's right about one thing," Powell said. "You're lucky you're not dead. And you're lucky that little girl's not dead just like her father."

"You think Shawn Finley's dead?"

"It's been, what, over a week since she talked to him? No trace of him? And he might've been in deep with these chumps? I'd say he's floating face down someplace."

"I don't have the heart to tell her that," I said. "She wants me to keep reassuring her."

We turned onto the Bay Bridge. I envisioned Shawn Finley lying somewhere beneath it. I pressed the ice pack lightly to my temple. The cold did a decent job of numbing the pain. It felt like I was growing another head.

"Charlie, that little girl's got no business on a stakeout with you," Powell said.

"I know. Ryan said the same thing."

"And this is the last time I'm gonna tell you. If you wanna drive that fruit basket on wheels, you better make sure nobody sees you."

"I know. I got too aggressive."

I'd known Powell for six years. He'd always driven the same truck: a black 4x4 Dodge Ram crew cab with a menacing brush guard. It was a fortress of badasssery befitting his personality. Nobody got inside his head. It occurred to me that I didn't know much about him other than his résumé. The *Chronicle* did a nice profile on him when he won the Medal of Valor. It probably looked nice in a frame next to the Silver Star he'd received as an army captain in Kuwait. I'd met his wife, Jackie, at the ceremony. His sons, James and Reggie, were nice guys, quiet and thoughtful just like their father.

Unlike Chief Mike Gramble, Inspector Dwayne Powell was the real thing. He had served his country and his community honorably and admirably. To that end, he had no time for bullshit.

"Charlie, I'm letting you go," he said.

"Second time I've heard that tonight."

"No. I'm firing you."

"Look, I know I screwed up, boss. But I really need the extra cash right now."

"Your family needs you alive," Powell said.

We'd reached the edge of San Francisco from the bridge. To our right, a maze of brightly lit skyscrapers blinked at us through a thin fog. To our left were Oracle Park and McCovey Cove. A few hours earlier, a collection of paddleboats would've been drifting offshore in anticipation of a thunderous fly ball, waiting patiently like dogs under a dinner table. We wound our way onto Fremont and passed Salesforce Park, its lush, romantic greenery concealed by darkness. Below, just south of Market, a row of homeless tents crowded the sidewalk.

"Dystopian, isn't it?" I said.

"Very," Powell said.

Neither of us spoke again until Powell turned his truck onto Stockton and parked in front of my house. The curtains were closed and the lights were off.

"Can I at least keep the ice pack?"

"Sure," Powell said.

"Thanks. For the ice, but mostly for saving my ass tonight. Ryan's the smart one. We won't starve."

"I've got a business and a reputation to protect, Charlie. I can't have my employees getting into fights, getting arrested. It's taken a long time to build what I've got—as a soldier, as a cop, as a business owner."

I nodded.

"But that's not why I'm letting you go."

I pushed the seat up and stretched my shoulder. The dull nerve pain had been replaced by a general soreness. The aspirin wasn't helping yet.

"I'm letting you go because as your employer, I'm responsible for you," Powell said. "You *are* too aggressive. It's the same mistake you made as a reporter. You get any more aggressive and something bad is gonna happen. I'm ultimately responsible for what happens to you and what happens to your family. You've got a beautiful wife and daughter upstairs asleep right now. You want me having to knock on their door one night, tell them you got yourself killed?"

"No," I said.

"That's the damn road we're heading down," Powell said. "I hired you for some routine investigations. Nothing too crazy, nothing truly dangerous."

"I'm just trying to help a girl find her dad."

"I know. And she's gotten you into some shit. She didn't mean to, but here we are. Now you've gotta decide what's more important."

It was the most I'd ever heard him swear in one conversation.

"I know what's more important," I said. "But a guy's life might be at stake, and there's something up with his bosses. Did Friday send you the pictures of the cars parked out back of the bar?"

Powell flashed the Hate Smile.

"Yes, and I'm done talking about this," he said. "I looked up Ross Dunne's rap sheet. He's one crazy dude. His brother Colin is no saint either. They're both bad news. You can't get mixed up with them. The girl can't get mixed up with them. They've given you a free pass to back off and pretend this never happened. Use it."

Despite my body's best wishes, I unbuckled my seat belt, grabbed my stuff, and hopped out of the truck.

"Thanks again, boss," I said.

"Rest up, clear your head, get some distance from this, help that girl find some other family or at least find her way back home," Powell said. "Then come talk to me."

I nodded and closed the passenger door. My phone buzzed again. This time it wasn't Friday.

# CHAPTER 22

>Is this Charlie Shaw?

Yes.

>This is Tate. The bartender at the Rock. We met a few days ago.

I remember. Hi, Tate.

>I heard what happened behind the bar tonight. Are you okay?

I'm fine, thanks.

>Are you out of jail?

Yes.

>I may have some info on Shawn Finley.

I'd like to hear about it.

>Can we meet tonight? It's kinda urgent.

Dwayne Powell had made a convincing case to stay the hell away from the Dunnes or anyone connected with Shawn. I set my phone down in the kitchen and tiptoed past Friday asleep on the couch and past Ryan asleep in our bed. Sleep looked enticing. In the bathroom I brushed my teeth in the dark. I took out my contacts and put on my glasses. I went back to the kitchen for a water bottle. I glanced at the couch. Friday had rolled from her side to her back. For the first time, her face looked peaceful. In the morning, with her father still missing, the peaceful look would vanish. Her face would return to a familiar expression: a blend of worry, anguish, and pain.

I picked up my phone and texted Tate.

Sure, I can meet.

Keys in hand, Mango parked on the street, my head, neck, and shoulder begging for a soft pillow, I found myself back on the road toward India Basin at a quarter to one in the morning.

It wasn't until I reached Addison Lane that I considered this might be a trap. Maybe the Dunnes weren't really interested in a truce. Maybe she was loyal to her employers and gave them my business card tonight. Maybe Ross and Colin told her to set up an ambush at her place. I might be asking for another gun in my face.

Powell said I was too aggressive. He was right. The first rule in reporting was "Get the damn story." There was a story behind this case whether I found Shawn Finley or not. I liked finding stories and seeing where they led. I was also following Powell's first rule in investigating: "Use your instincts." I remembered the look on Tate's face in the bar when I met Colin. My gut said this wasn't a setup.

At a quarter past one, I parked two streets from Tate's address and walked the rest of the way. The fog had thickened and the temperature had dropped below fifty. Back in Texas it was a quarter past three and probably just below one hundred. In some ways, moving to California still felt like discovering a new planet. I zipped up my windbreaker. My mind flashed back to the Jericho in Ross's track jacket. I wished I'd brought my own. I grew up around guns but didn't like them. I wasn't a hunter or a collector or a killer. My father taught me that guns were an instrument for protection, nothing more. Ryan always thought I'd need one at some point doing this type of work. She was right. She was always right.

I checked the crib app on my phone. Callie was sleeping soundly in sort of a sprinter's stance: her head and torso arched forward, her left arm reared back and her right arm parallel with her right knee, pumping forward in acceleratory motion.

*Crawl before you can walk and walk before you can run, little one.*

I wondered how much she dreamed at this stage of her life. One day I'd ask her and actually receive a coherent response. I both looked forward to and dreaded the thought. It meant she'd be growing up. I wanted her to be my tiny little angel forever.

Tate's house was a tiny brick bungalow with a tiny front porch and a five-step concrete staircase to the front door. The rest of the street contained similar modest shotgun houses. The front lawn was the size of a golf cart and covered mostly in weeds, though someone had planted some cheerful iris bulbs along the sidewalk.

Gingerly—embarrassingly gingerly for a man in his early thirties—I climbed the steps and rang the doorbell. The door cracked open. A big blue eye peered out at me through the space. I smiled. The door widened.

"Come on in," Tate said.

I was immediately greeted with the unassailable musky smell of weed. The entire place wasn't much more than eight hundred square feet, with a tiny kitchen to the left and a tiny den to the right. It was neat except for some ashes on the coffee table in the den. A single roach had been put out in the ashtray. A single wineglass sat beside it.

Tate must've just gotten home. She was barefoot but otherwise provocatively dressed in careful makeup, a tight mauve miniskirt, and a tiny black tank top cut above her pierced belly button. Her long bleached blond hair was middle-parted with curtain bangs. The only thing she'd changed out of were her black heels. They lay on the carpet.

"Have a seat," she said, and pointed to a ratty couch behind the coffee table.

"Thanks."

"Can I get you anything?"

"About eighteen hours' sleep and a Vicodin drip."

"You look pretty good for getting into a brawl and spending half the night in jail."

"Looks can be deceiving," I said.

Other than the couch, the room was inexpensively but tastefully furnished, like a model space you'd see at IKEA, with a couple of potted fake plants and a gray oversized chair and ottoman opposite the couch. A decorative velvet pillow shared the word *Faith* in flowing script.

Tate dropped into the oversized chair.

"Apologies for the smell," she said. "I usually need something to help me come down after a shift."

She sat in the chair and sipped her wine with both hands like a communion taker. The silver cross was around her neck again.

"Wanna smoke? I've got a little left. Might take the edge off."

"I'm good. Thanks."

"You really beat the shit out of Ross tonight," she said, and laughed.

Her voice had a sexy feminine raspiness that might have been aided by the joint.

"How bad?"

"Colin had to help him back into the bar. Couldn't put any weight on his leg and his face was swelling up."

"Good."

She laughed again and sipped more wine.

"You liked seeing Ross beat up?"

"He's a dumbass," she said. "He's mean too."

"What about Colin?"

"Colin's all right."

"Is he a good boss?"

"He's all right."

"Are y'all friends?"

She eyed me for a few seconds, either suspiciously or seductively. I couldn't tell which. I could never tell which.

"'Friends,'" she repeated. The word made her laugh a little. "Yeah, I guess we're friends."

I didn't see any signs of a guest in the house. The kitchen was clean except for one bowl and spoon on the counter.

"You live here alone?"

"Yeah. Not much room for anyone else."

"Are you from Derryville?"

"Modesto. I did a couple semesters at USF, dropped out. Met Colin at a club. He needed bartender help."

"How long ago was that?"

"Couple years. Colin opened the bar a couple summers ago."

"When did Shawn Finley start?"

"Sometime last summer, I think."

"What can you tell me about Shawn?"

She stared at me again, this time non-seductively. It was more of that fearful look she'd shown at the bar.

"I wanted to text you the other day," she said. "When you slipped me your card."

"Why didn't you?"

She reached for her wine and downed the rest of it.

"I can't tell you too much," she said.

"I just want to find Shawn. I don't really care about anything else."

She hesitated, then nodded to herself.

"Shawn and I worked the bar together for a while. Colin hired me first. Then Ross hired Shawn. Both of us used to work the bar only. Colin took care of the finances. Ross handled most of the other staff—waiters, waitresses, cooks."

"Then what happened?"

"Ross and Colin, they started to . . ."

She paused.

". . . expand the business," she said. "They put me in charge of a lot of the day-to-day bar stuff. They got Shawn involved in some other things."

"What other things?"

"Other aspects of the business."

"What does 'the business' entail besides drinks and bar food?"

She looked down at her hands and ran two fingers over the silver cross.

"They hold this poker game on Thursday nights," she said. "In the back room."

"Did they play tonight?"

"Yeah."

"I saw those three cars parked out back," I said. "Who are they?"

"I don't know names."

I stared at her.

"Seriously," she said. "It's all arranged by Ross and Colin. The guys park in the back, walk down this little hallway, and into a back room. If they want drinks, Colin texts me the order and I leave a tray by the door."

"Very hush-hush," I said. "You've never seen the players?"

"Not once," she said. "And they've been doing this on Thursday nights for close to a year."

"What about the cars?"

"I've seen them when I go out back for a smoke break."

"Always the same cars? Black Ferrari, aqua blue McLaren, red Maserati SUV?"

"That sounds right."

"Was Shawn involved in this Thursday night game at all?"

"Not that I know of," Tate said. "It was strictly Ross and Colin's thing."

"Big-money stakes?"

"I told you, I really have no idea."

"But we do know the Dunnes are into underground gambling on some level."

"Yes."

"Where else did they 'expand the business'?"

She looked away again.

"Girls? Drugs?"

"Look, I don't know everything, okay? I just know Shawn helped Ross and Colin do some of the under-the-table stuff."

"And now Shawn is gone."

"I haven't seen him in a week or two," Tate said. "He just stopped showing up to work."

"Did you try to contact him?"

"Couple times, yeah."

"Nothing?"

"No."

"Do you have any idea where he might be?"

Tate shook her head.

"I overheard Ross and Colin tonight," she said. "Before they ran into you. They were whispering about something. Then Ross said something like, 'I wanna give him a proper send-off tomorrow night.' Colin laughed and said, 'A gold watch?' And they kept laughing."

"You think they were talking about Shawn?"

"Maybe. A gold watch means maybe they're talking about someone who works at the bar, right?"

"Maybe. How many are on staff?"

"Six, I think, counting me and Shawn."

I sighed. This wasn't as helpful as I'd hoped. My eyes felt heavy. Tate rubbed her cross. Must've been a nervous tic.

"Do you think they'd have any reason to hurt Shawn if they knew where he was or where he ran off to?"

"I don't know, maybe."

"Why?"

She shook her head.

"Did Shawn double-cross them?"

She shrugged. She wasn't giving me everything.

"Do you know if they've made other people disappear before?"

She shook her head again.

"Do you think there's a chance they already killed Shawn?"

"What? No. I mean, fuck, I don't know. I have no idea. That's why I'm asking you. I'm worried about him."

"Do you have any idea where I should look next?"

"I don't know for sure. But Ross and Colin have this tradition Friday nights where they hit up this casino."

"Where?"

"The La Rousse casino. Outside Sonoma."

"I've heard of it. It's new."

"It occurred to me that maybe . . . well, maybe Shawn found a job at the casino and they found out about it."

"Are they going this Friday night? Tomorrow night?"

"Yes."

She blinked her eyes. I looked at my phone and tried to hold back a yawn. Quarter till two.

"Have you thought about calling the cops?"

"About Shawn?"

"Yeah."

She laughed.

"They own the cops," she said.

"In Derryville?"

"Yeah."

"Chief Gramble?"

"The guy with the mustache? Especially him."

"How'd they pull that off?"

She started to speak, then thought better of it.

"Like I said, I don't know everything, okay? I just know they've been building things up for a while."

"Other aspects of the 'business.'"

"Yeah."

"But you want someone to help Shawn."

"Yeah. He's a good person. You've talked with his daughter, right?"

"Yes. She doesn't think he's a good person. But he's her dad."

"When she came into the bar the other day, I wanted to say something. The poor girl. She looked so scared."

"Why do you think Shawn is a good person?"

"He talks about her . . . what's her name?"

"Friday."

"Friday, yeah. How could I forget a name like that? He talks about her all the time. Shows me pictures of her. He's been trying to get sober. Trying to get himself right before he sees her again. He was planning to go see her earlier this year."

"What happened?"

"He slipped."

"With the bottle?"

"And other things. It happens."

"And you know something about that," I said.

Tate's blue eyes widened, then sank to the floor.

"Yeah," she said.

I looked at the empty wineglass. I glanced back at Tate. She was looking at it too.

"I've been clean almost a year," she said. "With the hard stuff, at least."

"Must be tough bartending."

She nodded.

"Shawn's been going through the same thing. We'd talk about it."

"Talk each other through it?"

"Yeah. It was . . . I dunno. Cathartic."

"Sounds like you were a good team," I said.

"Yeah. He looked out for me, more than Colin or Ross would. The guy's great with cars. Fixed a flat for me one time. Gave me a jump before. Told me I needed a new battery and put it in himself."

"Former mechanic," I said.

"Right."

"What about you and Colin?"

"What about us?"

"You said you and Shawn are close. You also said you and Colin are friends."

She looked at her hands.

"Are you and Colin more than friends?"

She shrugged.

"Depends on the week," she said.

"Do you love him?"

It was a personal question, but I'd gotten this far and figured it was worth a shot. She also was inebriated on two fronts.

"No," she said to her hands. "But he takes care of me. He's been pretty good to me."

"That's something at least."

"But this whole thing has gotten out of control. All the shit they're into. I don't even really know who he is anymore."

"And you want out."

She looked up from her hands. She wasn't crying, but a stress tear had formed in her right eye. She wiped it away. She nodded and rubbed her cross again.

"Are you religious?"

It was another personal question. She gave me a puzzled look. She glanced down at her necklace and back at me.

"Oh. No, not really," she said. "My dad was. He gave this to me when I was little, before he died."

There was a hard knock at the door. *Boom, boom, boom, boom, boom, boom.* Six knocks in succession. Powerful.

"Tate," a muffled male voice said.

"Oh shit," she said, and jumped to her feet. She grabbed me by the arm and pulled me off the couch.

"You have got to get in this closet right now," she whispered. "If he sees you, he'll kill you."

"Who?"

"Bosh," she said.

# CHAPTER 23

I crammed myself into the coat closet by the front door. Coats and jackets smothered me. A naked metal hanger jabbed into the back of my neck. I had no space to lift a finger. It felt just like home.

I heard the heavy sound of boots hitting the white tile just inside the doorway. The door slammed shut.

"It's late," Tate said. Her voice sounded tired and irritable. "What's up?"

I didn't have time to ask her who "Bosh" was before she shoved me in the closet. Didn't matter. I knew the voice. "Bosh" was Snake Tat.

"You're not answering your phone," he said to Tate.

His voice sounded even huskier two feet away. I took a deep breath, swallowed hard, and tried not to move. The edge of the metal hanger pressed hard on my neck. My hands began to clam up. I wondered how long this would last.

"It's two o'clock in the fucking morning," Tate said.

"Colin sent me over here," Bosh said. "Wanted to make sure you're okay."

"I'm fine."

"And he has a message for you. He wants you to open the bar in the morning."

"Fine," Tate said. "Whatever."

"Is anybody else here?"

There was a pause. It felt like an eternity. I imagined Tate pointing to the door, the literal trap they'd laid for me. I'd walked into it like a dog after a Milk-Bone.

"No," Tate said. "Just me."

The closet door didn't open.

The heavy boots battered the tile again. I heard the front door open and slam shut and a few moments later a car engine start and tires squeal.

The closet door opened. I was free.

Tate had her hands behind her head. She inhaled and exhaled in slow, measured puffs, trying to control her breathing.

"Sorry about that," she said.

I peeked through the blinds. Black Escalade. I still couldn't make out the plates.

"Bosh," I said.

She nodded.

"Got a full name?"

"No. That's what they call him."

"Do you know where he lives?"

"No idea. I think Ross hired him. He started showing up around the bar a few months ago."

"Is he there much?"

"Hardly ever. When he is, he either goes straight to the back room or the office or stays outside and picks up Ross or Colin. It's shady as fuck."

"I saw Bosh in Sausalito a couple nights ago," I said. "Ross and Colin were with him. He got out of his Escalade and beat a guy half to death. Guy's name is Scottie Coburn. Worked for Rivet Security in San Francisco. Got fired this week for sleeping with a very wealthy man's wife."

I showed her a picture of Scottie on my phone.

Tate shook her head.

"No. I've never seen him."

"What exactly does Bosh do for the Dunnes besides hurt people?"

"I don't know for sure," Tate said. "When I first saw him, I thought he was the new bouncer in the bar. But like I said, he's almost never around."

"You think he's doing some of their under-the-table stuff?"

"Yes."

"Like Shawn did?"

"No. Different from Shawn. This guy is legitimately scary. I think he's a fucking psycho or something. He wears fucking combat boots. Gives me the creeps that he knows where I live. Did you park in front of the house?"

"No. Couple streets over."

"You've gotta get out of here. Jesus, I've probably told you too much. I don't even remember everything I've fucking said."

"I'll let you know if I find Shawn," I said. "Take care of yourself."

She was done talking. The door shut hard behind me. I went down her front steps and glanced around for the Escalade. It was gone. I walked the two blocks back to Mango and drove home.

# CHAPTER 24

The most-recent best moment of my life came on March second. Callie had just passed the two-month mark. It was the first time she truly recognized my face, not just my voice. I didn't realize that a baby's sight wasn't fully developed for the first few months. Until then, she probably saw Ryan and me in fuzzy gray bits and pieces.

On March second, I was strapping Callie into her stroller for a morning walk on the Embarcadero. I was a foot from her face, close enough for full cognizance at her age. Suddenly her eyes widened. Her mouth dropped open. She didn't make a sound. She just stared at me in toothless wonderment.

"Hi, precious," I said.

I finished strapping her in and backed away. She stared out at the morning sunshine. Her eyes scrunched and her mouth widened into a voiceless roar, like a lioness presiding over her savanna. It was the most joyous thing I've ever seen.

At six thirty Friday morning, Ryan and I were back on the Embarcadero pushing Callie's stroller. We'd beaten most of the car and bike traffic and, most importantly, the tourists. I'd gotten the best forty-five minutes of sleep of my life. I'd crawled into bed at three, listened to my head thump for an hour, listened to Callie cry for an hour, then felt Ryan nudge me at five forty-five.

"Surprise," she said. "I'm on PTO today. Callie's up again. Wanna take her for a walk?"

"I got home at three," I murmured.

"Come on," she said. "It'll be fun."

So we did. Grace Chen made us some coffee on the way out. Friday Finley, after all the fun we'd had in Derryville, was still asleep on the couch.

The sun's warmness felt good on my face. The sun's brightness did not feel good on my eyes. I'd taken more aspirin with my coffee. It hadn't kicked in yet.

Ryan had her hair in a bun. She wore her Stanford hoodie over black spandex pants and white sneakers. She was lean and athletic and undeniably lovely. I wondered if the monthlong no-sex thing was really still a thing.

"How'd your presentation go?" I asked.

"Good," Ryan said. "They approved the storyboard and budget for a new commercial."

"Can I be in it?"

"No."

"I've been thinking," I said. "We could sign Callie up for some baby modeling gigs, like the Gerber commercials, and *she* could be the family breadwinner."

"I'm not letting our daughter be a child actor," Ryan said. "Can you believe this is Grace's last day?"

"Nope."

"I think it's been worth the money."

"Absolutely."

"Callie slept seven and a half hours straight last night."

"All it took," I said, "was her learning to suck her own thumb."

"It's called self-soothing."

"Couldn't we have figured that out on our own?"

"Did we?"

"No. You're right, Grace is amazing."

"She cooks, she cleans, she vacuums," Ryan said. "God, I don't want her to go. If it came down to you or her, tough call."

"Funny," I said.

"That reminds me. We've gotta get Callie some new clothes.

These onesies are getting tight on her. She probably could wear a six-to-twelve-month size at this point."

"Okay."

"And we're running low on formula again. I swear she drinks a gallon of that stuff a day."

"Okay."

"I don't feel bad anymore about going to formula so quickly. Remember our first night with her at home? God, that seems like a lifetime ago. You were so sweet going to find some in the middle of the night. Was better than her starving. I just couldn't pump anything out. Looking back, I was probably feeling too much pressure. My God, the cries she was making. Poor thing. I think I had nightmares about them for weeks."

"I got arrested last night," I said.

Ryan stopped the stroller.

"Excuse me?"

"Well, more like detained."

"What are you talking about?"

"Let's keep pushing. She'll start crying if we stop."

Ryan acquiesced but kept her eyes on me as we walked.

"Charlie Shaw," she said, "what the fuck?"

I pointed to the stroller.

"*Fudge*," Ryan said. "What the fudge?"

"It's a long story. We were in Derryville. Friday and me."

"Derryville?"

"Yeah."

"You're lucky you didn't get shot."

"Well . . ."

"You got shot?"

"No. Almost. I got in a fight with a guy we were staking out."

"Who?"

"One of the guys that Friday's dad worked for. At a bar called Cashel Rock. His name's Ross Dunne. He owns the bar with his brother, Colin."

"This guy Ross pulled a gun on you?"

"Yes. He said we were trespassing. We got him, uh, subdued. I told Friday to take off and she did, just before the Derryville police chief showed up and hauled me away. Just me, interestingly enough. Not Ross. Powell came to the station and took me home."

"Are you okay? Your face looks okay."

"I'm okay."

"Is Friday okay?"

"Yes."

"Did you have to post bail?"

"No."

"What did they arrest you for?"

"Assault. No charges. The Derryville police chief said he was protecting me from getting killed."

"What do you think?"

"I think the Derryville police are as crooked as my shoulder."

We were walking south toward the ballpark. Ryan stopped in front of the Hi Dive bar and pushed the stroller to a bench facing the water. The morning sun stretched its legs.

Ryan peeked inside the stroller.

"She's asleep. I've got to sit down."

I sat with her. Ryan took a deep breath and exhaled slowly.

"I was just about to lift your suspension," she said.

"Because I look so good in these short shorts?"

"Now's not a great time to flirt with me."

"Sorry."

"But yes, you look good."

"You too."

We watched the water together.

"I thought your last job was creepy and a little scary," Ryan said. "Covering all those awful crimes. This is . . ."

"Worse?"

"Much. You're not just writing about it. You're living it. Can't you go back to reporting? Call up Maggie at the paper? I'm sure she'd hire you back."

"I don't want to go back," I said. "Not right now, at least."

"Because you have a client?"

"There was this one case I wrote about a couple years ago," I said. "Family on Capp Street. The father came home, got in an argument with the wife. Pulled a gun. Shot her. Shot her mother who was living with them. Then he shot himself. The only survivor was his six-year-old daughter. The mother had shielded her before taking a bullet in the head. I still remember pictures of the girl's face. I don't know what happened to her."

"I asked you the other night about your sister," Ryan said. "I asked if you're helping Friday because you're still grieving for Sophie. You told me no."

"I did."

"I don't believe you. I think you grieve for her as much now as you did then."

"You didn't know me then."

"I know you better than you know yourself."

"That's probably true."

"Am I right about Sophie?"

"Yes."

"It still hurts?"

"Yes."

"And helping Friday eases the pain a little?"

"Yes. And helping Friday is what I would do for Callie. To the ends of the Earth."

We watched the water for another minute. Then Ryan pulled the stroller around to face us. Callie was zonked out. Her head drooped. The bottom of her chin pressed against her chest. A thin line of drool hung from her lower lip. Ryan wiped it away carefully with her sweatshirt.

"Friday has her mom's ashes in her roller bag," Ryan said. "In a little urn."

"You went through her stuff?"

"Yes. Her first night here."

"Ryan . . ."

"I wanted to make sure she wasn't a danger to any of us."

"She's not."

"I know that now. I haven't had a chance to interact with her much. I've been so busy with work this week. But she seems like a wonderful girl. Smart, pretty, helpful. Grace raves about her."

"They've hit it off."

"The poor girl's got a crappy life. You're doing your best to make it a little less crappy."

Ryan pointed to Callie.

"But this girl is our prize," she said. "She is irreplaceable. And so are you. Nothing comes before us."

"I know."

"Then please, let this go."

"Powell said the same thing."

"He's right."

"Friday saved my life," I said.

"What?"

"She grabbed her baseball bat from the car and hit Ross Dunne with it. Made him drop the gun."

"She's kind of a badass, isn't she?"

"A complete badass. She knows how to handle herself. Sophie was the same way. When we were kids, she got a black eye riding her bike into a fire hydrant. Shrugged it off like it was nothing. When I first saw Friday's face, the black eye, it was like looking at Sophie. Is any of this making sense?"

"Yes," she said.

"It's not easy for guys to talk about their feelings."

"I know. So you're saying you owe it to Friday to keep looking into this?"

"I'm saying I want to finish what I started," I said. "Or at least try. I have a lead."

"On finding Friday's dad?"

"Maybe. Tonight at that new casino near Sonoma."

"Will these Dunne brothers be there?"

"Yep. It's my educated guess that they're into some bad stuff. And that they're paying off the local police. And that they want to knock off Friday's dad, if they haven't already."

"Why is it an educated guess?"

"I found a source."

"Like the sources you had at the paper," Ryan said.

"Yep."

"What kind of 'bad stuff' are we talking here?"

"I think the Dunnes are into multiple illegal activities. Underground gambling is one of them. Turns out they were hosting a high-stakes poker game last night at the bar. Three very expensive cars parked out back."

"Did you recognize them?"

"Nope. I got the license plates but haven't run them yet."

Ryan took another deep breath.

"You don't think Friday's dad disappearing is much of a coincidence, do you?"

"Not one percent," I said.

"I don't want you to go tonight."

"I'll be careful. More careful than I was last night."

"Can Mr. Powell come with you?"

"He fired me last night."

"Why? Because you got arrested?"

"Because he wants me off this case."

"Maybe you should listen to him," Ryan said.

"I definitely should listen to him."

"But you won't."

"Not yet."

"If you don't call Mr. Powell, then I wish you'd call Tex," Ryan said.

"Friday asked me to leave the cops out of it."

"But you guys could've been killed last night."

"She's my client."

"She's sixteen, for fuck's sake."

"*Fudge.*"

"Sorry."

"It's not really SFPD's jurisdiction anyway," I said. "And it's pretty obvious the Derryville cops are on some kind of payroll. They wouldn't investigate a damn thing."

Ryan's eyes stared into mine.

"I told you that you needed a gun," she said.

"I won't need a gun tonight. I'm just gonna surveil."

"Better than you did last night?"

"Much better. Besides, I'll be in a very public place."

"Are we even safe at home right now?"

"Yes. The Dunnes are leaving town today. Besides, I don't really think they want any more trouble. They know who Powell is and they know he's got connections to the cops."

"They're hoping you'll leave this alone?"

"I told the Derryville police chief that I would."

"But you won't," Ryan said.

"Not yet."

"I'm texting you tonight. Every twenty minutes."

"Okay."

She took my hand and kissed it and snuggled in close to me. She looked down and noticed the back of my forearm. Ross Dunne's teeth had turned my skin puffy and red-and-bluish.

"Jesus," Ryan said. "Did you fight a rattlesnake too?"

"The guy bit me."

"I can see that. Any other battle scars?"

"Caught a fist right here," I said, and pointed to my head.

Ryan touched it gently. It still stung.

"Feels like a fucking tennis ball," she said.

"*Fudge,*" I said.

"Oh, shut the fuck up. She's asleep."

We looked at Callie again. I knew Ryan was thinking what I was thinking. *How did we make something so perfect?*

"You'll miss dinner tonight," Ryan said. "Grace is cooking."

"I know. Save some for me."

"You'll need a nap before you leave."

"Let's walk home, then."

"You promise you'll take care of yourself?"

"Yes," I said. "I'll bring the bat."

# CHAPTER 25

"Take the bat," Friday said to me.

"For luck or protection?"

"Both."

We were sitting on her bed for the week. For four straight mornings she had straightened her sheets and moved the foldout under the couch and arranged the cushions exactly as they'd been when she arrived.

"You don't have to do that," I said.

"I'm kind of a neat freak. My mom was the opposite."

"We appreciate the attention to detail. But it's your bed. Make it as messy as you want. I do with mine."

"It's kind of a good luck thing."

"Making the bed?"

"Yeah."

"You believe in luck?"

"Kinda. Maybe it's my Irish side. My dad would always say, 'My luck's about to turn, my girl Friday.' Except it never really did."

"But you still believe."

"Mainly I'm just trying not to be a slob around here. You guys have enough to deal with."

"Ain't that the truth."

"You ever notice that your mind's fresher when you first wake up every morning? Before your brain has time to kick into anxiety mode?"

"Always. The older you get the less fresh it gets."

"I'm just always a little more optimistic about things when I first wake up. Before the world has time to beat me down."

"I know what you mean."

"I wake up and think, 'Maybe we'll find him and this will be my last day here,'" Friday said. "And when I go, you guys won't have to clean up after me. Things can just go back to the way they were. For you guys and for me. No offense."

"None taken."

She was wearing a new classic rock tee under her denim jacket. The Clash.

"I'm sorry you can't go tonight," I said. "It's twenty-one and up only."

"It's okay."

"And after last night, I can't risk your safety again."

"It's cool, really."

"You sure you're okay after last night? I should never have put you in that situation."

"I'm fine. I'm not the one who got bashed in the head."

"I mean emotionally."

"I'm all right," she said. "I just want to know."

"You deserve to know."

"And I trust you'll do everything you can to find out."

"I will."

"But I don't trust those guys," she said.

"Me either."

We'd run out of things to say. I noticed she'd set the wool heart pillow upside down on the couch. I fixed it.

"Maybe you are a slob," I said.

She smiled. The dimple below her right cheek resurfaced.

"Whoops," she said.

"Clash today, huh?"

"Yeah."

"What's your favorite song?"

"Probably 'Train in Vain.'"

"Mine too. When I was growing up, I used to think instead of 'Rock the Casbah,' they were saying 'Rob the Cash Bar.'"

Friday laughed. If I couldn't find Shawn Finley, I'd settle for that small victory once every couple of days.

"Speaking of getting robbed," I said, "the repair shop called."

"Did they find the parts they needed?"

"Yeah. Might take a day or two."

"How much do I owe you?"

"I'm not telling."

"It's a lot, isn't it?"

"It's not a little. But it's on Ryan and me."

"Is she okay with that?"

"Sure."

"I'm paying you back," Friday said, "if it takes me twenty years."

Ryan was in the shower. Grace entered the kitchen wearing her night nurse uniform.

"We're officially down for our nap, and it's officially Chef Grace time. Got an apron?"

"Bottom drawer by the fridge."

"Thank you, sir."

"What's on the menu?"

"Tomato-egg stir-fry with scallion pancakes, a family treat. Ryan and Friday are going to help me."

"You might regret that," Friday said.

"Sorry again about missing out," I said to Grace.

"Don't think of it. Duty calls. I have a positive feeling, a real positive energy, that it's going to be a good night all around. Ooh, this is a cute apron."

The apron read *I Don't Know What I'm Doing*.

"Grace," I said, "have you ever had a bad day?"

"That's entirely up to me. And for that reason, no."

I zipped most of the bat into my backpack, which Ryan had already packed with snacks. She'd folded a note inside.

*Be fucking careful. I love you.*

"I'm gonna head out before she tries to talk me out of going," I said.

"Best of luck," Grace said.

"Yeah," Friday said. "Good luck."

I held out my fist for a bump. Friday hugged me instead.

I walked to Callie's nursery, blew a kiss to the door, and headed downstairs to Mango.

The Friday night traffic made the drive closer to an hour and a half than an hour. La Rousse casino was a sprawling five-hundred-thousand-square-foot property between Sonoma and Santa Rosa on a quiet stretch of the 101, neighbored only by a small hospital and a senior living home.

The twenty-story property was brilliantly lit and not-so-subtly inspired by the flamboyant casinos of Monte Carlo: creamy stucco, fabulously ornate doors, perfectly symmetrical windows. A grand fountain, surrounded by lush landscaping, stood regally in the circle drive to the main doors. The place was decidedly European except for the Super Walmart–sized parking lot the length of ten football fields extending out toward the highway. It had become the top gambling destination—the top *legal* gambling destination— for most people in the Bay Area, and for tourists, it was a short drive to wine-tasting destinations in Santa Rosa to the north and Sonoma to the east and Napa farther to the east. One glance at a dreamy vineyard off SR 37 would make them forget all about the eight hundred bucks they'd blown on craps.

I'd never been inside the hotel. The main lobby had an airy luxe look, with Corinthian columns and potted plants and ornate velvet and linen upholstery. The casino had all the normal trappings: a thousand dopamine machines and tables dressed up by a garish decor. The floors were carpeted in loud and earthy colors in wild circular patterns. They meshed well with the endless dings and bings from the slots and the endless supply of interior oxygen. An insomniac's wet dream.

Walking in the place, you'd expect every man to be dressed like

007 and every woman to be dressed like Halle Berry. Instead it was a hilarious mix of jeans and jorts and suits and dresses and leggings and heels and flip-flops. My attire was somewhere near the median: brush-cotton tan pants, an untucked black button-down and black-and-white Jordan 1s. I'd also worn a black cap and sunglasses, not so much to channel Phil Hellmuth but to avoid detection by my Derryville friends.

My watch read just after eight. I walked a lap around the maze. I didn't like to gamble. I wasn't very good at it and I didn't enjoy donating money for noncharitable reasons. Living out here made me realize just how many people had no income at all, much less disposable income. Blackjack was particularly evil. I sat at a blackjack table in Oklahoma once and lost eighty bucks in eighty seconds. I also managed to piss off the guy next to me because apparently I hit when I shouldn't have. I didn't know it was a team sport.

The place was pretty full and would get fuller in the next two hours. I saw no sign of Ross Dunne or Colin Dunne or Shawn Finley. I thought about Tate's theory and wasn't sure I bought it. If Shawn Finley found another job as a casino dealer or a pit boss or a bartender, why would he leave without notice? Perhaps he simply had no professionalism, no tact. The way his daughter described him and the way his rap sheet read, I could buy unprofessional. Perhaps he didn't like or respect his employers. I wouldn't blame him for that. Perhaps he had reason to fear them. That seemed plausible too.

At the very least, Shawn Finley would've said goodbye to Tate. They'd become confidants, co-counselors through the hellscape of addiction. Ghosting her on purpose seemed unlikely. I didn't like that he'd disappeared without explanation. I didn't like the conversation Tate had overheard between Ross and Colin Dunne.

I sat at the bar a few feet from a set of slots and ordered a beer. Unsurprisingly, a video poker screen was available at each seat. Before Callie was born, Ryan said she always did pretty well at these in Las Vegas. The key was finding a "Jacks or Better" machine with a progressive jackpot. The screen in front of me offered both. I ignored it.

On cue, twenty minutes after I'd parked and told her I made it safely, Ryan texted me again.

>How's it going?

Bored.

>Seen anyone yet?

Nope.

>Is the casino nice?

I guess.

>Dinner was amazing.

Wish I was there.

>Me too. Don't gamble.

You know I won't gamble.

>A big pack of diapers costs $48.50.

I know.

>Friday said you got a report back on her car.

Yes.

>How much will that cost?

More than the diapers.

>Be careful.

I will.

>And don't gamble.

The bar had a view of the poker room down the tiled walkway. I kept an eye on the entrance for a while. No one I knew came in or out. A gray-haired woman in too-tight jeans sat next to me and ordered a Bloody Mary. The bartender was not Shawn Finley.

"Having any luck?" the woman asked me.

"None," I said.

"Me either until I played that Monopoly Big Spin over there," she said, and pointed behind us. "Two hundred smackeroos."

She showed me her chips.

"Guess that means you're buying."

She guffawed.

"Sure thing, honey," she said. "You're cute enough."

I thanked her for the beer but couldn't let her distract me. I made another lap. Halfway back to the bar, I spotted two guys sitting alone at a blackjack table. I could've recognized that forehead from Napa. It was Ross Dunne.

# CHAPTER 26

Colin Dunne sat next to Ross at the blackjack table. They both wore their customary attire: Colin in a pink button-down open at the chest, Ross in a white track jacket also, unfortunately, open at the chest. Ross had a beer. Colin had a cocktail with a tiny straw. Each boasted a respectful chip stack. I sat at some generic slot machine twenty yards away and pretended to play.

Ryan texted me.

                                                          Still okay?

Yes. Can't talk now.

                                        Did you find them?

What part of "Can't talk now" isn't clear?

                                                            Asshole.

Sorry.

I watched the Dunnes play blackjack. The brothers didn't look alike. They acted differently too. Colin was subdued, serious, calculated. He studied his hand and the dealer the way he'd studied his computer at Cashel Rock. Ross talked incessantly at an unpleasant level. He constantly fiddled with his chips. He laughed like a prepubescent jackal. If he wasn't Colin's brother, Colin probably would've choked him. I thought about going over there and doing it myself.

Ten minutes later a man walked up behind the Dunnes and put his arms around them. He wore a beige linen suit with a matching beige vest. It was a lighter, more summery look than the dark suit he'd worn in his office. The beige matched his tan skin. A white handkerchief matched his white shirt. He wore no tie tonight, but his soccer haircut was still impeccably moussed and styled.

Ross and Colin stood up and hugged Dalton Crawford, founder and CEO of Rivet Security.

"Scottie Coburn's ex-boss," I said to the slot machine. "Didn't see that one coming."

Ross and Colin invited Crawford to join them at the table. He did. He moved smoothly, confidently, as a man with a five-thousand-dollar suit should. He smiled, revealing his extraordinarily white teeth. His apricot face was completely unwrinkled, as if somebody had ironed it. He set a bill on the table. The dealer accepted it and presented him with chips, probably a hundred bucks' worth. I continued to fake-play the slots.

Crawford and the Dunne brothers stayed on blackjack for the next half hour. Colin's stack dwindled a little. Ross's stack crumbled. Crawford's stack continued to grow. From this distance I couldn't hear a word any of them said over the casino racket. Only Ross's laughs and hollers were audible. At one point Colin got up to use the restroom. I turned my back as he walked past me. I moved to a different slot machine set back a few feet from the walkway with a view of the table. It would be highly disappointing for them to spot me now.

At a quarter past nine, Ross set down his cards and picked up his phone. He appeared to be reading a text. He nudged Colin and showed him the screen. Colin smiled. Ross put his phone away. The brothers folded their hands, tossed a few chips to the dealer, stood, and headed down the walkway together.

Crawford didn't watch them go. He continued playing Heads-Up against the dealer.

I set down my warm beer and followed Ross and Colin through the path of restaurants and roulette tables and bewildering sets of slot machines out through the front entrance and into the parking lot. Ross wasn't moving so good. He wore a black walking boot on his right leg. I smiled and thought of Friday.

*Pretty good slugging percentage, kid.*

Ross and Colin walked the long distance toward the back of the parking lot, near the access road to the highway. They stopped at the driver-side window of a blue Toyota Corolla and spoke to someone behind the wheel.

I crouched behind a Buick two rows back from the Corolla. I couldn't see the driver and I didn't recognize the car. It was an older model with California plates. Its engine and headlights were off. Colin said something to the driver and walked with Ross to the rear of the car. They glanced around suspiciously. The lot didn't have many parked cars this far back.

Satisfied they weren't being watched, Colin popped the trunk open.

I couldn't see inside, but the Dunnes appeared satisfied with the contents. They smiled and fist-bumped each other.

Colin closed the trunk and patted the top of it twice. The driver got the message. The Corolla's engine started. The headlights flipped on.

As the Dunnes started back toward the casino, I tried to remember where the hell Mango was. For once, the bright-yellow paint came in handy on a stakeout. I spotted her a few rows behind me. I peeled away from behind the Buick, tiptoed to the correct row, and sprinted to her, praying my footsteps fell out of earshot.

The driver did me a favor by not leaving right away. I had enough time to start up Mango just as the Corolla turned onto the access road that fed into the 101 south toward San Francisco.

Of course, Ryan texted again.

Still okay?

"Yes, but still can't talk, sweetie," I said to Siri.

> Sorry. Friday wanted to know how things are going. She's having a hard time with all of this. Harder than I am.

"I know. Tell her I'm doing my best and I miss you guys. Kiss Callie for me."

> Love you.

"Love you too."

There was a decent amount of traffic at nine thirty on the 101. I was thankful for it. More cars allowed me to hang a few lengths back. The Corolla was doing exactly the speed limit and I hoped it would stay that way. Mango did pretty well on the highway for a senior citizen, but I didn't want to test her at eighty-plus miles an hour for long stretches.

I had nothing to do while driving in the dark except keep my eyes on the Corolla and try to think. My head still throbbed from last night and the endless casino buzz didn't help. Sitting in the car and the bar and at the slot machines made my shoulder ache. The lack of sleep made me yawn. At least Ross's bite marks had stopped stinging. I popped a couple of aspirin from the bottle Powell gave me. Man, I was getting old.

*Think, Charlie.* What would Powell do in this situation?

Powell said he would've dropped the case right after Derryville. I didn't believe him. He was too competitive and too prideful and too damn good at his job. I was competitive and prideful, at least.

I could call Tex at the SFPD and tell him what I had seen. I could at least give him the car's plates. But what exactly did I see? Two guys opening a trunk? Maybe they'd ordered custom golf clubs. Or a case of Opus One from the vineyard. I had nothing to go on besides circumstantial evidence that these guys were total creeps.

Ten miles up the road in Petaluma, the Corolla got off the highway and stopped for gas. I parked Mango behind some trees at the restaurant next door. I got out, crouched between two trees, and waited.

The man called Bosh got out of the Corolla.

He had on the same black combat boots I'd seen outside Scottie Coburn's houseboat and heard outside Tate's closet. He wore the same hooded leather jacket over torn blue jeans. His face had the same feral glower that sent a little shiver through my nervous system.

Bosh made a couple of selections at the pump and inserted the nozzle into the Corolla's tank. He removed an object from his jacket pocket and tossed it in the trash. Then he lumbered inside the convenience store.

I jumped from behind the trees and hustled to the pump, which was parallel to the store entrance. I fished the object from the trash. It was a cell phone. I stuffed it in my pants pocket and threw a glance at the entrance. Nothing. No other cars were around. Bosh had left his unlocked.

I took a deep breath and tried the trunk. It clicked open.

I stared down at a lifeless body, a man's, with dark shoulder-length hair, lying in a fetal position.

# CHAPTER 27

I grabbed the body by the shoulders the way I usually pick up Callie, except two hundred pounds heavier, and pulled it from the trunk. I held it upright, pressed against me, and closed the trunk with one hand.

Bosh was still inside the store.

I lifted the body over my decent shoulder and speed-walked back to Mango. A pulse of hot magma shot through my arm. Something dripped down my neck. I dropped the body into a sitting position behind the trees and tried to control my breathing. The whole sequence had lasted maybe a minute, but it felt like an hour had passed. I hadn't heard a single sound in the moment, not even the faint wisp of breath from the body.

I crouched down close to Shawn Finley and felt for a pulse. It was faint too, but it was there.

I rubbed the side of my neck and then my wet fingers. Shawn had a small gash on the top of his forehead where it met his hairline. Blood had dripped down the side of his face and onto his gray tank top.

A moment later, Bosh exited the store with a plastic sack in one hand and a can of beer in the other. He replaced the pump, closed the gas cap, threw his bag inside the Corolla, started the engine, and drove back toward the highway.

My body shuddered and released every ounce of adrenaline. I looked over at the broken man. His face didn't entirely match the old picture Friday had given me. He was heavier now, unhealthier looking, with longer, stringy hair. The blood from his forehead had seeped into his gray-flecked stubble.

I pushed myself up and retrieved a water bottle from my backpack, poured some onto my hands, and lightly slapped his cheeks. His body stirred and his nose sniffed. I slapped him a little harder. His dark eyes twitched and then opened slowly. He let out an atrocious cough and spat on the pavement.

"Shawn Finley," I said. "Charlie Shaw."

The man coughed some more and spat again.

"Ohhhh," he moaned.

"You're welcome," I said. "We've gotta get out of here before that son of a bitch realizes he left a body behind."

"Who are you?"

"I work for your daughter."

"You work for my . . ."

"Daughter. Friday. Come on."

I picked him up by the shoulders again. This time he wasn't completely dead weight, but that didn't give my own shoulders much of a break. I put his left arm around my neck and helped him into the passenger seat.

A young couple stared at us as they walked from the restaurant to their car.

"Rough night at the casino," I said.

They nodded dubiously and kept walking.

"Make me one promise," I said to Shawn Finley. "Don't bleed all over this car. It's a classic."

I stripped down to my undershirt, rolled my button-down into a ball, and handed it to him.

"Pressure," I said.

He nodded and pressed it over his cut. I got behind the wheel, put Mango in drive, and headed south for home.

# CHAPTER 28

"I think the bleeding stopped," Shawn Finley said.

We'd been quiet for half the drive back to San Francisco. I had many questions for Friday Finley's father. I also had little interest in talking to a deadbeat dad who'd almost gotten me killed on this fucking goose chase.

"Thanks for getting me out of there," he said. "You're a sweetheart."

I didn't respond.

"Where are we going?"

"We need to get you to a hospital. Get your head checked out. Then I'm calling the police, even though I made a promise I wouldn't."

"Promise to who?"

"Your daughter."

"I don't need a hospital. And no cops. Please."

"I don't see any other way."

He'd been slumped in the passenger seat with his eyes shut for a half hour. For a while I thought he'd dozed off. He sat up slowly and grunted as he readjusted his seat belt.

"Riding in a trunk's hard on these old bones," he said.

He had the gruff voice of a perpetual smoker, though he didn't smell like smoke. He didn't smell particularly good in general. There was a faint scent of booze on his breath and his clothes.

"How do you know my daughter?"

"I'm a private investigator. I met her in San Francisco a few days ago. She hired me to find you. She's been staying with my wife and me in the meantime."

"Where?"

"North Beach. She doesn't understand why you've ghosted her for two weeks. Ever since her mother died."

"Hey, I love Friday. And I loved Patricia."

"Sure you do."

"What do you know, anyway?"

"I know I've acted more like her father in the past few days than you have in years."

He didn't have a response to that, so he focused on himself.

"Aren't you gonna ask me how I wound up in the back of a guy's trunk?"

"We'll get to that," I said.

"You got anything in here besides water?"

"Nope."

"Got a smoke and a light?"

"Does this look like a car I wanna smoke in?"

"Guess not. Hey, this is a pretty nice ride. Ninety-two Bronco?"

"Eighty-five."

"I've done work on some of the sixties models. Those damn things go for two hundred K now. How 'bout some Advil or something for this headache?"

I tossed him the aspirin bottle and reached into my backpack for another water bottle.

"Thanks. What'd you say your name was again?"

"Charlie Shaw."

"Charlie Shaw, you're quite a guy."

"Friday's car is in the shop," I said. "She almost totaled it trying to find you."

"Oh, shit. What was she driving?"

"Her mom's 4Runner. She's all right, though, if you're interested."

"Of course I'm interested."

My phone buzzed and the screen brightened.

"Is that Friday?"

"My wife. Making sure I'm not dead yet while I'm out looking for you like a kid who's lost his puppy."

I prompted Siri and sent Ryan a text back.

All good. Be home in a little while. Love you.

"You're not gonna tell her about all this?" Shawn asked.

"First I want some answers."

"About Friday?"

"About Friday, about your riding buddy Bosh, and Ross and Colin Dunne and Tate from Cashel Rock."

"Damn," he said, "you've been busy, haven't you?"

"Very."

"So you're a PI, huh? Like the movies?"

"Just like."

"How's the pay?"

"Your daughter's broke. So, not great."

"I wasn't 'ghosting' her," Shawn said. "I'm trying to protect her."

"From what?"

"Me."

Shawn Finley and I rode in silence for a stretch. Mango was a bumpy ride even on residential streets. I'd put bigger tires on her a few years ago, thirty-three-inchers with no lift. Highway riding meant we had to raise our voices a little, even with the music off.

"Guy who winds up in the trunk of a psychopath's car has made some interesting life choices," I said.

"Now you're catching on."

"What'd you do?"

"I'd rather just show you."

"Show me what?"

"In Oakland," Shawn said. "Not far from my old place."

"You want me to drive you to Oakland tonight?"

"Please. One more favor for your old buddy Shawn."

"Your last known address was in Eastmont."

"That's right."

"Where the hell have you been staying, anyway? I've been looking everywhere."

"I made a deal with a motel over there. After I got hired at Cashel Rock. The motel let me keep a room for a fixed rate. They needed the business, I guess. Got room service every day, free washer and dryer."

"Sounds like the Taj."

"Buddy, if you've lived like I have for the past few years, you'd think it was."

He coughed again. It sounded like a lung was trying to work its way up.

"Did Bosh break any ribs?"

"Just here," Shawn said, and pointed to the cut at his hairline.

"Where'd he find you?"

"I'd been staying in some dump outside San Rafael. Know a guy who manages the place. Thought I could trust him. I opened the door and Bosh must've hit me with the butt of his gun. Threw me in the back like a fucking carry-on. Guess he wanted to show off his catch to the boys tonight."

"Bosh must be pretty good to have tracked you down."

"I'm sure he had help."

"From who?"

"Derryville cops, man."

He said it derisively, as if I should've known the answer.

"I've met Chief Gramble," I said.

"He's a peach, isn't he?"

"He said he'd never heard of you."

Shawn laughed. "And you bought that?"

"No."

"That town is something else," Shawn said.

"So you've got the Dunnes and half the Derryville PD after you."

"First time in my life I've felt special."

"You still haven't told me why."

"Drive me to Oakland," Shawn said. "It'll make sense."

We were fifteen minutes outside San Francisco. Oakland was another fifteen minutes away. My body begged for sleep. My legs and my ass felt numb from sitting so much. My shoulder was a lost cause. I'd seen a video once of a crab casually ripping off his injured claw so he could grow another one. I envied that crab.

"I'm serious about calling the cops," I said. "The real cops, not Derryville. Bosh ain't gonna shrug his shoulders over this and say, 'Oh well.'"

"Cops will be interested in what I've got," Shawn said.

"Evidence?"

"Something like that."

"Fine. We'll go to Oakland, then the police. Oh yeah, and your daughter, who's worried sick about you."

Shawn said nothing and looked straight at the road.

"Deal?"

"Deal," he said.

"When's the last time you saw Friday?"

"In person? Too long."

"She was trying to reach you about coming up for the service. That's how this all started."

"Friday's never had the most patience. I think it's because she's so smart. She gets bored easy."

"I think she's got patience. More than she should. I think it just ran out."

Shawn looked at me.

"Could be," he said.

The brake lights in front of us acted as rectangular red beacons guiding us through the darkness, two strangers with nothing in common, connected only by a child's sorrow. Soon the south tower on the Golden Gate Bridge emerged to the right and then around a curve it faced us indomitably. Sometimes at night, depending on my mood or the level of the fog, it felt like driving through the mouth of hell.

"I've lived a lot of places," Shawn said. "Never seen a place that had so much right and so much wrong all at once."

"Home is what you make it," I said.

"You don't sound quite like you're from here."

"Texas."

"I should've known. You're full of Southern hospitality, Charlie Shaw."

"'Politeness is half good manners and half good lying.'"

"I didn't think she'd drive all the way down here."

"Friday?"

"She was always pretty stubborn, even as a little girl. Impatient *and* stubborn, now that I think about it. When she was six or seven, she got on the neighbor's trampoline and jumped on that damn thing for hours, into dinnertime. I went over there, told her to wind it up, time to eat. She kept going like the damn Energizer Bunny. She yelled at me, 'No, Daddy!' and kept jumping. Didn't realize she was getting too close to the metal edge. Did a face-plant right onto it. Cut her forehead up pretty good. Three stitches, I wanna say it was. Stubborn as hell. She got it from her mom. Her mom was a good woman. She just . . . lost her mind. No other way to put it. We didn't have the money to get it . . . you know."

"Diagnosed?"

"Yeah, diagnosed. How long does it take for aspirin to kick in?"

"Probably fifteen minutes or so."

"I could use a drink."

"Water will do."

"Yeah, sure. Water's great. I love it. Anyway, Patricia was a good woman. She was good to Friday. She and I just took it as far as we could, you know? The tank ran empty."

"So you took off."

"Hey," he said. "I had my reasons."

"And you found yourself down here. Working for these assholes."

"It's what there was. I did some odd jobs for a while, trying to stay afloat. I ain't exactly got a portfolio. I met Ross while doing an overnighter last year."

"In Derryville?"

"Yeah. He was at the station. Probably handing them a payoff, now that I think about it. He liked my name. 'Strong Irish lad,' he said. We talked about growing up on the coast. I was a foster kid, bounced around shelters for a while. He did too. Told me to come see him when I got out."

"They needed a bartender."

"Yeah. I know how to work on cars and I know how to make drinks. Did it years ago before I met Patricia. Tate helped me pick things up pretty quick. Money wasn't great but it was something."

"Till you got promoted."

Shawn eyed me again.

"'Promoted,'" he said. "That's a funny way of putting it."

"That's what happened, right? They gave you some illegal work to do? Just like Bosh?"

"I never hurt anybody," Shawn said. "Bosh was the real muscle."

"Muscle for what?"

"Good old racketeering," Shawn said. "Just like the movies. *Goodfellas* is my personal favorite."

"And you were their Henry Hill."

"Wasn't like I had much of a choice."

"You could've left."

"They would've killed me. I knew too much. I signed up to tend bar, man. That's it."

"You thought it was honest work."

"That's right."

"That's why last year you told Friday that you'd found a job."

"I wanted her to know I could get it together. I always planned on going up there again. Her mother and I weren't ever getting back together, but at least I could've been close."

We'd changed bridges, and this time we were on I-80 between San Francisco and Oakland. Until I moved here I didn't know the Bay Bridge was four times longer than the Golden Gate. The brilliant LED lights made the eastern span shine like a diamond pyramid.

"What I don't understand," I said, "is how a couple small-time thugs like Ross and Colin built an operation that appears to be fairly profitable. Don't they have any competition?"

Shawn laughed through his vile cough.

"Easy to wipe out competition," he said, "when you've got the police chief in your pocket."

"How'd they do that?"

"Gramble wants to run for public office someday. Can't do that if you've had a scandal."

"Has he had a scandal?"

Shawn nodded. "They got pictures of him."

"Doing what?"

"Playing Candy Land. What do you think?"

"Extramarital affairs?"

"You got it."

"So, it all filters down from there," I said. "Cops fall in line. Maybe even round up any competition out there."

Shawn looked out the passenger window.

"And they look the other way with everything," I said. "Including those little underground poker games at Cashel Rock."

"I don't know anything about that," Shawn said. "I swear. That was all tight-lipped. All I know is the blinds were big and the Dunnes took a nice rake off the total winnings."

"I saw three cars there last night. Know any of the players?"

"Nope."

I took out my phone and pulled up an online picture of Dalton Crawford, CEO of Rivet Security.

"What about him?"

"I told you, I don't know nothing about poker. Ask Ross or Colin. It's their little side hustle."

"Got any idea how Ross and Colin attracted rich whales to their little dump on the east side?"

"No idea."

I shrugged and put the phone down.

"I've always wondered that, though," Shawn said. "Not just the poker part, but how Ross and Colin got the money to buy the bar in the first place, do all the renovations. They're from Derryville, man. Probably grew up with nothing. Ain't like they've got a trust fund. You've met them, right?"

"Sort of."

"They ain't rocket scientists. I should know. I ain't one either. Hey, you happen to find a phone in that trunk?"

I pulled it out of my pocket and tossed it to him.

"Hey, you're a pal," Shawn said. "Take this next exit. We're getting close."

# CHAPTER 29

I exited 580 just north of Mills College and wound along a little two-lane road bordered by lumpy hills and thick grass and tall trees. Occasionally a house or apartment building with faint porch lights and picket fences would interrupt the darkness like pops of color on black brocade fabric.

"This is Mountain Boulevard," Shawn said. "Place is up here a little ways."

"Looks familiar," I said.

"Leona Heights. Used to work at Leona Lodge."

"I've driven people here for Uber. They do weddings, showers, stuff like that."

"Yep. I was a waiter till they fired me."

"For what?"

"Drinking on the job. Park here."

The street curved down and to the left. I stopped on the shoulder along some wood fencing. Fifty yards ahead the fence ended and was replaced by a metal cattle gate that blocked a clearing for a dirt road.

"That area's monitored," Shawn said. "At least they say it is. The lodge is a quarter mile up the road. There's probably an event tonight. Follow me and don't make a bunch of noise."

We got out of Mango and hopped the wood fence to our left and trudged our way through thick brush. A heavy branch struck me in the face and reminded me of Tate's closet hangers. Finally we reached some open space.

"How's your head?"

"Fine," Shawn said. "You got a flashlight on that phone?"

"Yeah."

"Turn it on. My battery's almost dead."

I did and a dim outline of trees emerged. Three Monterey pines formed a rough triangle, their branches touching. Shawn walked beyond them, reached into the next line of brush, and pulled out a shovel.

"Couple months before I skipped town," he said, "I was staying at that motel, drinking myself to sleep, all alone except for some occasional companionship, if you know what I mean. One night I got real blitzed on Jim Beam and maybe some other accessories and I got paranoid Ross or Colin was gonna send Bosh after me. Convinced myself he was gonna break down the fucking door."

"Prophetic," I said.

"So I came out here and decided to protect my investment. Shine the light right there."

He walked to the center of the triangle and punctured the earth with the shovel.

"What'd you steal?" I asked.

"When I sobered up, I figured it wasn't such a bad idea to hide some of it. So I'd come out here every now and then and . . ."

He grunted as he lifted up the first load of dirt and grass.

". . . add to the pile."

"Shawn," I said, "what'd you steal?"

Shawn continued to dig. It didn't take long. After about three feet he stopped and grunted and lifted a blue duffel bag out of the hole.

"A few days ago, Tate said the Dunnes might be getting wise to me. I never told her what I was doing. She either saw me or just sensed it. So, I got the hell outta Dodge. Didn't stop by the motel to get my stuff. Didn't have time to come back here."

The area was quiet except for our voices and the sounds of crickets and an occasional car passing on the road behind us. Shawn dropped the bag on the ground next to the hole and sat cross-legged next to it. He touched the laceration on his head and checked his fingers for blood.

"Fucker got me good," he said. "But he didn't get everything."

I kept the flashlight on him. He unzipped the bag and took out stacks of bills bonded by rubber bands. He tossed one to me. They were a mix of ones and fives and tens and twenties. Some were new and crisp. Others were rumpled.

"Collection money," I said.

"Collection money, cash from the register, anything they let me handle personally."

"How long you been skimming?"

"Last few months."

"They never noticed?"

"Like I said, these guys ain't rocket scientists. The money started coming in after they got the operation rolling. I skimmed in small drips."

"What's their operation consist of besides gambling?"

"Like I said, some of the old-school shit you might read about or see on TV. They ran protection for some businesses. They started a little escort service for clients."

"What else?"

Shawn shrugged.

"Drugs?"

"Like I said, I skimmed a little. And I did a little business on my own."

"Explain that."

"Couple guys were dealing on the north edge of town. Had a system set up, big client base. Ross wanted to scare them off. So he puts Bosh on it and tells me to go with him. We pay them a visit at some dry cleaning place they claimed to run. One of the guys says something smart and Bosh caps both of them. Dumps them in a fucking laundry hamper."

"I'm gonna take a wild guess and say the police investigation went nowhere."

"Bingo."

"So the Dunnes took their stash."

"And their source, and their clients. But I kept some of the stuff for myself. Bosh didn't notice. Mostly pills, weed."

"You dealt outside Derryville?"

"That's right."

"How much is there?"

Shawn dumped out the entire bag. More stacks tumbled onto the ground.

"Close to thirty," he said. "It ain't a fortune, but it's enough."

"Enough for what?"

"Enough for my baby girl to buy a new car for her Sweet Sixteen. Or start a nice little nest egg for college. Whatever she wants."

"You stole all this for Friday?"

"I'm not proud of it," he said. "It's the least I could do. For not being there."

"I think she'd rather have your head attached to your neck. If you stole a cookie from Ross Dunne, he'd cut your throat."

"You've seen the movies. Once you're in, you're in. You ain't ever getting out."

"These guys aren't the Corleones," I said. "They're punks who probably watched too many movies."

"You found me in a trunk, didn't you?"

"Yeah."

"They're the real thing. Bosh especially."

"Then let's end this."

"How?"

"I have friends at the SFPD," I said. "So does my boss. All the way to the top. You can make a deal. A good deal. You didn't sign up for this. You signed up to be a bartender. They should be sympathetic to that. We can put these guys away and you won't have to run from them. Or your daughter."

Shawn frowned when I said "daughter."

"But you might leave out the part about dealing on your own," I said. "And you're gonna have to get clean for her."

"I know."

Shawn picked up one of the stacks and flipped through it. Some of the blood from his hands smeared onto the bills. The flashlight app was draining my battery. I got a crib notification. Callie was squirming around in her sleep.

"You got kids, Charlie?"

"Yeah. A daughter."

"How old is she?"

"Six months, ten days, and thirty minutes."

"Then you know you do what you gotta do for them."

"First thing you can do," I said, "the best thing you can do, is just be present. She's a wreck, Shawn. She just lost her mother. She's been preparing herself to lose you. Wake up, man. You wanna be in her life or not?"

He nodded slowly. Then he tossed the stack into the bag.

"She been doing okay? My girl Friday?"

"She's the toughest kid I've ever met."

He smiled.

"Sounds like my girl. Y'all been looking out for her?"

"Best we can. You wanna see her?"

"More than you can imagine, Charlie."

"Come on. I'm running out of flashlight."

I tossed him the stack he'd shown me and stood and headed back toward Mango.

Then everything went black.

# CHAPTER 30

I walked into my old cubicle at the *Chronicle* to change Callie, but she was sitting in my desk chair, fully dressed, fully grown. Her face was blurry, but she had the same hairstyle as her mother with natural brown curls at the tips. She talked seriously, directly to me, but no sounds emerged. As she talked, she morphed into Ryan. Her face and voice became clear. She asked me how I was doing, if I was safe, if I was coming home. I said I'd be there soon.

A moment later I was paddling out to the middle of a dirty pond. The water was freezing. The pond was littered with trash and moss and algae. Some of it stuck to my arms and face. Friday Finley was sitting cross-legged in the center of a circle, floating on the water. She stared at me, expressionless. I told her I'd be there soon.

My eyes opened. I stared into darkness, as dark as sleep. Then the pain started. A rush of it to the center of the back of my head. My vision blurred in the darkness and I tried rubbing it clear with cold fingers. I lay still for a moment with my eyes closed. The pain continued but the dizziness stopped. I was on my back. I tried sitting up. The pain overwhelmed me and I vomited violently. That helped a little.

Something buzzed next to me. I swatted at it. The buzzing stopped. A couple of minutes later it buzzed again. I swatted down at the ground and felt plastic. Phone cover. I picked it up and turned it around to the screen side. It was ten past midnight. I still had a little battery left. I also had three missed calls and five missed texts from Ryan in the past hour.

# Stakeouts and Strollers

> ETA?
> You said you'd be home soon. I'm getting worried.
> Please call. You're starting to freak me out.
> Hello?
> I'm calling Mr. Powell. Please please respond.

Staring at the screen made my eyes feel like they'd gotten jabbed by hot pokers. The blurriness started again.

> Don't call him I'm ok be back soon.

Against my better judgment I scrunched my knees and pushed off the ground. Standing took a couple of tries. Finally, I got there. I turned on the flashlight and squinted and scanned the area. Shawn Finley wasn't around, but he'd left his blue duffel bag next to its shallow grave. The shovel now lay a few feet away next to a new, smaller hole. It was empty too.

I bent down to pick up the bag and got lightheaded again. I leaned against the tree in the middle and closed my eyes until the sensation passed. I zipped open the bag. The money was still there, or at least the majority of it.

I slung the bag over my shoulder and plodded through the brush. Another branch hit me in the face. What else was new.

The road was quiet when I got to Mango. I could hear the faint sound of music from the lodge. I took a moment to catch my breath, using Mango as a brace as I'd done with the tree. My keys and wallet were still in my pocket. At least he hadn't stolen my car.

Driving home was an adventure too. The streetlights hurt my eyes and the bumps in the road made me nauseous. I couldn't see shit until I reached the highway lights and headed west. I drove thirty miles an hour the whole way back. Cars honked at me on the bridge. I wanted to scream something back but decided against anything that took unnecessary effort. The thing I really wanted was sleep. Or death. Whichever came first.

Somehow I got back to the house just after one in the morning. My phone had died on the drive back. No telling how many times Ryan had messaged me in the past forty-five minutes. Didn't matter. She was waiting for me at the top of the front steps.

"Hi, sweetie," I said. "Not sure I can climb those."

"Are you drunk?"

"Concussed, I think."

"Oh my God."

She met me at the sidewalk and put the palms of her hands on my cheeks. Something fluttered in the blinds on the second floor. Grace, wearing her night nurse uniform, peered through the window. I could hear Callie wailing inside.

"You've got dirt on your clothes," Ryan said.

"Yeah."

"And some scrapes on your face."

"Yeah."

"And your breath smells like puke."

"Love you too."

"Let's get you inside."

She put her arm around my waist. I used her and the railing as my latest brace.

"Where were you hit?"

"Back of the head. Shovel, or a shovel handle. One of the two."

"Shovel? Were you at a fucking cemetery?"

"Kinda."

"Who hit you?"

"Now, that's an interesting story."

Friday met us in the doorway at the top of the steps. She, like Ryan, was dressed for bed in shorts and a T-shirt. She looked terrified, the way people look in movies when the doctor announces whether their loved one will make it out of surgery.

"Hang on," I said. "I left something in the car."

"Jesus, Charlie. What is it?"

"My backpack. And a duffel bag."

Friday and Ryan exchanged glances.

"I'll get it," Friday said.

I handed her the keys and she ran barefoot down the steps to Mango. I'd parked on the downhill slope close to the stop sign at Chestnut. For a moment I'd left the car in drive and almost slid into the intersection.

"Do you need a doctor?" Ryan asked.

"I don't think so."

"Let's just get you inside and sit down first. My God."

Friday ran upstairs with the backpack and duffel bag slung over separate shoulders and we all went inside together. In the living room I fell into the accent chair opposite the media lounger.

Friday set both bags next to the chair. Grace held Callie in her arms.

"Oh my, Charlie, are you all right?" Grace asked.

"I've been better."

Callie voiced her disapproval with this little caucus.

*"Oh-wah! Oh-wah! Oh-wah!"*

"That," I said, "is not helping my head."

"Poor baby can't sleep," Grace said.

"None of us can," Ryan said. "I may never sleep again."

She went to the kitchen for some ice. Friday searched the pantry for pain meds. I tried to stand to check on Callie and blood rushed to my head and the dizziness returned and a thin film of yellow covered my vision. I sat back down.

When the yellow dissipated I peered into the kitchen. Four women from six months to sixty years old stared at me. It felt like an intervention.

"What's in the bag?" Ryan said.

"Snacks you packed. Couple of waters. Friday's bat. Wish I'd used that tonight . . ."

"The bag, not the backpack. Don't fuck with me right now, Charlie."

Everyone's eyes widened. Callie continued to wail.

"I'm gonna take her into the nursery," Grace said, "and let you guys talk."

"What's in the bag?" Ryan asked again, her voice raised. "And what happened to you?"

Friday stared at the floor.

"Did you find my dad?" she asked, just above a whisper.

"I wanna hear this too," a male voice said.

Dwayne Powell stepped into the kitchen from the hallway that led to the guest bathroom. As usual, he was dressed business casual, no matter the time or place. He stood beside Ryan and Friday in the kitchen.

"Boss," I said. "I didn't see your truck on the street."

"How many fingers am I holding up?"

"Somewhere between one and five."

"That's why."

Ryan brought me some water, four aspirin, and a ziplock bag filled with ice from the kitchen. I'd become the authority on ice.

"I called Mr. Powell because I was worried," Ryan said. "Obviously I had a good reason. Look at you."

"I didn't lose any money, at least."

"Stop joking around. Why are you stalling?"

"Because I don't want to say what I have to say."

Friday looked up.

"Is he . . ."

"No," I said. "Your dad's alive."

"You found him?"

"Yes."

"Where is he?"

I rubbed my eyes again. The pain behind my head had regressed to a constant dull ache. The room swayed a little like a boat in a current. Callie's cries were muffled behind the closed nursery door.

"You're my client," I said to Friday. "Guess I owe you the truth, don't I."

"Yes, you do," Powell said.

I glanced at Powell, then at Ryan, then at Friday.

"I don't know where he is," I said. "But he's alive. He's been hiding from our friends in Derryville."

"The Dunne brothers?"

"Yes, and the man with the snake tat. They call him Bosh. He's a hired killer. I got Shawn away from them tonight."

"How?"

I told them about my casino visit and explained how I found Shawn Finley in the trunk of Bosh's car.

"The Dunnes planned to kill him," I said. "For stealing their money. Now they might figure out I have it and come for me."

Friday looked at the duffel bag. Her face went white. Powell shot me a look that would've stripped paint off a fence.

"Oh my God," Ryan said.

"We need to get everyone to a safe place," I said. "Callie especially. Maybe your parents' house, Ryan."

"They can stay with me," Powell said.

"You got room?"

"My mother-in-law lived with us for six years. I'm owed a favor."

"This is like fucking nightmare fuel," Ryan said. "Am I dreaming this? You're saying we are no longer safe in our own house? You want us to pack and leave tonight?"

I nodded. She looked at Powell.

"He's probably right," Powell said. "They know where you live. They know Charlie's been poking in their business."

"I thought you said they wanted a truce," Ryan said.

"They did, but now someone's messing with their money," I said. "They're not gonna let it go."

"Wonderful," Ryan said.

"I'll make some calls," Powell said. "You got the license plate on that car?"

I told him and he headed back down the hall.

Friday picked up the duffel bag.

"Is the money . . ."

"Yes," I said.

"How much?"

"Close to thirty grand."

"Why do you have it?"

"The money's for you. Your dad was hiding it, saving it for your birthday, for college, for your future. He showed me the spot where he buried it. I thought he'd come back with me and surprise you. I thought wrong."

"So he hit you with a shovel?" Ryan asked.

"That or a bear knocked me out. When I woke up, he was gone."

"But he didn't take your car or the money."

"Nope."

Friday's face went from white to red. She rushed for the front door, threw it open, and slammed it behind her.

# CHAPTER 31

"I can't," Ryan said. "I'm literally speechless over this whole thing."

"Hang on," I said. "I'll be back."

"You can barely stand."

"I'll manage."

I dragged myself up and out of the chair and out the front door and down the steps. Friday had turned left, away from the Bay. She sprinted up the slope on Stockton and across Lombard. No cars got in her path. I walked in pursuit.

"Friday!"

She turned.

"Please don't make me run up that damn hill. It's been a long-ass night."

She stopped, her hands on her hips, her bare feet on the cold pavement. She sat on the bench outside the little market on the corner. The neon beer signs in the store windows were off. Nothing moved on the street except me muddling my way up Stockton. For a second, I thought about driving Mango the single block south, but that seemed like more trouble than it was worth.

Friday sat on the bench, her head down, her sleeveless goose-bumped arms crossed. She shivered a little against the wind.

"I'm so sorry he did that to you," she said.

"Don't be sorry. I'm sorry I couldn't bring him home."

"I told you he was a loser."

"He's your dad. You had every right to look for him."

Tears began to form in her eyes, as they had the day we met. She could no longer control them. She could no longer wipe away one and shield the rest with Gen Z armor. This time they flowed down both her cheeks. She began to cry into my chest.

"He didn't hit me because he wanted to hurt me," I said. "He hit me because he doesn't want to face you. He's probably ashamed. But more than anything, he doesn't want you to get hurt because of the things he's done."

Friday's sobs grew louder, uncomfortably loud, even with her head buried in my sternum.

"He said he loved you," I said. "And your mom. But he's got real problems."

Then I shut my mouth and patted her arm and let her cry. Like a hand to a hose valve, the tears slowly let up and stopped.

"He thought he could buy me off with dirty money," she said.

"In his mind he thought he was doing the right thing."

"How can you defend him? He could've killed you tonight. Or gotten you killed."

"I'm thinking how a father would think about his daughter."

"You would never leave Callie."

"No, I wouldn't."

"And you wouldn't have joined a gang, or whatever the fuck they are."

"He told me he didn't know what those guys were into when he took the job. He just got caught up in it all."

"You believe him?"

"Yes."

She sniffled.

"Doesn't change anything," she said.

"I know."

She wiped her nose with her arm and her tears with her shirt and sniffled some more.

"Tell me about the garden," I said.

"What?"

"At your mom's house. The one you worked on together. I wanna hear about it."

"Not much to tell. There's all kinds of flowers."

"Tell me about them."

"Before she got sick, we'd just finished with some new pots. Mixture of purple kale and multicolored pansies. Yellow blotch, white blotch, and pure violet."

"I know kale. They look kinda like cupcakes. Makes me hungry."

"I thought they got too big and started looking like cabbage."

"That makes me less hungry."

She laughed a little.

"Before she died, my mom wanted to plant a mix of calibrachoa, petunias, and some asparagus fern. It likes heat and sun."

She wiped away the last of the tears. The swelling around her injured eye was gone. The discoloration was now almost all yellow except for one little streak of black and blue.

"I want you to go with Powell," I said. "And once this is over, you're welcome to stay with us as long as you like."

"You're kidding, right?"

"No. Why?"

"Ryan probably hates me for this. For you getting hurt. All the trouble I've caused you guys."

"No, I don't."

Ryan stood on the curb, her arms crossed, shivering too.

"Got room for one more," I said.

She sat on the bench with Friday in between us.

"It's really gotten cold," she said.

"Because y'all are dressed for July in Texas."

Ryan reached out and patted Friday's thigh. Her hand hovered in the air for a moment first as if she was debating the move. Callie had done a pretty good job of busting up Ryan's shell, but she still had her defenses up against Friday.

"I had no idea this would happen," Friday said. "I'm so sorry. For everything."

"No," Ryan said. "I'm sorry. I lost my cool in there. I needed a few minutes to process everything."

There was an uncomfortable silence, interrupted by Friday's sniffles and the sound of a car rolling through the stop sign on Lombard.

"I'm just scared," Ryan said. "For Charlie, for Callie, for Grace, for Mr. Powell. And for you. I admit I've had reservations about the work Charlie's been doing. And about taking on another houseguest. We're crammed in there as it is. Most importantly, we've got a six-month-old child to protect. This is an unusual situation, to put it politely."

"I know," Friday said.

"It has to be awkward for you too. But you've been very helpful to us and very kind to Callie. And the truth is, I can't be angry about what happened tonight, because I've been supportive of Charlie through this whole thing."

"Eh, sorta," I said. "With a stipulation or two."

"I told Charlie to go tonight," Ryan said. "What happened is not your fault."

"But it is my fault," Friday said. "I told Charlie that my dad was probably up to something illegal or dangerous or both. I didn't want the cops involved."

"I don't think we can avoid the cops anymore," I said. "The real cops. Not the posers in Derryville."

"I know," Friday said. "I just wanted to find him."

"Like any daughter would," Ryan said. "Friday, I was lucky. My dad was mostly around except for some work trips. Lately I've been thinking about what it would've been like if I'd grown up without him. And I've been imagining what it would be like for Callie to grow up without Charlie. It's unimaginable. So, I've been torn between wanting to protect us and wanting to help you."

Friday nodded.

"I'm very sorry this has happened to you. And I still want to be in your corner. But we need to get the authorities involved."

Friday nodded again.

## Stakeouts and Strollers

"Callie and I are gonna go stay with Mr. Powell," Ryan said.

"You're okay with that?" I asked.

"Do I love it? No. Is it better to be safe than sorry? Yes."

"I love you."

"I love you too."

We reached across Friday and clutched hands.

"I've asked Grace to go on home," Ryan said. "She's done more than enough for us and her contract ends in the morning anyway. I'm going back inside to pack for Callie and me. And Charlie's gonna get his head looked at."

"I think I'm fine," I said.

"I think you've had enough bumps on the head. Friday, we'd like you to come with us."

Friday stared at her bare feet. None of us spoke for a minute.

Ryan yawned. I yawned. Friday yawned.

Finally, without looking up, Friday said softly, "Okay."

# CHAPTER 32

"I can stay with Ryan and Callie till this is all over," Grace said, holding her travel bag. "I don't have another job lined up for two weeks."

"We can't risk your safety," I said. "We just can't do it."

"I've spent twenty-eight years around thousands of screaming crying newborns, dozens at the same time. It doesn't get any scarier than that."

I held out my hand to Grace.

"Thank you for everything. You're a superhero. I thought Callie might sleep in twenty-minute spurts for the rest of her life."

"It's all about finding that thumb."

"And that's your superpower."

She dropped her bag and brushed away my hand and hugged me. Then she hugged Ryan and Friday.

"I want a rematch in Go Fish," she said. "One day."

Friday smiled. "I'd like that."

"You have so much to offer this world. Don't let your past cloud your future."

"I won't."

They hugged again. Ryan dabbed at something in the corner of her eye. She'd probably claim it was dust or allergies. Powell sat at the kitchen counter with his arms folded and a cup of coffee beside him.

"We all need to get moving," he said.

Grace picked up her bag.

"Thank you for everything you've done for this community," she told Powell. "And thank you for watching over my friends here."

"Yes, ma'am," Powell said.

They shook hands.

"I better go before you guys get Callie up," Grace said. "Try some raspberries when it's time to eat. She hated them the first couple days, but I think she's come around. That girl is so smart. She studies everything. Yesterday she was processing the aerodynamics of my finger moving back and forth. I think she's gonna be an engineer."

"Sounds perfectly safe and completely boring," I said. "Fine by me."

"Charlie, you take care of yourself, please. And them."

"Yes, ma'am."

Grace glanced around the tiny living room and kitchen once more. Then she softly opened and closed the door. We watched her climb into her car without incident, start the engine, and drive away.

"I'm gonna miss her," Ryan said.

"Me too."

"Time for us to go too," Powell said. "Ryan, are you about packed?"

"Almost. Need to grab a couple more things with Callie and then I'll scoop her up."

"Good. I'll call Reggie. You'll follow him to my house."

"You sure he's okay with this? It's two in the morning."

"He's a marine. And he's my son. He's used to early wake-up calls."

"So am I," I said, "working for you."

"You insist on staying here?"

"Yes."

"Fine. Once they're off, we're heading to the ER."

"Wonderful."

"Got to be done."

"Please explain something to me," Ryan said. "What's the point in us hiding out if you're just gonna stay here and get your head blown off?"

"I'm not gonna let these guys come here and destroy this house," I said. "This is our home. This is my daughter's home."

Ryan looked at Powell.

"I'll stay with him," Powell said. "James and Reggie can keep watch at my house. I talked with SFPD. They agreed to meet with Charlie and me at the station tomorrow to talk about all this."

Ryan's face still twisted with anger and confusion. Powell walked toward her, leaned down, and whispered something in her ear. They locked eyes for a moment.

"All right," she said. "If Mr. Powell wasn't tougher than John Wick, I'd say no."

I put my hand on top of hers.

"He's not *that* tough," I said.

"Yes," Powell said, "I am."

Ryan kissed me. She gently ran her fingers through my hair.

"Does that hurt?"

"A little."

"Are you still dizzy?"

"A little."

"Go see a doctor, please."

A single honk sounded downstairs. Powell walked to the window and peeked through the blinds.

"Reggie," he said.

Callie was already strapped into her baby car seat, sound asleep, her head down, her bottom lip out in a pouty face, dreaming about something, perhaps another round with Sheldon the seahorse. Everyone told me babies were easy to read. *They cry when they're hungry, when they're tired, when their diaper's full, when they want attention.* All of that was true but oversimplified. Callie was a seventeen-pound riddle. Her little brain never stopped moving at warp speed—always processing, sponging.

I kissed her forehead and kissed Ryan once more.

"I'm sorry," I said.

"I know," she said.

I yawned. She yawned.

"Y'all be safe," I said. "I'll check in along. We'll all be okay."

It took three trips downstairs to get all of Ryan's things and all of Callie's things into the Highlander. Ryan gave me one last look before driving away. I blew her a kiss. She flipped me off. Then she blew one back. I knew she was only half joking. We waved to Reggie. Both cars drove away.

I moved Mango into the garage out of sight—a stern suggestion from Powell—and he drove me to UCSF Medical Center. The front desk and the nurse and the doctor asked me what had happened. I told them I slipped and fell backward into a wall. After three hours of waiting, form-filling, and test-taking, I learned what I already knew: I had a mild concussion. The ER doctor also prescribed antibiotics for the gnarly bite marks Ross Dunne had gifted me. Powell and I got back in his truck at five a.m., just before the sun began to peek over the city skyline.

"I thought you had to stay awake for twenty-four hours after a concussion," I said.

"That's a myth," Powell said. "But they suggest having someone with you while you sleep."

"Sleep sounds pretty good. 'Pretty good' as in 'I've never wanted something so much in my entire life.'"

"How's your head?"

"Better."

"Good. I've got something to show you when we get back to your house."

"You think James and Reggie can handle things at your place?"

"I raised them, didn't I?"

"Answer me this," I said. "And be honest. If you were me, would you have helped Friday find her father?"

"I wouldn't have let her stay with me," Powell said. "Conflict of interest."

"That's not what I asked. Would you have stayed on this till you got an answer?"

Powell turned left onto Stockton and we passed the usual band of early-morning joggers and dog walkers in Washington Square. The loungers and picnic crowd would arrive a few hours later and spread out across the healthy green summer grass.

"Probably," Powell said. "But I would've gotten the job done faster. And I wouldn't have let some drunk blast me with a shovel."

# CHAPTER 33

The house on Stockton felt hollow and desolate without Ryan and Callie and Friday Finley and Grace Chen. No crying, no laughter, no gossip, no diaper smells, no *House Hunters*. Sometimes, even with only four or five people, our thousand-square-foot home felt like Levi's Stadium. Not anymore.

I grabbed two water bottles from the fridge. The pain meds from the hospital helped my head and my shoulder and my arms and legs, but my mouth felt dry. I handed a water bottle to Powell. He removed his Beretta from the pancake holster on his waistband and set it on the kitchen counter.

He took out a binder from his work bag.

"A little more dirt on the Dunne brothers," he said.

He'd found the owners of the three luxury cars parked behind Cashel Rock on Thursday night. Their names and headshots were listed beside the license plate pictures I'd taken in the parking lot.

"I thought you said you weren't interested in this case," I said.

"I lied," Powell said.

He flipped through the pages and read the text aloud.

"Eric Maniet, founder and CEO of Enspire, an employee management software company. Drives a curaçao blue McLaren 570S, license plate 2GLW342.

"Ram Khatri, president and CEO of Radiant, a cloud-based content management system for business clients. Drives a red Maserati Levante, license plate 2DEN590."

I pointed to the last name and picture.

"Dalton Crawford, founder and CEO of Rivet Security, drives the black Ferrari. The guy who hired and recently fired Scottie Coburn, Deborah Wellington's boy toy."

"I thought his picture might pique your interest," Powell said.

"I went to the Rivet offices in the 5M district this week," I said. "Crawford wanted to personally thank us for uncovering Scottie's affair with Mrs. Wellington. Said it was a PR nightmare for one of his top executives to disgrace one of San Francisco's most prominent families. He also said he knew nothing about Scottie getting assaulted."

"Maybe he's a liar," Powell said. "Obviously, he knows the Dunnes. The question is, how?"

I studied the profiles of the three men. "These guys all went to MIT together?"

"Yep. Crawford, Maniet, Khatri all graduated in the same class. Computer science majors. I'll ask again: What's the connection between them and Cashel Rock?"

"Poker," I said. "Underground poker. Thursday nights in a back room for the past year."

"Who told you that?"

"Girl named Tate, a bartender there. And Shawn Finley, before he blasted me with a shovel."

"Big-money poker?"

"Sounds like more than the average throwaway game in your basement."

"How long has it been going on?"

"About a year. The Dunnes set it up. They invite these same three guys every Thursday night. And Crawford was with the Dunnes last night at the casino too, playing cards. Apparently it's a Friday night tradition."

"Just Crawford? Not his college pals?"

"Just Crawford. Then Ross and Colin met up with Bosh in the parking lot. Took a peek at Friday's dad unconscious in Bosh's trunk."

Powell looked over the pictures again.

"SFPD might be interested to know why Derryville lowlifes are hanging out with San Francisco tech executives who all report annual revenue north of three hundred million," he said. "Crawford, specifically. I find it very interesting that he's playing cards with the Dunnes a couple days after their enforcer assaults one of his employees."

"I find it very interesting too. What else did you dig up about him?"

"Nothing super extensive. He's self-made. Grew up in Nevada, got a full ride to MIT, graduated with honors. Worked at a profitable start-up in Boston for nine years. Moved to San Francisco two years ago and started Rivet Security with a generous round of Series A funding from a venture capital company. In Year Two, Rivet doubled its revenue from Year One. This year, it quadrupled its revenue to four hundred million. He made your old newspaper's 'Top 40 Under 40' list for entrepreneurs in San Francisco. In the article, he admits gambling is a hobby. Said he wants to play the World Series of Poker next year."

"Guess he's got enough to cover the entry fee," I said.

"We're meeting with SFPD about the Dunnes in a couple hours," Powell said. "What do we know?"

"We know that the Dunnes hired Bosh to kidnap and kill Friday's dad, presumably over thousands of dollars in stolen money. We know that the Dunnes—who happen to be friendly with Scottie's old boss, Crawford—were with Bosh when he assaulted Scottie outside his home. And we know the Dunnes are reaping profits through illegal gambling. According to Friday's dad, it's a hell of a lot more than that. Girls and drugs too."

"Would be nice if Mr. Finley were around as, you know, an actual witness," Powell said. "You'll learn that proof is kind of important to an investigation."

"He took off because he's afraid to face Friday."

"Better than a bullet in the head from Bosh or the Dunnes."

I felt a yawn come on and couldn't stop it.

"Go sleep," Powell said. "I'll keep watch."

"Just like your soldier days?"

"Yeah. Kuwait and North Beach. Can't tell the difference."

I went to bed and dreamed about Callie asking for a new car. Powell woke me up at ten thirty. Ryan had texted me.

> What did the doctor say?

Mild concussion.

> I guess that's good news.

It is. I'll be fine.

> We're all settled here.

Good. Keep me posted on you and Callie and Friday.

> I will.

She wants a new car.

> Friday?

No. Callie. In my dream, anyway.

> We'll be dealing with that before we know it.

Love you.

> Love you too.

I showered and changed clothes. Powell was having coffee at the kitchen table.

"We're out of aspirin," I said. "I've been popping them like Skittles."

"What about the bottle I gave you?"

"That's empty too. I'm gonna walk over to the Lombard market."

"I'll go with you."

"I'm good. I just need fresh air. It's literally two hundred feet that way."

"I'll go with you," Powell repeated.

"Fine."

Powell put his gun back in its holster and concealed it under his untucked collared shirt.

Outside, the morning fog had cleared and the sun was shining. Our neighbor two houses up had bought a used Volkswagen Beetle with temporary paper tags. His last car had been broken into. Parking the new one on the street was an interesting choice.

As we approached the Beetle, I heard a quick succession of footsteps behind us and a thud against Powell's back. He made a grunting sound and lurched forward, stumbling up the hill.

It was Bosh. He'd clubbed Powell with his two oven mitts for hands.

Bosh grabbed Powell by the back of his belt and hurled him into the Beetle's windshield like a discus. Powell crashed into it on his right side. The glass cracked like a spiderweb. I felt something press against my back.

"Walk," Bosh said, "or you bleed out right here."

Powell groaned on top of the car. Bosh and I turned and walked in the opposite direction downhill on Stockton. A red Honda Civic was parked at the Chestnut intersection. Bosh opened the driver-side door. He'd acquired a new ride since the Corolla.

"Get in," he said.

I got in the Honda. Bosh got in the back seat on the opposite side, facing me. He held his gun in one hand and the ignition key in the other.

"Start it," he said. "Drive."

# CHAPTER 34

"Where is Shawn Finley?"

Bosh had instructed me to turn right on Stockton and right on Bay Street toward the Embarcadero. I assumed we were working our way back to the Bay Bridge and eventually to Derryville.

"I don't know what you're talking about," I said.

"So he climbed outta the trunk on his own?"

I could feel the sweat bubble on my hands as I clutched the steering wheel. Bosh tapped the gun's muzzle against my right arm.

"I'll ask again. Where is Shawn Finley and where's the shit he stole?"

"I told you. I'm sorry, but I don't know what you're talking about."

Bosh sneered. His gravelly voice sounded even deeper than before. He'd probably been up all night too. Seeing him up close, no longer in darkness, his hair and chin strap beard were a lighter brown than I had thought. His eyebrows furrowed. His big dark pupils burned. His black Henley shirt and denim jacket bulged so tight against his massive chest that I thought the seams might burst, Hulk style. His thick neck was almost parallel with his ears. He was the most intimidating person I'd ever encountered—even more than Callie at the doctor's office.

"I know you've been snooping around Cashel Rock," Bosh growled. "I offered to clip you a couple days ago after you tangled with Ross. He and Colin said no."

"Guess they changed their minds."

"You guessed right."

We were approaching Bay Street. The Honda smelled like fast food. Trash and old receipts littered the dashboard and floor mats.

"One more time," Bosh said. "Where's Shawn Finley?"

"I hate to give you the same answer, but I don't have a clue. Have you contacted Chief Gramble with Derryville PD? I'm sure he'd be happy to help."

Bosh laughed. It sounded about as pleasant as a power saw.

"All right," he said. "If you don't know nothing about Shawn Finley, then you're worthless to me. Let's just find an empty parking lot. I'll put two in your head and be on my way."

It occurred to me that I didn't have my phone. I'd left it in the house when Powell and I went downstairs. Didn't make much difference. Reaching for it in the car might have tested Bosh's trigger finger.

*Think, Charlie.*

I could drive the Honda into a ditch or a light pole or another car, but that wouldn't do me much good either. I didn't have a seat belt on. I was unable to come up with a plan that wouldn't result in death or serious injury by crash or bullets. As long as I was driving us around, Bosh probably wouldn't shoot.

*Okay then, Charlie. Just keep talking.*

"This car sucks," I said.

"What?"

"I said this car sucks. Yours is much nicer."

"What the fuck did you just say?"

"You know, your Escalade? The one out front of Scottie Coburn's place in Sausalito a few nights ago? I watched you beat the shit out of him, threaten to kill him."

"You were there?"

"Yeah. Following Scottie for another case I was on. Why'd you warn him to stay away from Deborah Wellington?"

Bosh was quiet. I glanced at him through the rearview mirror. He appeared to be gritting his teeth. He probably wanted to kill me right there but couldn't. It was his idea to have me drive.

We caught the light at Bay Street. I braked to a stop three cars behind the intersection. Traffic was piling up near the Embarcadero.

"Scottie's got a really nice place," I said. "We talked for a while after you left him on his back in the parking lot. I helped him inside, found out where he worked. Funny how his boss, Dalton Crawford, knows your bosses. Small world, huh?"

Bosh pressed the muzzle hard against my neck.

"Who's Dalton Crawford?" he said.

"You don't know?"

The light on Bay turned green.

"Doesn't matter," he snarled. "Turn left."

"The Embarcadero's to the right."

"Shut the fuck up and turn left."

I turned left. Bosh's cheeks were infectious red. His face glowered. His breathing through his nose got heavier.

"Change of plans," he said. "Get on Watercrest. We're going to Sausalito. Pay Scottie a little visit. Take care of two problems at once."

The rest of the drive took about fifteen minutes. We passed the spot on Watercrest where Friday had wrecked her car. We merged onto the 101. We hit a pothole just before the Golden Gate Bridge and something toward the back of the Honda rattled.

"When I'm done with you two," Bosh said, "I might just go back to your pretty little house and set it on fire with your wife and kid and Finley's daughter inside. Then I'll go find your boss and finish him off too."

My jaw clenched. I glanced at Bosh through the mirror. He laughed again.

"Surprised? We've been checking up on you too, Charlie Shaw."

He leaned back in his seat with the gun pointed in my direction, more casually than before. He now had a plan. He'd get to Sausalito, put Scottie and me in a room together, tape our mouths shut, shoot us dead. He wouldn't find Shawn Finley or the money, but he'd take care of two whistleblowers. For that, he'd get a nice pat on the head from Ross and Colin Dunne.

As expected, weekend traffic in Sausalito was thick. It would've been a good day for Uber fares. Would've been better than driving around a lunatic with a gun. Per Bosh's instructions, I pulled into the Herring Harbor parking lot and found a spot toward the back with no neighboring cars.

"Hand me the keys," he said. "Slowly."

I dropped the keys into his left hand. The key chain also had a silver charm in the shape of a cross.

"Take your hands off the wheel and slowly get out of the car," Bosh said. "Meet me at the trunk. I've got the gun on you. If you make a run for it or if you call for help, I will shoot you. Don't think for a second I won't do it."

I did as he said. We met at the trunk. He had the gun concealed in the right-hand pocket of his hooded denim jacket.

"Now walk to the entrance. I'm right behind you. Make any move besides a straight line and you're fucking dead."

Bosh's combat boots crunched the pavement behind me. No one joined us in the parking lot. The spaces were maybe a third full with cars. Most residents were probably out enjoying their Saturday, doing normal, legal, pleasant things. Shopping, sailing, biking, hiking, drinking. Scottie might be doing one of those things too, if his ribs had healed up enough. I had no idea where he was.

An older man with a dog on a leash came through the security gate just as we approached. He held the gate for us. He looked at Bosh as if he'd encountered a grizzly bear.

Bosh and I walked the wood-paneled corridor, turned left at the corner, and stopped three houseboats down at 12 Central Dock. Bosh felt almost conjoined to me, no farther than a half step behind.

"Knock," he said.

I did three times. We waited. Nothing. From the corner of my eye, I thought something fluttered in the window blinds to our left.

"Again," Bosh said.

I could feel his hot breath on my neck. I knocked three more times. We waited some more. Nothing.

"Scottie!" Bosh barked.

I let out some air and closed my eyes, thought of Powell and hoped he wasn't hurt too badly. I thought of Shawn Finley and hoped he would come to his senses. I thought of Friday Finley and hoped she would find peace, if not her father. I thought of Ryan and wondered if she was trying to reach me right now. I thought of Callie and hoped she would grow up proud of her father for what he'd tried to do.

Something stirred behind the door. The sound of a latch relenting. The creak of a door moving free of its frame, if only temporarily. I swung my right foot upward and backward as violently and forcefully as I'd moved anything in my entire life. My foot caught Bosh somewhere in the groin. He stepped back and grunted in pain. The door swung wide open. Scottie Coburn held a double-barreled shotgun.

I dove to the ground just before thunder roared from the mouth of the shotgun. I heard a louder groan from Bosh, then the thump of his knees on the ground, then the thud of his body falling face forward. The gun fell from his hand and clacked on the pavement. Like a dueling gunfighter, he'd been too late on the draw.

I checked for a pulse but there was no need. A growing pool of blood covered the back of his denim jacket. Blood dripped from his mouth. His eyes were open and empty. I looked up at Scottie. He was still holding the shotgun, trembling, staring down at his assailant.

"Thanks for being home," I said.

# CHAPTER 35

The tranquil seaside parking lot morphed into a morbid afternoon laser show. The Sausalito cops sent a fleet of Ford Expeditions, sirens wailing, blinding red and blue and white lights whirling on their grilles and roofs and side mirrors. Two ambulances joined them. I'd called 911 with Scottie's phone. I told them I was a private investigator and my friend had shot an intruder in his doorway in self-defense.

The police arrived in six minutes. Scottie and I waited for them outside his house.

"Don't touch the body," I told him.

"Okay."

Scottie had set the shotgun on the ground next to Bosh. His hands, now empty, continued to tremble.

"You all right?"

"Yeah. I saw you guys through the window. Told you I'd be ready if that guy ever came back."

"I remember."

I probably wasn't the only person who heard the shot and dialed 911. My ears still rung from the blast. My headache returned. Two men and a woman passed us while we waited. They gaped at Bosh's body. We tried to explain what had happened. The woman cupped her hand to her mouth and squealed. One of the men put his hand on her shoulder. They ran from us toward the parking lot.

"Better get out while they can," I said. "Cops will shut down this whole area."

I was right. Cones and crime scene tape blocked access to the lot and to Scottie's home. Three officers approached us in the doorway with guns drawn. Scottie and I raised our hands. I had my detective's license and driver's license already out.

"I'm the guy who called 911," I said, and handed my cards to the first cop.

They patted us down. They asked us if we knew whether Bosh was deceased. They asked us if we were injured. They asked if anyone was inside Scottie's home. They separated us. Scottie went inside. I went to the parking lot and sat on a bench by the entrance and gave one of the officers a brief statement. He asked me to stay put and wait for the detectives to arrive.

I watched the grim procession under a cloudless pristine sky. Three Sausalito cops walked toward the back of the lot, where I'd parked the Honda. Two medics from the ambulance wheeled a gurney toward Scottie's houseboat. I stretched my shoulder and closed my eyes and tried to rest until my next interrogation. The sunlight made my headache worse. The sounds I'd heard were unshakable. Finally, I drifted off. Sometime later, a tap on the shoulder woke me from an unmemorable dream.

"Charlie."

Dwayne Powell stood over me. Beside him was Tex, wearing a tan suit and powder-blue tie. Beside Tex was a woman in a cranberry pantsuit.

"You and Inspector Powell never showed up to our little meeting at headquarters," Tex said. "Now I know why."

"Sorry, Tex. Boss, you okay?"

"Was gonna ask you the same thing," Powell said.

"I'm all right."

"That's what I was hoping to hear," Tex said. "Charlie Shaw, meet Detective Rivera with the Sausalito Police Department. I'm here to assist her and the SPD with this investigation."

Detective Rivera and I shook hands.

"While you were napping on this nice little bench, Detective Rivera, Inspector Powell, and I spoke with Mr. Coburn," Tex said.

"Thanks for letting me catch up on some sleep," I said.

"Figured you needed it," Tex said.

He checked his notebook.

"Mr. Coburn was surprised to learn that you were a private investigator and not his neighbor, a . . . Lenny Poffo."

"Lanny," I said. "He butchered a perfectly good pro wrestling alias."

"You pretended to be his neighbor when you were investigating him and Arthur Wellington's wife?"

"Maybe."

Tex shook his head and stepped away to speak with the Sausalito officer who had taken my statement. Another Sausalito officer asked Detective Rivera to walk in the direction of the Honda.

Powell eased into the spot next to me on the bench.

"Back's a little sore," he said. "I've had worse. Bosh hurt you?"

"Nope. Just kept a gun on me. And said a lot of mean things."

"He's dead?"

"Very."

"Sorry I didn't see him on the street."

"Don't apologize for a damn thing, boss."

Powell handed me my phone. I had eight missed calls and fourteen unopened text messages.

"I talked to your wife," he said. "She knows you're okay."

"Good," I said. "I don't think I have the energy to explain this to her *and* Tex right now."

Tex pulled another bench over to mine. He sat down facing me and removed a pen and memo pad from his jacket pocket. He was an earnest-looking man with expressive brown eyes. He seemed much younger than a guy who'd turned thirty-five a few weeks ago.

"Any injuries?"

"I wouldn't wanna check my blood pressure right now," I said. "Other than that, no."

"Feel like telling your story again?"

"Whatever you need."

Tex clicked his retractable pen.

"Then let's get started," he said. "I got some of the backstory from Inspector Powell on the way over here, but I want your account of things."

"Might take the rest of the day."

"What's the short version?"

"Two small cases combining into one big shitstorm."

"Okay. Let's start with Mr. Coburn and the deceased. Mr. . . . ." He read off his notepad. ". . . Vandenbosch."

"Bosh's name is Vandenbosch?"

"Yep."

"First name?"

"Tyler. Tyler Vandenbosch."

"I only know him by a nickname. Bosh. He worked for Ross and Colin Dunne, owners of the Cashel Rock bar in Derryville. I've been trying to find another man who worked for them—Shawn Finley, a bartender who hasn't shown up to work in a couple weeks. He is Friday Finley's father. Remember her?"

"The girl with the busted-up 4Runner?" Tex said. "The one we tracked down from Oregon a few days ago?"

"She's down here trying to find her dad," I said. "Turns out he was running from the Dunnes, his bosses. He stole money from them. The Dunnes are wannabe wise guys running some type of illegal operation in Derryville. The bar appears to be a front. Last night I found Shawn alive but unconscious in Bosh's trunk. He took me to the money he stole. Then he blindsided me, ran off, left me the cash."

"Why?"

"So his daughter would get the money and he wouldn't have to face her like a man. The money's in a duffel bag at Inspector Powell's house. Bosh figured it was me who found Shawn. He grabbed us this morning. Said the Dunnes ordered the hit."

"Why didn't you come to me sooner about all this?"

"Because Friday asked me to find her dad without the police if possible. She knows he's a lousy crook."

Tex gave me a long stare. It was the first time I'd ever seen him truly irritated with me.

"Inspector Powell briefed me about the Dunne brothers," Tex said. "We've got officers out to speak with them. Let's start at the beginning. Give me everything you've got."

I explained to Tex that this whole fiasco started in this same parking lot a few nights ago, where I'd tailed Scottie and Mrs. Wellington, and where my future client, Friday, had tailed Bosh and the Dunnes from Cashel Rock.

"That's where you saw Miss Finley for the first time in the parking lot," Tex said.

"She'd met the Dunnes at the bar. Asked about her dad. They weren't helpful, so she followed them to see what they were up to. Bosh picked them up at the bar, drove them here."

"And in separate cars, you and Miss Finley watched Mr. 'Bosh' Vandenbosch assault Scottie."

"Yep."

"And he said to Scottie, quote, 'Stay the fuck away from her'?"

"Yep."

"Meaning stay away from Mrs. Wellington?"

"I assume so, yes."

"Why?"

"No idea. Scottie had no idea. He said Bosh was a total stranger. But I just learned that Scottie's former boss, Dalton Crawford, is a frequent guest at Cashel Rock. An apparent friend of the Dunnes."

"So maybe Crawford asked them to assault Scottie that night? Scare him straight?"

"I dunno. I met Crawford this week after we wrapped the Wellington case. He was a perfectly likable guy. I showed him a picture of Bosh, asked if he'd ever seen him before. He said no. And he claims he fired Scottie *after* Arthur Wellington got my pictures and told him about the affair. Wellington recently invested in his tech company."

"Let's recap here," Tex said. "Case Number One, your stakeout on Scottie Coburn and Mrs. Wellington, led you to Case Number Two, Miss Finley and her search for her father, Shawn."

"Correct."

"And your search for Miss Finley's father led to what you call this 'shitstorm': an investigation of Shawn Finley's bosses, the Dunne brothers, and your final encounter with the Dunnes' hired gun, Mr. 'Bosh' Vandenbosch."

"Yep."

"Tell me more about the Dunnes."

I went through my unpleasant encounters with Ross and Colin:

- My ugly fight with Ross outside Cashel Rock.
- Derryville Chief Mike Gramble's "subtle" warning for me to leave town.
- The Dunnes' Thursday night poker game at Cashel Rock with three tech executives, including Dalton Crawford.
- And the Dunnes' Friday night casino trip with Crawford, where I found Bosh holding Shawn Finley in a trunk.

"The Dunnes are apparently into gambling, drugs, girls, maybe more," I said. "Last summer they hired Friday's dad and coerced him into handling some of their illegal dirty work. Somewhere along the way they also hired Bosh as their enforcer."

"To enforce what?"

"I dunno. Anything from collections to executions."

"Including a murder attempt on you and Scottie today."

"Yep."

"Your man here has been busy, Inspector Powell," Tex said.

Powell nodded. He sat next to me on the bench in silence, arms folded, watching the cops and medics and forensic experts comb the area. A couple of San Francisco police cruisers arrived to assist with the scene.

"Why do you think the Dunnes want you dead?" Tex asked.

"Because I've been pissing them off lately."

"Investigating their more discreet activities?"

"That's a nice way of putting it."

Tex jotted down some more notes.

"A couple things here seem really off," he said.

"Just a couple?"

"I don't understand how these upstanding members of the San Francisco business community—Dalton Crawford, in particular—got hooked up with these guys," Tex said.

"Us too."

"We'll have a talk with Mr. Crawford."

Tex scribbled some more notes. He asked more questions. He wanted to know exact times, exact locations, license plate numbers.

Detective Rivera returned and whispered something to Tex. He closed his notebook and stood up.

"Hang here for a minute," he said.

They walked back toward Bosh's Honda. I closed my eyes. A hungry seagull squawked somewhere nearby. I remembered that I hadn't eaten all day. My stomach growled and confirmed this.

Powell's eyes were still fixed on the parking lot.

"You're lucky Bosh decided to make a pit stop here," he said.

"Yep."

"And you're lucky Scottie had a gun ready inside the house."

"Scottie told me if Bosh ever came back, he'd shoot him."

"Tex didn't ask an important question. Why would Bosh stop here? Their business with Scottie was over. He had nothing to do with Friday's dad."

I shrugged.

"I have a theory," Powell said.

"Your theories are usually correct."

"You steered Bosh over here, didn't you."

"Yep."

"To buy yourself some time."

"Yep."

"How?"

"I goaded him. I told him I saw him beat up Scottie a few nights ago. Told him I knew his bosses were connected to Scottie's boss. Told him I knew something fishy was going on."

"That was a gamble."

"Bosh was gonna kill me anyway."

"He could've killed Scottie too."

"It was a chance I had to take."

Powell didn't answer. After a minute I glanced over at him. His eyes were closed too. After a while Tex returned.

"Come with me," he said.

We walked to the back of the parking lot. The red Honda's trunk was open. We peered inside.

"Can you identify this woman?" Tex asked.

"Yes."

# CHAPTER 36

"Her name is Tate," I said. "Like Shawn Finley, she was a bartender at Cashel Rock."

The past tense seemed appropriate. Tate was lying on her back in the sort of peaceful sleep pose I'd seen Callie deploy in her crib. Only Tate wasn't sleeping. Her big blue eyes stared into nothing. The silver cross still dangled from her neck.

"Looks like she was strangled," Tex said.

I'd reached my limit on dead bodies in a single afternoon. A wave of nausea bubbled up from my stomach. I ran to the shrubs behind the Honda and got sick. Powell came over and patted me on the shoulder. I wiped my mouth and rejoined Tex at the trunk.

"Car is registered to a Tate Wilson. Addison Lane, San Francisco," Tex said.

I glanced at Tate's body again. She was wearing bedtime clothes: black T-shirt, white athletic shorts.

"She and Shawn Finley were friends and coworkers," I said. "I met her at the bar the first time I went to ask about Shawn. I gave her my card. She reached out a couple days later."

"When?"

"Thursday night after my fight with Ross. Early Friday morning, actually. Inspector Powell had just given me a ride home from the Derryville police station. She texted me and said she had info. I drove to her apartment. She told me the Dunnes would be at the casino last night. She was worried they might hurt Shawn."

I could feel Powell's eyes on me.

"You went to Tate Wilson's apartment?" Tex asked.

"Yes."

"What information did she provide?"

"She'd overheard the Dunnes talking at the bar. Sounded like they were plotting something on Shawn."

"What did they say?"

"Something about giving Shawn a 'proper send-off.'"

"How did she start working at Cashel Rock?"

"She said Colin hired her a couple years ago. They were . . . involved. Off and on."

"Lovers?"

"Yes."

Tex took more notes.

"Anything else?" he asked.

"Yeah. Bosh showed up at her apartment while I was there."

Tex glanced up from his notebook.

"Bosh was there?"

"Yeah."

"And thirty-six hours later he's driving her car with her dead in the trunk?"

"Yeah."

"Why did he go to her apartment in the early hours of Friday morning?"

"He said she wasn't answering her phone. He said Colin had some work instructions for the following day."

"Where were you during all this?"

"Hiding in the coat closet."

Tex shook his head as if to say, "You poor pathetic bastard."

"Did you have any contact with Tate after visiting her apartment?"

"No."

"You didn't tell her you found Shawn Finley?"

"No."

"You didn't warn her that Bosh might be a threat?"

I started to feel sick again.

"No," I said.

Tex made more notes.

"If we search Tate's apartment we might find your fingerprints on doorknobs, maybe some coats?"

"You might."

"You think Bosh killed her after Shawn escaped from his trunk?"

"Yes."

"You think Colin ordered that too?"

"Probably. They might've assumed she was ratting them out."

Tex closed his notebook.

"I'm gonna ask one of the Sausalito guys to drive y'all home."

"Thanks."

"Keep your phone on, stay in town, the routine stuff. I might have more questions. I'll let you know if we find the Dunnes."

"Don't count on the Derryville cops for help," I said. "You ever meet Chief Gramble?"

"No," Tex said.

"Word is he's running interference for these guys."

"Why would he do that?"

"One, because it's Derryville," I said. "Two, Shawn said the Dunnes have dirt on the chief."

"Blackmail?"

"Yeah."

"We'll keep an eye out. Next time, maybe give me a heads-up sooner."

Powell and I started back toward the front of the parking lot.

"Pretty girl," he said.

"She was trying to get her life together," I said.

"Too late for that."

"I already feel sick enough, boss."

My phone buzzed again. I went back to the bench by the entrance and answered.

"Charlie," Ryan said. "Thank God."

"I promise I'm okay. No bumps, no bruises, no scratches, no more concussions."

"That's good news," she said. "I have some bad news."

"What?"

"Friday's missing."

# CHAPTER 37

"Missing as in, she said goodbye?"

"Missing as in, she's gone," Ryan said. "Said she was gonna take a nap in one of the guest bedrooms about two hours ago. I just walked in. She's gone. Her luggage is gone. The window is cracked open."

"Did she leave a note?"

"No. I can't find the money her father stole from those nasty people either."

"That duffel bag?"

"It's not here. I looked everywhere."

"So we have no clue where she went?"

"No. I'm sorry, Charlie."

I sat back down on the bench. I felt the pain in my head start to resurface like an angry ocean swell.

"I thought this might happen," I said. "We couldn't keep her cooped up in another house for long. She believes this whole mess is her fault."

"Should we call the police?" Ryan asked.

"Powell and I are finishing up with Tex. I'll call you when I get home."

"You're both okay?"

"I'm okay. Powell is indestructible."

"I love you."

"I love you too."

I called Titan Auto Repair.

"Hi, this is Charlie Shaw. I'm having some work done on a silver 4Runner for a Miss Friday Finley."

"Yes, Mr. Shaw. We just finished up yesterday. Miss Finley already came by and picked it up."

"Miss Finley left with the car?"

"Yes, sir."

"When?"

"Last hour or so."

"Did she pay the balance?"

"Yes, sir, she did. In full. Paid in cash."

"She didn't happen to mention where she was headed, did she?"

"No, sir, she didn't."

"So everything's fixed? The axle?"

"Yes, sir. We offered to fix the damage on the bumper, replace the paint where it had been removed on impact. We do that sort of work too. She declined."

"She'll have no problems getting back on the road, then."

"No, sir. It's an older model, but she runs fine."

"Thank you."

I called Friday three times. She didn't answer. I left a message, assuring her I wasn't angry and asking her to confirm she was all right.

I told Tex and Powell about Friday. Then Powell and I went home in the squad car. We were quiet on the ride back. My neighbor's new Volkswagen with the broken windshield was no longer parked on Stockton.

"Poor guy," I said. "He'd just bought that car."

We thanked the officer for the ride and got out. I looked at Powell.

"I know," I said.

"You know what?"

"When you fired me Thursday night after I got arrested, you told me to stay away from these people. And what did I do? I went straight to Tate Wilson's house and kept pushing. And now she's dead."

"I told you to stop," Powell said, "because at that point you still had a chance to stop. Now I've got your whole family hiding in my house. We need to wrap this up. I need my personal space."

He scanned the street for any sign of trouble, his eyes sharp and penetrating.

"What did you whisper to Ryan?" I asked.

"When?"

"Just before she packed up Callie and left the house."

"I promised that I wouldn't let anything happen to you," he said. "And I asked her to trust me."

"Thanks," I said. "Even though you fired me."

"Some good that did," Powell said. "Look where we are now."

"So now what? Should I go upstairs and hide under the bed?"

"No. We're both gonna try to get some rest. Then we're gonna help the police expedite this investigation. I look out for you, and you look out for me. Deal?"

He held out his big right hand. I shook it.

"Deal."

"I'll talk to the department about sending a patrol car through here, keep an eye on things," Powell said. "We don't know what the Dunnes will try next."

"Where do you think they went?"

"Probably split when they didn't hear back from Bosh. Where do you think Friday went?"

"Home to Oregon, maybe."

"Not much of a home."

"No, but it's all she has."

"Maybe she likes personal space too," Powell said, and delicately started up my front steps.

I went inside and called Friday again. She didn't answer. I went to the kitchen and made a sandwich. I ate two bites and set it down. I wasn't hungry. My head hurt. I took a forty-five-minute hot shower and changed clothes and went into the living room. Friday had made up the couch on her last day in the house, just as she said she would. Powell now occupied the space with his feet up and his gun resting on the coffee table.

    I swiveled the media lounger around to face the front door and closed my eyes and thought about Callie and Ryan and Friday Finley and Tate Wilson. At some point my mind gave up, and I slept undisturbed for sixteen hours.

# CHAPTER 38

Tex called the next morning.

"Looks like Ross and Colin Dunne skipped town," he said.

"You checked Derryville?"

"Yeah. They share a house in the nice part of town."

"On Garden Grove. I've seen it."

"Nobody's home. We went to Cashel Rock. The bar's closed. We tried calling. No answer. The Dunnes probably figured it was too hot in the kitchen when they didn't hear from Bosh."

"Bosh and Tate worked for the Dunnes, and now they're both dead," I said. "And Tate and Colin Dunne had an intimate relationship."

"Not a great look," Tex said.

"Got an APB out?"

"Yeah."

"Search warrant?"

"Yeah. Sausalito's letting us lead the case. We've got more resources and we've got jurisdiction over some of this anyway."

"Talk with the Derryville police?"

"Chief Mike Gramble said Ross and Colin Dunne are terrific guys. Said he didn't know Bosh or Tate. Said it's a terrible tragedy what happened. Said his department will help any way they can."

"Do you believe that?"

"No."

I had the *Chronicle*'s website pulled up on my laptop. The headline and deck read:

## Sausalito Home Intruder Killed

### Woman Found Dead in Car Trunk; Two Men Wanted for Questioning

The story didn't include names or headshots except for Ross and Colin Dunne. "The owners of the Cashel Rock bar in Derryville are wanted for questioning about a deceased woman and deceased man believed to be Cashel Rock employees. Prior to his death, the man attacked a bystander at the corner of Stockton and Chestnut and forced another man into a red 2014 Honda Civic at gunpoint. The car was registered to the deceased woman. Police found her body in the trunk. Police are asking for the public's assistance in finding the Dunne brothers, who are not currently suspects but could have information critical to the investigation."

"Dalton Crawford might know something," I said. "He's the last person I saw with the Dunnes."

"Spoke to Crawford and his two college buddies, Khatri and Maniet," Tex said. "They all insist the Dunnes are poker acquaintances, nothing more, and they have no knowledge of the Dunnes' activities and no idea where they might be. Crawford also patently denied any prior knowledge that the Dunnes would assault Scottie Coburn a few nights ago during your little stakeout on Mrs. Wellington."

"Just a big coincidence," I said.

"You think Crawford hired them to do the job?"

"Maybe," I said. "Anything new on the deceased?"

"Yeah. Bosh is Tyler Vandenbosch, forty-three years old, Derryville address. Drove a black Escalade. Mr. Vandenbosch was born in Tulsa, Oklahoma. Ex-military, army. Went AWOL and was dishonorably discharged two years ago. Incredibly, no criminal record."

"Got one now," I said.

"He had a cell phone on him at time of death," Tex said. "We're going through it. The blue Corolla you found Shawn Finley in was reported stolen, by the way."

"Figures. What about Tate?"

"Didn't find much family. Her parents are dead. Her mother lives in Modesto. Taking care of her grandson."

"Tate's son?"

"Yep."

"How old?"

"Three."

"Jesus."

"Your turn to report," Tex said. "Any luck finding Miss Finley?"

"Nope. Not answering her phone. Repair shop says she picked up her car yesterday. Paid in cash."

"With the stolen money?"

"Yep."

"I'd like to have a statement from her."

"I'd ask you to put out an APB, but she's probably long gone."

"Back to Oregon?"

"If she's smart," I said.

"What about her dad?"

"Her dad ain't worth finding. Speaking of pains in my ass, what's gonna happen to Scottie Coburn?"

"He cooperated fully," Tex said. "He'll probably be fine. He shot Bosh in self-defense. Castle doctrine."

"Good."

"You and Powell still feeling rough?"

"My body is rested. My mind is not."

"Don't blame yourself for Miss Finley leaving."

"I'm not. I blame her dad for that. I'm blaming myself for Tate's murder. And for my family having to hide like rats in the daylight."

"How long before you bring them home?"

"Not until we find the Dunnes."

"I got this case because I know you and Powell pretty well," Tex said. "But that also means my boss is watching me close. He and Powell go way back."

"They do."

"And my boss knows you've got contacts at the *Chronicle*."

"The *Chronicle* fired me," I said.

"SFPD just doesn't want sensitive information compromised," Tex said.

"I understand."

"I can't tell you everything, but I'll keep you in the loop best I can."

"And if I find anything that might be helpful, I'll let you know."

"We got a car watching your neighborhood for now," Tex said. "Gives us another reason to have a police presence. Too many break-ins there this summer."

"Thanks."

"Don't get yourself killed," Tex said.

I peeled myself off the media lounger and relayed the info to Powell over eggs and toast. He drank coffee. I drank tea. During my second cup I got another phone call.

"Maggie Salvetti," I said. "Still managing editor at the *Chronicle*, or did they fire you too?"

"You weren't fired," Maggie said. "You were furloughed and you never came back."

"You guys hurt my feelings."

"Poor baby. How's Callie, the real baby?"

"She's starting on solids. Mostly on her face and bib, but making progress."

"I called you a couple times last night," Maggie said.

"I was asleep."

"For twelve hours?"

"Sixteen, actually."

"Did you happen to see the story in today's paper about an assault on Stockton between Chestnut and Lombard?"

"I didn't read the paper when I *worked* for the paper."

"You still at the same address?"

"Yep."

"It happened two doors down from your house. A man fitting former police inspector Dwayne Powell's description was thrown into the windshield of a car."

"Wow."

"Then the attacker, this huge guy with a snake tattoo on his neck, pulled a gun on another man and forced him into a red Honda Civic at the corner of Stockton and Chestnut."

"Crazy."

"The other man fits your description."

"According to who?"

"An eyewitness."

"Did you ask the cops?"

"They haven't released names."

"What happened to the attacker?"

"Shot to death in Sausalito. Tried to break into a houseboat."

"That's nuts," I said.

There was a pregnant pause on Maggie's end of the line.

"You're fucking with me," she said.

"I'm not."

"You didn't hear about this at all?"

"I was probably asleep," I said.

"Bullshit. Parents of six-month-olds don't sleep. It's an oath they take after conception."

"We hired a night nurse last week. Callie's sleeping. We're sleeping. All's well."

"So you're telling me," Maggie said, "that yesterday morning around eleven, you were not forced into a car at gunpoint by a guy that looked like Conan the Barbarian?"

"Unless I dreamt it," I said, "no."

Maggie paused again.

"Thanks for the time," she said. "Keep your doors locked."

I FaceTimed with Ryan and Callie and told them I'd made it safely through the night. Ryan said Callie had settled in okay at

Powell's house. They'd brought down Reggie's old crib from the attic. Callie hadn't yet figured out the phone screen. She pressed her face to it like a hippo with its nose against aquarium glass.

Powell's wife, Jackie, stepped into view and smiled and said hello. She didn't seem concerned about the mess we were all in. She was, after all, married to Dwayne Powell, which was like being married to Rambo. Ryan did look concerned. I could always spot her stress signals. She'd clench her jaw and bunch her lips together and speak in measured tones. I told her that she and Callie were safe with Powell's sons, and that Tex and the police were making progress, and that I missed my girls very much.

After lunch, I decided to call Friday Finley once more. It had been over twenty-four hours since she left Powell's house. Even if she had made one overnight stop, she'd had enough time to reach Oregon by now.

The phone rang four times and sent me to voicemail.

"Friday, it's Charlie again. I'm gonna repeat myself and say we hope you're home safe and please let us know where you are. There's also something I didn't share with you this past week about my sister, Sophie. She died when she was your age, sixteen. She'd just gotten her license. She went to a party with some guys in the city she didn't know, and she got assaulted by a stranger. I never found out who.

"Sophie got depressed. Wouldn't eat, wouldn't leave her room. Felt like it was her fault. Too ashamed and too scared to tell my parents. Finally she told me, her protective older brother, after I promised not to tell Mom and Dad or our younger brother or the police. It kept me up all night. The next morning, I decided to go to our little police station in town. Our parents weren't home, so I skipped school and filed a report. I knew it was worthless; I didn't have any details. But it felt like the right thing to do—the only thing I could do.

"Sophie said she was staying home sick that morning. When I got back to the house, she was dead. It's taken me years not to blame myself anymore. It's taken me years to see the world in a positive light again. Ryan has slowly helped me see that. Callie has given me a real purpose. Nowadays, I just wish my sister could've seen that her life would eventually move out of the darkness—that there was a shimmer of light in the far distance. If we don't meet again, I want you to keep this in mind: Nobody in this world controls your happiness or your future but you. Not your mom, not your dad, not me. Just you."

# CHAPTER 39

My phone buzzed an hour later. The name "Friday Finley" appeared on my caller ID.

"Hello, stranger," I said. "Where are you?"

"Are you alone?"

The caller was most certainly not Friday Finley.

"Yes," I said.

"Listen to me very carefully, or she dies very painfully," the voice said.

# CHAPTER 40

Ross Dunne's voice was quite distinctive. It was viciously impish, as if he'd stolen it from a twelve-year-old in detention.

"I'm only gonna tell you once," he said. "The first thing you're gonna do is forget about the cops. If you call them, or if I even start to think you've called them, she's dead. You got that?"

"Yes," I said. "Is Friday okay?"

Ross ignored my question.

"Is Bosh dead?" he asked.

The forcefulness in his tone counterbalanced his high-pitched voice. If I weren't shaken by the subject of the call, I would've laughed.

I took in a deep breath and said, "Yes."

It occurred to me that I didn't recognize my own voice. It sounded parched and throaty now, as if I'd just finished a race. My breath no longer came involuntarily. I forced myself to inhale and exhale short, distressed wisps.

There was a long pause from Ross. Then he said, "You kill him?"

"Scottie in Sausalito killed him. Bosh took a side quest to the kid's house after he grabbed me. Got himself shot."

Another long pause. I took the opportunity to catch my breath.

"Fuck it," Ross said. "Doesn't matter. Our boy Shawn Finley . . . where is he?"

"I don't know where Shawn is."

"Bullshit."

"I found him in Bosh's trunk, and then he ran off like a stray puppy. That's the truth. If you have Friday, you also have the money Shawn stole from you. She took it with her when she left us."

Another pause. I envisioned him communicating silently with his brother, Colin. Powell stood up and went to the kitchen. He rummaged through the drawers and found a pen and notepad. He scribbled something and handed the paper to me.

"Fuck the cash," Ross said. "Shawn's got something else we want."

"What is it?"

"He'll know."

I read Powell's note aloud. "I want to speak to Friday. I want to hear she's okay."

"She's fine. For now," Ross said. "You've got till midnight to round up Shawn. Tell him I've got his little girl. In exchange, I want what's ours. Don't ask the cops for help. Don't call this number. I'll call you at midnight and we'll set up a little meet. If I call and you say you don't have Shawn and what he stole, his daughter dies."

"What'd he steal?"

"None of your business."

"I may need a little more time."

I was talking to myself. Ross had already hung up.

# CHAPTER 41

I stared at nothing. I heard Powell's voice but no words. I imagined Friday walking through the door with my family, unharmed, smiling. She had a wonderful smile when she felt like using it. Her life hadn't given her much to smile about. I wondered if she'd ever have reason to smile again.

"Charlie!"

Powell snapped two fingers three inches from my face.

"Sorry," I said.

"Was that the Dunnes?"

"Yeah. Ross. The short, ugly one."

"Tell me everything he said. As close to verbatim as possible."

As I spoke, Powell scribbled onto the notepad. When I finished, he set the pen down.

"Fourteen hours," he said.

"Yep."

"Not much time."

"Nope."

"When you last saw Shawn, did he give any hint where he might be headed?"

"You mean, before he line-drived me with a shovel?"

Powell opened his eyes and glowered at me with a ferocity that transcended professional focus. The stare made my eye twitch. I looked away.

"Sorry," I said. "No, I don't have a clue where Shawn went."

Powell stood up from the couch and stretched his injured back.

He began to pace the room with a soldier's gait, upright and efficient.

"Ross gave away a couple things on the phone," he said.

I rubbed my forehead, a futile attempt to ward off another headache.

"Remind me," I said.

"He asked if you were alone," Powell said. "So he's not watching this house."

"Good. I'd prefer not to get picked off like skeet."

"Ross also said 'we.'"

"Meaning him and his brother?"

"Unless they recruited help. Who else was in their crew besides Bosh?"

"I don't know. I'm guessing they had a couple low-level pushers. But Bosh and Shawn were their main guys."

Powell went to the kitchen and returned with some water.

"We shouldn't have left her with that money," he said. "We should've put it away someplace. Or given it to Tex."

"Nobody was thinking straight," I said.

"It's my job to think straight," he said.

"How do you think they found her?"

"Maybe she found them."

"Why?"

"Bribe off the Dunnes," he said. "Give them the cash, ask them to leave everyone alone."

"Who in their right mind would do that?"

"A sixteen-year-old," he said. "A grief-stricken sixteen-year-old who felt guilty about this whole situation. Maybe she thought the money could fix things. For her dad. For you."

My hands were clammy. I wiped the perspiration onto my jeans.

"When I was ten or so," I said, "Sophie and I stole a couple packs of gum from the local convenience store. It was that Bubblicious gum, real thick and sugary. My mom wouldn't buy it for us. When we got home, I tore into my pack. Fit like three pieces in my mouth at once. Soph got this look on her face. A wave of guilt came over her. She grabbed her pack and what was left of mine, hopped back on her bike, and returned them to the store. Admitted what she'd done. Got a big spanking from my dad. Grounded a month."

"Did she tell on you?"

"No."

Powell let me reflect in silence. Then he said gently, "We've gotta get moving, Charlie."

"We don't even know if Friday's alive," I said.

"You think Ross would kill her?"

"Yeah."

"Would Colin?"

"He's no angel either," I said. "Or rocket scientist. But he's the cooler, smarter head."

"He'd convince Ross to use her as bait?"

"Probably."

"For whatever they want from Shawn?"

"Probably."

"If it's not about the stolen cash," Powell said, "what's it about?"

"The hole," I said.

"Hole?"

"There was a second hole in the ground the night Shawn knocked me unconscious. I tripped over it walking back to the car. He dug up the money in front of me. While I was passed out, he must've dug up whatever the Dunnes are looking for."

"Did he mention he had anything of unique value to them?"

"No. Just the money for Friday."

Powell glanced at his phone. "We now have thirteen hours and fifty-three minutes to find Shawn," he said, "unless we find the Dunnes first. We could try Dalton Crawford's office, ask him if he knows where his boys went."

"He'll probably just repeat what he told Tex," I said. "And we'll have wasted an hour of precious time."

"We could ask Tex to bring Crawford in," Powell said. "Apply some pressure."

"Ross Dunne explicitly said no cops."

"They always say that."

"Kidnappers?"

"Yep."

"You've dealt with kidnappers before?"

"Been around hostage situations before."

"And?"

"The cops could help us find Shawn. They could also help us run a trace on the Dunnes. Maybe find their nest."

"Ross said don't call. He said he'd call us at midnight. And to be honest, boss, I can't live with anything that might happen to Friday because we tried to get cute."

Powell closed his eyes again and cleared his throat. He seemed entirely too relaxed for the moment.

"Then we better find Shawn," he said.

"Brilliant," I said. "How?"

"Think," he said. "Hard."

"Closing your eyes like that," I said. "Does it help the thinking process?"

"Helps me."

"Meditation?"

"Meditation's for TikTok slack-asses," Powell said. "We grown-ups call it 'taking stock.'"

"All right," I said. "Let's take stock."

I closed my eyes. I was still seeing floaters since Shawn Finley's RBI single to my cranium. Yellow ones, like little amoebas dancing across the darkness. My temple twitched. I tried to ignore it. I tried to think of something pleasant, something that would quell my anxiety and relax my brain. I thought of Callie the first time she saw a dog on a walk. It was a Cavalier King Charles spaniel tugging on its leash. Callie squealed in excitement. I smiled to myself. Then I tried to narrow my focus completely, the way I locked in on home plate when I was an average college pitcher. I tried to rewind through the past week. I replayed every conversation with Friday Finley since we met and recalled every word Shawn Finley said to me after I saved his life.

I opened my eyes. Powell opened his.

"I just took stock," I said.

"And?"

"And it's a pretty effective trick."

# CHAPTER 42

Pacifica was a mellow surf town thirty minutes south of San Francisco on the PCH, known for its waves and its fog. Drive thirty more minutes south and you'd see a great deal more sunshine. I learned about fog belts and microclimates when I moved out here. There are no microclimates in a Texas summer. Just searing heat.

Powell drove us in his formidable Dodge Ram. Halfway there he stopped at a gas station and sat idle for a couple of minutes to gauge whether we'd been followed. Satisfied, he put the beast back in drive and continued on.

Above us, stringy clouds clumped together like a sheath of ice, dulling the sun's luminescence. A batch of low fog greeted us as we exited the PCH. Neither of us spoke. Powell played Miles Davis's *Kind of Blue* at a placid volume. I liked Miles Davis. I liked jazz. Ryan and I enjoyed the Fillmore Jazz Festival every year. But jazz or blues or Beethoven's Ninth wouldn't do much to calm my nerves now.

We parked in front of the visitor center and a string of white clapboard storefronts a block from the ocean. Powell checked his rearview mirror. After a long moment, he gave a thumbs-up sign. No tail.

"You tell Ryan about all this?" he asked.

"I'll tell her later. You gonna tell Jackie?"

"Much later," he said. "Let me see that picture again."

I texted him the photo Friday sent me the first time we visited Cashel Rock. Powell studied the picture of Shawn from six years ago.

"You really think he's here?" Powell asked.

"No idea. He might be in a ditch a hundred miles from here."

"If we strike out here, we're calling for help. Can't screw around too long."

"Fine. How should we play this?"

"Divide for now and hopefully conquer," Powell said. "I'll take the beach. You take the buildings."

Powell unbuckled his seat belt, opened the center console, unlocked a steel case, and took out his Beretta. He holstered the gun on his hip. Then he stepped out of the truck and zipped up his windbreaker.

"If I find him," he said, "I'll try my best not to shoot him."

I watched Powell head toward the seawall until he turned right and out of sight. He was tall and angular with broad shoulders and perfect posture. He always moved with undeniable purpose and poise, like a championship boxer or a Hall of Fame quarterback who'd seen every possible blitz. He appeared to be favoring his back a little. It was the first time I'd seen him favor anything. There was a time when I assumed he was hardwired by circuitry, not flesh and bone. He rarely showed emotion besides occupational indignation. Mostly, he was as animated as the gun at his waist.

I had almost reached my breaking point, ready to break down or break things or both. I wondered how Powell could remain so composed. I decided it came cumulatively with years of practice: at blood-soaked battle sites, at gruesome crime scenes, at grim hostage standoffs. He wasn't numb to it all. Experience had made him fearless.

"'A man is not made for defeat,'" I said to myself.

I slung my backpack over my shoulder and started along the avenue. I stopped inside various storefronts: a gift shop, a coffee shop, a day spa, a minute clinic, a wellness center, a wine bar. No one recognized Shawn Finley, or at least the younger, cleaner Shawn Finley portrayed in the picture. No one thought they'd encountered an older, grungier Shawn Finley in person.

I checked with the Inn at Rockaway and the Sea Breeze Motel. At both places, the concierge apologized and said they were not permitted to disclose whether Shawn Finley was a guest.

I tried Nick's Seafood Restaurant next to the motel. The hostess and the bartender didn't recognize Shawn in the picture. The bar was empty and the pre-dinner crowd was small. The dining area smelled like fresh fish and buttered bread. Any other day, I'd stop and order a crab sandwich. I wasn't hungry. I went back outside.

Rockaway Beach was a narrow strip of rocky beach bordered by two small cliffs, one on each side. The cliffs rose just high enough to create an inlet, like the opening of a book. The landscape looked more like New England than boilerplate California: moody, soupy, earthy, craggy. I'd heard it was a good spot for whale watching and for surfing big waves if you knew what you were doing. Beginners were encouraged to try the calmer waters at Linda Mar Beach a couple of miles down the coast.

I stopped at the seawall and compared the picture to the current setting. It was the exact spot Shawn and Friday had chosen years ago: standing together against the railing, arm in arm, backed by a cluster of rocks and the foamy tide and, well beyond, the foggy outline of one of the twin headlands. I imagined the scene: Shawn smiling, asking a fellow tourist if they'd mind taking a picture of him and his precious daughter; Friday, shy and reserved, forcing a smile in front of a stranger, finding comfort in her father's embrace.

An aggressive wave crashed against the lower rocks. I put my phone away.

I unzipped my backpack and took out my binoculars. Below, the beach had a decent crowd for a summer Sunday afternoon. Couples and kids spread out across the coffee-colored sand. Some laid down blankets. Some brought beach umbrellas of varying colors to protect themselves from cloud-constrained sunrays. Some sunbathed. Some collected rocks. Some threw a football around. Little brown birds hopped around the beach on two feet as if they had been shoelaced together, their mouths pried open, chirping at each other with obnoxious zest. They acted like teenagers trying to decide which house to hide the keg in. One bird had flown on top of an umbrella and sat in regal repose facing the ocean. King of the world.

I could see Powell making his way through the group of people, checking and crossing off faces. He was having as much luck as I was.

It was a pleasant day, upper sixties, with a hassle-free breeze wafting off the shoreline. In the far distance I could see the flat blue profile of the Pacific. Much closer, I could see four surfers snagging waves. I trained my binoculars on each surfer. None of them was Shawn Finley. Any hope of the contrary was ridiculous. Shawn Finley couldn't walk a straight line, much less pop up on a board.

I put the binoculars away and sat on a bench and waited for Powell. I checked my notifications. No new calls from Friday's phone. Ryan had texted me a picture of Callie enjoying a sweet potato puree. About 90 percent of it had landed on her cheeks and in her hair.

> How are you and Mr. Powell?

Just relaxing.

> Heard from Friday?

No.

> I bet she went home.

Probably.

I hated lying to Ryan about anything. In this situation, I believed it was the right decision. If I told her the truth, she'd insist on helping. I needed her and Callie inside and safe. Friday had left the house, and now her life was in danger. When this was all over, I may never leave the house again.

Powell joined me at the seawall a few minutes later. He sat beside me on the bench and took off his shoes and shook out intrusive bits of sand.

"No Shawn," he said, as he retied his laces.

"No Shawn," I said.

"Tried the hotel and motel?"

"Yeah. They wouldn't confirm or deny he's a guest."

We sat for a few minutes. I knew Powell was mulling our next move. How long should we stay? Should we risk involving the police? Was Shawn long gone? Or dead?

A week ago, Friday had been asking the same questions about her missing father. A week later, we'd walked ourselves in a deadly circle with abject collateral damage. Shawn was missing again. Friday had been abducted by his former employers, and two of his former coworkers were dead. Maybe Callie's insomnia wasn't the worst thing in the world.

Powell checked his watch.

"I'll go talk with the motel desk, explain our situation," Powell said. "Cheap motel rooms are Shawn's style, right? Bosh found him in one."

"Unless the second thing Shawn stole was more cash," I said. "Maybe he's staying at the Waldorf in Beverly Hills right now."

Powell patted my shoulder. "Why don't you keep watch out here?" he said.

"Sure. I gotta hit the bathroom. Want a crab sandwich to go?"

"No thanks. Not hungry."

"Me either."

I went back inside Nick's. The restaurant was humid and dimly lit. The coastal fog stunted the natural light outside. I returned from the restroom and sat at the bar and asked for a water bottle. I could see the street through a mirror installed above the cash register. The bartender had gained two patrons: a sullen-looking couple in their midthirties. He poured them two beers on draft, then retrieved my water bottle from a mini fridge.

I was reaching for the last ten-dollar bill in my wallet when I saw him.

## CHAPTER 43

If I hadn't seen him, I would've smelled him. The irresistible tag-team stench of booze and body odor. If I hadn't seen or smelled him, I would've heard him. Unhinged, incomprehensible shouting, the kind you hear at a football tailgate between drunken rival fan bases. At the surface level, it might've sounded amusing except for the hint of malevolence in its tone. Some drunks drank because they were running from something: loss, depression, stress. Running was Shawn Finley's specialty.

He was dressed for the occasion in a stained white tank top and white boxer shorts. The tank top was a size too small. It choked against his fleshy skin, revealing his potbelly. He wore no shoes or socks. He held a forty-ounce bottle halfway wrapped in a brown paper bag.

*Rock bottom at Rockaway.*

He stumbled up the street away from the beach, then stopped and decided the restaurant was a suitable destination for a man in his underwear. He burst through the door like an outlaw in a saloon.

"A fine wadder-ung hole," he yelled. He couldn't pronounce "watering."

His face looked worse than when I'd found him inside Bosh's trunk: greasy hair, neglected gray whiskers, distant bloodshot eyes. The cut on his head had begun to scab over, but it still looked pretty bad. The customers stared at him. I stared at him. He didn't notice me. He didn't notice anything but the bartender and the hearty light from the bar's neon-pink sign.

*Home away from home.*

He stood beside me and slammed his bottle down and hunched his arms over the bar as if he were preparing for a physical.

"Barkeep," he shouted, "is it happy-ower yet?" He couldn't pronounce "hour" either.

"Not here," the bartender said. "You're not dressed properly, sir."

The bartender wasn't rattled by Shawn's behavior. He had the look of a guy who'd seen this sort of thing before.

"Oh yeah?" Shawn shouted.

He ripped away the paper bag and smashed the butt of his bottle on the bar. Shards flew everywhere. The woman with the beer screamed.

I stood up and whirled him around to face me.

"What," I said, "no shovel?"

His bloodshot eyes widened. He lunged at me with the bottle. My grandma could've done it faster. I knocked it out of his shaky hand and grabbed him by the neck of his tank top and slammed him against the wall.

"It's Charlie," I said. "Remember me? Friday's friend. You're coming with me."

"Fuck you," he said, panting.

I slugged him as hard as I could in his flabby stomach. He groaned and doubled over and spit on the floor. I reached down and picked up the broken bottle with one hand. I grabbed him by the throat with the other.

"Hey," the bartender said. "What are you doing, man?"

"Back off," I said.

I raised the bottle toward Shawn's face. The blurriness in his eyes dissipated a little.

"I'm not her father, Shawn. You are. And if you don't come with me, the Dunnes are going to kill her in very short order."

"What?"

His eyes came into focus, like rain wiped from a windshield.

"Tate's dead and they kidnapped Friday, Shawn. I don't know how. It doesn't matter. What matters is we have a few hours before they call again. They want to meet with you, Shawn. They want something you stole from them."

His mouth dropped. He squinted and blinked his eyes, trying to process my words.

"She's . . ."

He gulped. His throat made an unpleasant ripple against the palm of my hand. I loosened my grip a little and he sank to the floor. He put his head on his knees and began to cry.

The bartender said, "I'm gonna call the cops."

I set the bottle back on the bar.

"Don't," I said. "We're just about done here."

Shawn's crying intensified. I crouched on my haunches and got even with his face.

"Look at me, Shawn."

He shook his head between his knees.

"I'm no good for her, goddamnit!" he shrieked. "Don't you see?"

He blubbered. It made his knees shake. I heard the restaurant door open. A party of three hustled outside, their unfinished plates still on the table. The couple at the bar followed. I didn't blame them. It was a volatile, pathetic situation.

"You can either stay here and drink yourself to death, which appears to be your plan, or you can come with me," I said. "We're running out of time."

He shook his head again.

"She needs you, Shawn. She needs her father. The father in this picture."

He raised his head high enough to peek at the photo on my phone. A moment passed, and slowly he lifted his head. He wiped his tears with his forearm.

"Where did you get that?" he asked.

"She gave it to me. To help me locate you. She kept it all these years."

"Is she all right?"

"I don't know," I said. "Let's go find out."

# CHAPTER 44

I gave the bartender my last ten bucks and apologized for the commotion. Shawn didn't have any cash on him. His boxers had no pockets.

I wheeled him outside by the arm. He needed assistance. His eyes had come back to Earth, but his walk remained unsteady.

Powell found us in the street. His eyes trained on Shawn.

"The Talented Mr. Finley," he said. "Displeasure to meet you."

"You won't believe this," I said. "He walked into the bar looking for a drink."

"He should've walked into a Kohl's," Powell said.

Shawn had been squatting in an old-model brown Buick parked in a garage a block away. It was obviously stolen. The car stank of cheap bourbon and cigarettes and BO. We gathered up Shawn's stuff: his phone, his wallet, and a pair of filthy pants.

"Where is it?" I asked him.

"Where's what?"

"The second item you dug up the other night."

Shawn shrugged and threw up on the garage pavement.

"You're just an absolute delight, aren't you?" Powell said.

"The item?" I said again to Shawn.

He grumbled and wiped his mouth. "I don't know, man. Somewhere in the car."

"Stay with him," Powell said. "We don't want him running off again."

I stood with Shawn while Powell checked the console and the

glove compartment. He checked under the seats. He shook his head. He popped the trunk and went around back. He pulled away a patchwork blanket, probably stored by the car's rightful owner.

Underneath was a box. It was a small iron strongbox and very old, the kind Wells Fargo might've used to carry cash by horse. Somebody had fitted a modern-day padlock over the lid. Powell handed me the box. It weighed maybe five pounds.

"You stole this from the Dunne brothers?" he said to Shawn.

"Yeah," Shawn muttered.

"You know what's in it?"

"No."

"You got the key?"

"No."

Powell shook his head in disgust. We got some pants and shoes on Shawn and walked him to Powell's truck. He put the child safety lock on Shawn's door. I sat beside him in the back. The strongbox sat up front with Powell.

"Roll the windows down, please," I said. "It smells like low tide back here."

"Who are you?" Shawn said to Powell, as if he'd just now appeared.

"Any day but today," Powell said, "I'd be your worst nightmare."

Shawn passed out on the ride back to the city. We arrived at my house just after four. Powell did a loop around the block first as a precaution. I woke Shawn and helped him up the stairs and inside. Powell carried the strongbox.

We did a quick sweep of the house for intruders. All clear, Powell set the box on the coffee table in the living room.

"Dump him in the shower," he said. "I can't take it anymore."

"With his clothes on?"

"Sure. They need cleaning too."

"Come on," I said to Shawn.

The booze and the stress had taken their toll. Shawn was half asleep and didn't fight me. I grabbed a stool from the hallway and sat him down in the shower with the water on warm.

When I got back to the living room, Powell was straightening a paper clip. My toolbox was on the coffee table.

"Found it in the garage," he said.

He folded the paper clip in two and clamped down the bent end with a pair of plyers. He inserted the bent end into the lock and began to jerk it around. Within a minute, the lock gave.

"Very impressive," I said. "Where'd you learn that, MacGyver?"

"A veteran investigator never reveals his tricks," Powell said.

"You saw it on YouTube, didn't you."

"Yeah."

He removed the lock and popped open the box.

# CHAPTER 45

"A few thousand in petty cash," Powell said, "and this."

He tossed me a black flannel drawstring sack. It looked like the bags that carry Crown Royal bottles. The sack weighed very little. I emptied its contents onto the table.

"What is it?" Powell said.

There were two matching men's gold signet rings with an emerald in each center. The emeralds gleamed under the ceiling lights. They looked like something Lex Luthor might've worn.

"Well," I said, "we know the Dunnes don't care about this cash. There's a lot less here than in the other bag of money Shawn stole from them."

"So, it's about the rings," Powell said.

"Guess so."

Powell picked up one of the rings and held it forehead-high under the light, examining all sides.

"Go fetch the klepto," he said.

I went back to the shower. Shawn sat bent over on the stool, running his wet hands through his hair.

"Feel better?" I asked.

"A little."

"You like coffee?"

"Yeah."

I tossed a fresh shirt and joggers over the shower door.

"I'll make some," I said. "Change into these."

I brewed two cups of coffee and added a little milk and sugar.

I handed one cup to Powell and set the other on the table. I went back to the kitchen and boiled some water for tea. By the time steam rose from the kettle, Shawn emerged from the bathroom wearing my clothes. The shirt clung tight around his midsection. He looked bad but better, bleary-eyed but lucid. He sat on the couch where his daughter had slept for several days. He stared at the open box and sipped the coffee.

"Good?" I asked.

"Yeah," he said.

"You're welcome," I said. "My head's better since you smashed it up, by the way. I'm sure you're very concerned."

Shawn set the coffee on the table and looked down at his beer belly.

"I'm sorry about that," he said. "I was in too deep. I had to keep moving. Friday, she . . . she's better off without me."

"Well," I said, "the Dunnes are forcing a Finley family reunion."

"Where's my girl?"

"Don't know yet. We're waiting on a phone call."

"Fuck that," Shawn said, and tried to stand. Powell's big right hand slapped Shawn's shoulder and encouraged him to sit. Shawn coughed his phlegmy cough.

"I need a drink," he said, "or a cigarette."

"Nope," Powell said. "Where'd you get this box, Shawn?"

"Dunnes' old storage unit, not long before I split town."

"Why?"

"I dunno, I was high. Ross and Colin weren't around. Box had a lock on it. Thought whatever's inside might be valuable—something I could pawn for cash."

"And the other bag you buried would eventually go to Friday."

"Yeah. After things cooled down a little."

"You didn't try to open the box?"

"I was going to after I . . ."

He gave me a side-eyed glance.

" . . . after we dug it up over in Oakland and I, you know, went on my way. But I got to Pacifica and started drinking and . . . forgot about it, I guess."

Powell tossed one of the rings to Shawn. His reflexes weren't optimal. The ring hit his belly and fell on the floor. He picked it up and stared at the green stone in the center.

"Ever seen the Dunnes wear one of these?" Powell asked.

"Never," Shawn said.

"Notice the engraving on the inside?"

Shawn held it up to the light. Powell handed him the other ring. Shawn studied that one too. All this effort was sapping whatever brain cells he had left.

"I can't read it," he said.

"Of course you can't," Powell said. "One says, 'R.D.' The other says, 'C.D.' Both rings have 'Poppa' written next to the initials."

"Ross Dunne," I said. "Colin Dunne."

Powell said, "And who's 'Poppa'?"

"How the fuck am I supposed to know?" Shawn said.

"Did they ever mention their father?"

"No. When I met Ross, he said he was a foster kid like me growing up."

"Got any idea why a couple rings might be so important to these guys?"

"Not a clue. Can we go find my daughter now? Is she alive?"

"If she's not alive, they don't get what they want," Powell said.

"How did they find her?"

"Our guess is she found them," I said. "Tried to pay them off with the money you stole for her. Probably hoping they'd leave all of us alone."

"And they killed Tate?"

"Bosh did," I said. "Strangled her. Probably for talking to me."

Shawn shook his head.

"Son of a bitch. I loved that girl too. This is all my fault, isn't it?"

"You can make it right," I said. "Some of it, anyway."

"How?"

"By sobering up and sitting quietly here with us. We don't move until they call."

"Great," Shawn said. "What now?"

"We've got a plan," Powell said.

"Did you call the cops?"

"We've got a plan," Powell repeated.

Shawn tossed his hands in the air and stared at us incredulously. We stared back at him silently.

"You guys are pretty calm about all this," Shawn said.

"Calm's a stretch," I said. "But we feel a little better now that you're here."

"Wonderful. How'd you find me, anyway?"

"Your cell phone."

"I had my phone on me, man."

"When I saved your ass from Bosh at that gas station, I fished your cell phone out of the trash. Your lock screen had the same picture Friday gave me. It was the only pattern I had to go on."

Shawn smiled faintly.

"Rockaway Beach," he said. "That was a good day."

Powell appeared to have lost interest. He reclaimed the rings from Shawn and went back to studying the engravings.

"What made that day so good?" I said to Shawn.

"It was the last quality time I got to spend with Friday," he said. "Trish and I had just separated, filed for divorce. I knew I wasn't gonna get custody. Couldn't hold a job. Couldn't keep it together. Trish let me take her down the coast for a couple days. I swore on Friday I'd bring her back safe. I don't know why Trish trusted me. I wouldn't have trusted me. But I stayed sober that whole trip, man. Friday loved the ocean when she was little, so I took her to a few beaches. I went to Rockaway as a kid. I liked how secluded it was. It wasn't your typical postcard beach. It was a little scruffier, had character. She loved it too. Right after we took that picture, a huge wave crashed over the seawall. Totally drenched us. She laughed so hard she was in tears. I can still hear it."

He leaned forward and looked me in the eyes for the first time.

"I don't care what you think," he said. "I love my child."

"Daughters are special," I said.

"That's right," Shawn said. "You know yourself."

"You left Friday with me to keep her safe," I said. "Then you went back to the beach. To remember her. Maybe to say goodbye in your own way."

Shawn frowned. His nose twitched. He blinked his watery eyes.

"Best memory I had of us," he said. "Memories are all I got left."

# CHAPTER 46

The countdown to midnight felt like days.

Shawn slept on the couch for most of the evening. He was a big guy and his feet hung off the edges. Powell and I shared a frozen pizza on the kitchen counter and kept an eye on the window to Stockton Street. He drank another cup of coffee. I drank three more cups of tea. We didn't talk about the looming showdown. Without a known location, there wasn't much purpose.

I glanced at the clock every minute. Ryan texted more pictures of Callie. Every picture made me long for a resolution to this mess. Part of me wanted to grab them from Powell's house and drive us all far away from here. Back to Texas, maybe. At least they'd be safe. The idea creeped into my mind more than once throughout the day.

Powell interrupted my thoughts as if he'd been reading them.

"You sure you want to do this?" he asked.

"Don't have much choice, do I?"

Powell set his coffee on the counter.

"There's something else I whispered to Ryan," he said. "Before she left the house with Callie."

"What was it?"

"I asked her to let you finish this because you need to."

"Why?"

"Because of your sister."

"Ryan told you about my sister?"

"I already knew."

"You did a background check on me when you hired me?"

"I did a background check on you when I was a cop and you were a nosy reporter calling me for information," Powell said.

"You think this whole thing is some kind of coping mechanism for me?"

"A little," Powell said. "I think down in your chest, you're a reporter who can't resist a big story. I think you're a new father who's got a soft spot for damsels in distress. And I think you're also carrying around a lot of grief."

"And saving Friday will fix things?"

Powell shrugged. He had another sip of his coffee.

"My brother got shot when we were kids," he said. "Cross fire. Riding home from school on his bike. Never found out who did it."

"I'm sorry."

"The pain never goes away. People don't understand that. You live with it the rest of your life. Some days it hurts only a little. Some days it's excruciating. But you try to live how they would've wanted you to."

Outside, a woman passed the house on a late-night stroll with her baby.

"Tonight's about as dangerous as it gets," I said.

"You can say no," Powell said.

"Would you?"

"No."

"I won't either."

"Why?"

"Because risking my life for strangers might make me a poor husband and father," I said. "But I've decided that walking away would make me far worse of a man."

"Fair enough."

"And," I said, "you promised nothing would happen to me."

"I'll do my best," he said.

At five minutes before midnight, Friday's number buzzed on my phone. The nasally voice spoke.

"You got Shawn?"

"I do, Ross."

"And the box?"

"Yes."

"Let me hear Shawn."

I looked at Powell. He shook his head.

"First, let me hear Friday," I said. "If she's not okay, the deal's off."

There was a long pause. On the couch, Shawn stirred from his nap.

A meek female voice spoke.

"Charlie?"

"Friday, are you okay?"

There was a pause, and then a very small, "Yes."

Shawn leapt off the couch like a tiger and tried to snatch the phone from my hand.

"Baby? Baby, it's me! I'm here!"

"Daddy!" Friday screamed.

The sound was so feral, so guttural, it made my stomach drop. Shawn was screaming too.

"I'm here, baby! We're gonna get you out of this!"

Powell pressed the mute button on my phone. He grabbed Shawn by the shirt collar violently but spoke to him in a serene tone.

"You make a bunch of noise, you threaten these guys, they're liable to hurt her. Grit your teeth and say, 'I'm here, Ross.' That's it."

Shawn swallowed hard.

"Do it," Powell said.

"Hello?" Ross yelled.

I unmuted my phone.

"We're here," I said.

Shawn hesitated, then said, "I'm here, Ross."

The words came out grudgingly, as if they'd been yanked from his mouth.

"Three a.m.," Ross said. "Back of the old department store on Mission and 6th. Just you two. No guns, no backup."

"The box for Friday," I said.

"That's the deal. Any surprises, she dies."

The line dropped. I looked at Shawn. Shawn looked at Powell. Powell looked at me.

"You heard the man," I said. "Just Shawn and me."

"Good luck," Powell said.

# CHAPTER 47

South of Market had seen its share of shuttered storefronts since the pandemic, but the open-air drug market was quite healthy. We passed a deal in progress on the way to our designated meeting spot.

Shawn walked beside me with the strongbox. His hands were shaking. I'd noticed they shook constantly whenever he was conscious. Physiologically, he probably needed alcohol as much as he needed air.

"Why'd they choose this place?" he asked.

"I don't know. My guess is they don't expect cops in the area. Police have been understaffed. In the summertime, they might have a larger presence around the tourist spots."

"This ain't just about the box," Shawn said. "You know they're gonna make a run at us. We need guns."

"My wife says the same thing," I said. "Promise me you'll stay cool through this, whatever happens, just like we discussed."

"What if they shoot at us?"

"In that case, duck."

The abandoned two-story building had been a chain store location that closed due to rampant retail theft. Its front windows were boarded up. Bright graffiti in many colors coated the store's exterior. Around the corner, an iron gate with a connecting door had been pried open.

I looked at Shawn. His eyes were wide with apprehension. I felt the same way. The pizza I'd eaten wasn't settling well.

"After you," I said.

Shawn handed me the strongbox and stepped through the opening. I slipped the box back to him and went in.

A single lamppost offered poor lighting. The area was empty. It smelled of trash and excrement. Twenty feet ahead stood some sort of scrap-metal partition, probably where the store had kept its dumpsters. The metal shed was maybe eight feet high. On our left was a boarded-up door to the building's first floor, and above that, metal stairs to a platform and a boarded-up door to the second floor. From there, a cat ladder led to the roof.

A rat scurried across the empty space in front of us. I heard Shawn inhale sharply.

"Ross," I shouted into the void.

A moment later, Ross and Colin Dunne appeared from behind the metal shed. Ross still wore his knee-high walking boot, courtesy of Friday's Louisville Slugger. He had on his customary fake-Mafia tracksuit with the jacket zipped up. Slung over his shoulder was the duffel bag Shawn had buried and left for his daughter.

Colin wore a hoodie over running shorts and sneakers. I couldn't tell if either guy was armed.

They stopped ten feet away. Colin's face was tight and expressionless. Ross grinned at us.

"Hey, fellas," he said. "Shawny Boy, you look like shit. Been on another bender?"

Shawn started to speak. I nudged him with my elbow and shook my head.

"Where's Friday?" I said to Ross.

"The box first," Ross said. "Shawny Boy, slide it over here."

Shawn did as instructed. Colin must've had the key in his palm. He knelt and tried the key. The lock gave. The box opened.

Ross kept his eyes on us while Colin riffled through the cash. Then he stood and handed Ross the flannel sack. Ross dipped a hand inside and fumbled around for its contents. He opened the sack and peeked inside.

"Good," he said. "Real good. Your daughter's a tough cookie, Shawn. Busted up my leg the first time we met."

"If you hurt her . . ." Shawn said, and his voice trailed off.

I could hear his breath. He was hyperventilating. I was too. It was a cool night, but I could feel sweat percolating on my forehead.

Ross grinned at us again.

"Settle down," he said. "First, I gotta say something to Charlie. That was a really sweet message you left on the girl's phone. The part about your sister killing herself? Man, what a shame."

I felt a sudden rush of blood in my cheeks. I clenched my fists involuntarily, then reluctantly unclenched them.

"You guys are a couple sad sacks, you know that?" Ross said. "Can't keep up with the women in your lives. Women are nothin' but trouble, if you ask me. Just like our girl Tate. Huh, Shawny Boy?"

Shawn's voice cracked. "I wanna see my daughter now," he said. "We had a deal."

"You're right," Ross said. "We did have a deal. You agreed to work for us and keep your mouth shut. You didn't do that. Even worse, you stole from us."

Ross took the duffel bag off his shoulder and dropped it next to the strongbox. He shifted his hollow eyes to me.

"And you," he snarled. "You and your little smart-ass mouth. You've been sniffing around our business for too long. Got our best man killed."

Sweat began to trickle down my forehead over my right eye.

"You know what?" Ross said. "Sorry, boys. Deal's off."

He snapped his fingers. For a moment, nothing moved in the still cool air. The silence was torture. Then a quick, precise, mechanical sound. The hammer of a gun sliding into firing position. Then the same sound again.

A moment later, the voice of Inspector Joseph "Tex" Whitmore boomed from above.

"Ross and Colin Dunne! This is the San Francisco Police Department! You are under arrest! Hands up!"

Both men stared up at the roof. I couldn't see Tex, just two shapes crouched in darkness.

"Hands up now or I'll shoot!" Tex shouted.

Ross swore and spat at the pavement. He raised his hands. Colin did the same.

"On the ground now!" Tex shouted.

They dropped to their knees and onto the ground, belly first.

I could now see Tex above us in the moonlight. He'd risen to his feet. His gun was in firing position. Dwayne Powell now stood next to Tex, his gun also trained on the Dunnes.

Suddenly, the metal shed in front of us rattled a little. Powell aimed his gun in its direction.

"Behind the shed!" he yelled. "Come out with your hands up!"

"Friday?" Shawn whimpered.

"Stay where you are, Shawn!" Tex yelled.

"Don't shoot!" Shawn cried.

He tried to run to the shed. I grabbed him by the waist, holding him back as if he were a squirmy toddler.

Just then, we heard something clatter on the ground behind the shed. Another agonizing moment passed. Two empty hands stretched out from the shed's entrance, and Mike Gramble, Derryville chief of police, emerged. He raised his hands, signaling surrender.

"On the ground, Mike!" Powell yelled.

Gramble knelt onto his belly beside his co-conspirators. He was dressed in civilian clothes: a dark baseball cap over his military-style buzz cut, collared shirt, jeans, and sneakers.

Shawn got loose from me. He sprinted past Ross, Colin, and Gramble to the metal shed. He peered inside, out of view.

I heard him say, "Sweetheart?"

He reappeared a moment later.

"She's not in there," he gasped.

# CHAPTER 48

Shawn and I searched the entire desolate area with Tex's flashlight while he read the Dunnes their rights. There was no sign of Friday.

Shawn unleashed a string of expletives. He kicked the metal shed. He threw an empty trash can. He stomped back to the center space where Gramble and the Dunnes lay. He kicked Ross in his injured leg. Ross shouted in pain.

"Where is she?" Shawn yelled.

"Hey," Tex said. "Stop, okay?"

"Ask them where the hell she is!" Shawn said.

I tried to grab his arm and he yanked free. He had a wild look in his eyes.

"Shawn," I said. "Please, calm down."

"Fuck that," he said.

Powell grabbed Shawn by his shirt collar and steered him over to a stack of rotted pallets. Tex finished his Miranda spiel and cuffed the three men on the ground. Ross winced at the cold steel cutting at his wrists. Tex instructed them to stay motionless. He asked them to share Friday's whereabouts. Colin spoke for the first time.

"We want our lawyer," he said.

"Is she alive?" Tex asked.

Ross swore under his breath.

"Lawyer," Colin said.

Sirens blared in the near distance. Moments later, police lights flooded Mission Street. Three officers placed the Dunnes and

Gramble in squad cars. Another officer retrieved Gramble's gun from behind the shed.

I sat next to Shawn on the pallets. I felt a sudden wave of nausea and fatigue as the adrenaline left my body. I rubbed my temples. Shawn lowered his head and ran his hands through his hair.

"What did they do with her?" he said. "What did they do to her?"

I knew he wasn't speaking to me. The questions were rhetorical. I patted him on the back.

"It's all my fault," he said. "It's all my fault. You said it yourself."

I patted his back again.

"What do we do now?" he said.

"We find her," I said.

"How?"

"I don't know. But Powell's the best there is. Tex is pretty good too. His whole department will be on this now. Missing girl, disgraced police chief. It'll be all over the news."

"Will you help?"

"Of course."

Powell walked over to us, holding his lower back.

"Long time for an old guy to sit around in stealth mode," he said. "No luck with Friday?"

I shook my head. Powell frowned. I knew what he was thinking. I didn't want to discuss it in front of Shawn.

"I knew Gramble was dirty," I said. "Didn't think he'd go this far."

"The Dunnes probably blackmailed him," Powell said. "That what you think, Shawn?"

Shawn still had his head in his hands.

"Probably," he said.

"They're dumb as rocks too," Powell said. "They gave us three hours to scout the area. Not one hour. Not two hours. *Three* hours."

Tex joined us. He set the strongbox and the duffel bag on the ground together.

"Thanks for the call," he said.

"Thanks for the help," I said.

"All this for a couple fraternity rings? I mean, don't get me wrong. They're nice. But they're not invaluable."

"Must have personal value," Powell said.

Tex leaned down in Shawn's direction and said, "Any idea what that personal value might be?"

Shawn looked up. There were tears in his eyes again.

"No, man. I told these guys. I don't know."

"But you worked for the Dunnes."

"Yeah. Am I under arrest?"

"No," Tex said, "but I'd like you to come to the station with me. We need more information about their operation. And I'd like to know more about your coworker Tate Wilson, the young woman we found dead."

Shawn jumped to his feet angrily.

"What I need," he said, "is my daughter back. Are you guys gonna do anything about that?"

He got within two inches of Tex's face. An officer saw and tried to intervene. Shawn punched him in the jaw, knocking him backward into Powell. Two more cops jumped on Shawn. He resisted. They wrestled him to the ground. He kicked at them with helpless legs. They cuffed him and routed him to a squad car as he screamed expletives and begged me to stop them. I stared at him as they led him away in my clothes.

"Guy's a loose cannon," Tex said. "Now he's in bigger trouble."

"He's strung out and he snapped," I said.

"Yeah, well, maybe he needs some time in the joint," Tex said.

He pointed to the duffel bag beside the strongbox. "This was the bag of money Shawn stole for his daughter?"

"Yes," I said.

Tex picked up the strongbox and started toward Mission Street.

"The paperwork on this will take me years," he said. "We'll put out an alert about Miss Finley. Good work, Inspector Powell."

"Glad to be of help," Powell said.

"I'll be in touch," Tex said. "You guys come up with anything, let me know."

I picked up the duffel bag. "What about this?"

Over his shoulder, Tex said, "I never saw it."

Powell sat on the pallets beside me where Shawn had been. "You okay?" he asked.

"I might throw up," I said.

"You did good."

"Not good enough. You think Friday's alive?"

"Wish I could say yes. Truth is, I don't know. It was never about an exchange. They wanted their stuff and both you guys dead."

"I know."

"But," Powell said, "we'll keep looking for her."

"Don't you have a business to run?"

"Perks of being my own boss," he said.

"Think Ryan and Callie can come home now?"

"Probably."

We sat there for a few minutes in silence. Powell stood and stretched his back.

"Mission," he said. "Mission and 6th."

"Yeah," I said. "That's the intersection."

"That's interesting."

"Why?"

"Dalton Crawford," Powell said. "He's got that fancy new office in the 5M district."

"Yeah. I've been there."

"Moved there from his old location," Powell said. "No more than a couple blocks from here."

# CHAPTER 49

Powell and I met Tex at Rivet Security headquarters just after nine. None of us had slept. None of us were in the mood for Dalton Crawford's plastic CEO smile. But there it was, glistening at us in the morning sunlight. He had on a single-breasted light gray suit with slim-fit tapered pants that stopped above his ankles. His white shirt had no tie. He wore all-white designer sneakers.

"Good morning, gentlemen," he said.

No one shook hands. Unlike my first visit, this wasn't a social call.

"Inspector Joseph Whitmore, SFPD," Tex said. "I believe you know Charlie Shaw and Inspector Powell from Powell and Associates. They're assisting me with the investigation into Ross and Colin Dunne."

"Absolutely," Crawford said. "Come on back. Mondays are a remote workday, so I'm the only one here."

We followed Crawford into his capacious office. Tex sat at the desk facing him. I sat next to Powell on the couch.

"I'll get right to it," Tex said. "We arrested the Dunne brothers early this morning, along with another one of their associates."

Crawford's eyebrows raised a little, but otherwise his tanned face had no discernible change in expression.

"Oh, wow," he said. "On what charge?"

"Kidnapping, among other things," Tex said.

"Good grief. What can I do to help?"

"The reason for our visit is a sixteen-year-old girl named Friday

Finley, from Oregon, who's missing," Tex said. "Abducted by the Dunnes after they allegedly abducted her father, Shawn, over some stolen items."

"Yes," Crawford said. "I remember you told me about the father when you contacted me about Ross and Colin's sudden disappearance."

"Mr. Finley has been found alive," Tex said. "But we are searching for Miss Finley."

He showed Crawford the Rockaway Beach family picture. Crawford shook his head.

"I'm sorry. I've never seen either of them before."

"When was the last time you saw or spoke to either Ross or Colin?"

"The La Rousse casino last Friday night," Crawford said. "As I've said, my only interactions with them are through poker games. I don't know them socially. I don't have intimate knowledge of their day-to-day activities."

"Did they ever make any mention of Miss Finley or her father?"

"No, never."

Tex glanced at Powell, who straightened a little on the couch.

"Mr. Crawford," he said, "it's urgent that we find Miss Finley. This is a matter of life and death. Are you telling us the whole truth?"

Crawford blinked his eyes. For a moment he looked a little defensive. Then he stored the expression away.

"One hundred percent the truth," he said. "Why would I have anything to hide? If I'd known these men were criminals, I never would've associated with them."

"See, that's my issue too," Powell said. "From what my colleagues tell me, you associate with the Dunne brothers quite a bit. At the casino up north. At their bar over in Derryville with two of your old college buddies. That's twice a week, correct?"

"I'm preparing for the World Series of Poker," Crawford said. "I'm sharpening my skills. I explained this to Inspector Whitmore a couple of days ago. Poker is just like pickup basketball. You meet people on the court or in the card room and you become friendly. I met Ross and Colin at the casino last year. They said they'd been discussing the idea of hosting a private game at their bar in Derryville. I invited Mr. Khatri and Mr. Maniet to join me. We're all computer guys from MIT, Inspector Powell. You might say we're computer nerds. The idea of playing a backroom game at a dive bar across the bridge is exciting to us. We've never seen any criminal activity at Cashel Rock. We've enjoyed the poker. Our relationship with the Dunnes ends there, however."

"Except the relationship doesn't end there," Powell said. "Or at least, it doesn't seem to. Did you order the Dunnes to assault your former employee, Scottie Coburn, a few days ago? For taking part in an extramarital affair that might've jeopardized your business with Arthur Wellington?"

Crawford's face reddened. Powell wasn't beating around any bushes. If I weren't sodden with stress and exhaustion, I would've wanted popcorn for this exchange.

"I absolutely, one hundred percent, did not," Crawford said. "I've already explained this to Inspector Whitmore."

"Just seems like an awful coincidence," Powell said. "We discovered another coincidence this morning. We apprehended the Dunnes during a ransom exchange at Mission and 6th. It's quite close to your old office location on Mission."

Crawford didn't reply. He seemed to be processing the information.

"Let's recap," Powell said. "In the past seventy-two hours, two of the Dunnes' colleagues have been found dead—a man and a woman. Another colleague, Shawn Finley, was abducted. Shawn's daughter, Friday, was abducted too, and she's still missing. It's a disturbing pattern of violence, Mr. Crawford. And yet, you say these guys are your friends."

"Acquaintances," Crawford said, his voice rising slightly. "Acquaintances only."

Tex jumped back in.

"Mr. Crawford, while apprehending the Dunnes, we found two items of great interest to them. Items for which they were holding Miss Finley for ransom."

He showed Crawford a photo of the two signet rings and their green emeralds.

"Ever seen these before?"

"No," Crawford said flatly.

"Did Ross or Colin ever mention these rings? Explain their significance?"

"Never," Crawford said. "I have a virtual meeting scheduled for nine thirty, Inspector Whitmore. There's simply nothing more I'm able to share about these men."

There was a long moment of silence. Then Tex rose from his chair.

"Thank you for your time, Mr. Crawford. You aren't leaving town on any business this week, are you?"

"No," Crawford said.

"Good, good. If you come across any information that would lead us to Miss Finley, please let us know."

"Absolutely," he said. "Thank you for coming."

On our way out, I turned to Crawford and said, "Poker's a funny game. I've never been good at calling out a bluff."

Crawford's tanned face made a very faint, nearly imperceptible twitch.

"Takes time," he said. "And experience."

# CHAPTER 50

The three of us stood outside Rivet Security headquarters, well out of earshot.

"I don't buy Crawford's act," Tex said. "But right now, I can't hold him on anything."

"We need the Dunnes to talk," I said. "Tell us what they did with Friday."

"They've lawyered up," Tex said. "My guys searched their house and the little poker room at their bar. Looks like they packed up any incriminating stuff and moved it. But we've got them dead to rights as perps or accomplices on Tate's murder and both Finley kidnappings. The casino parking lot has footage of them staring into Bosh's trunk last Thursday night. The gas station in Petaluma has footage of you pulling Shawn out of the trunk a few minutes later. Security cameras in Tate's neighborhood have Bosh's Escalade there last Saturday morning around her estimated time of death. Bosh's phone should connect some of the dots too."

"Dunnes have any family we can contact?"

"Not that we can find."

"Gramble talking?"

"Singing like a canary. Said the Dunnes have been blackmailing him for months. Said they had pictures of him with a woman at some escort service they're running in Derryville. But he doesn't know what the stolen rings are for, and he doesn't know where Friday is."

"Anything else we can do?" Powell asked.

"Anything you can to help the search," Tex said. "The Amber Alert for Miss Finley went out this morning. The media has the story. Hopefully we get some leads."

Powell and I thanked Tex, then walked to our separate cars.

"I'm headed home for a bit," Powell said. "Tired of rooming with you."

"Go see Jackie at your house," I said.

"Go see Ryan at your house," he said.

I was on my way when Maggie Salvetti from the *Chronicle* called.

"Got another eyewitness identifying you and Inspector Powell as the men getting assaulted on your street over the weekend," she said. "We've updated our report."

"Great," I said.

"I'm guessing you haven't read today's breaking news either," she said. "News that's gone national. A girl kidnapped? Derryville's police chief arrested along with these Dunne brothers—the same guys wanted for questioning in connection with two deaths and the assault on you and Powell?"

"I told you, Maggie. The only thing I read these days are picture books. Why don't you call your sources at SFPD?"

"You know our sources better than we do."

"Then you shouldn't have fired me."

"Furloughed. You know, Charlie, if you wanted to do some freelance work on this, we could figure out a nice little rate."

"Tell you what," I said. "Ryan and Callie just got back from a little trip. When they get settled, maybe we'll talk. In the meantime, I think you should play up this missing girl story as much as possible and stay on the police for info. Any coverage might help the search."

"You know her?"

"Nope. Just think that's the saddest part of all this."

"I don't believe you, Charlie."

"Maggie, I'm sorry, but after the week I've had, I don't give a damn."

I hung up in front of my house. Ryan's Highlander was parked on the street.

# CHAPTER 51

I parked Mango in the garage and went inside.

"Ryan?"

"In the kitchen."

I closed the door and snapped on the dead bolt. The house smelled like breakfast. Ryan had a quiche in the oven. She looked like she'd just showered. She wore her satin black bathrobe. Her hair was up in a messy ponytail and she wore no makeup. She had on white athletic socks and no shoes.

"Welcome home," I said.

She held a finger to her lips. "Callie's sleeping," she whispered. "Don't go in there. Took me an hour to get her down after Reggie helped me bring all our stuff inside."

She walked over to me from behind the counter and gave me a hard shove with both hands. I fell backward into our plastic trash can. Maybe she should've gone to last night's meet with the Dunnes.

"What was that for?" I said.

She hugged me hard and kissed my lips and pressed her hands against my face and chest and arms. She smelled like a summer citrus grove.

"Everything's still in one piece," she said.

"Why'd you push me?"

"For not telling me about Friday or whatever showdown you guys had with those Dunne creeps. It's all over the TV and radio. That Derryville police chief too. You were right about him."

## Stakeouts and Strollers

"I didn't want you to worry," I said.

She laughed. "Fat chance of that."

"Powell promised you we'd be okay. And we are."

"And now we're home," she said.

"Almost all of us," I said.

"Any word on Friday?"

"None."

I told her about my last twenty-four hours with Powell: finding Shawn Finley and the stolen rings, apprehending the Dunnes and Gramble and visiting Dalton Crawford's office, which wasn't exactly a lead on Friday.

"Maybe he knows more than he says," Ryan said.

"Maybe."

"And Friday's dad is in jail for assaulting a police officer?"

"Hopefully it'll sober him up."

"What do you think is the meaning behind the rings he stole?"

"I don't know," I said. "But somehow I think they're the key to finding Friday."

"Do you think she's alive?"

"I don't know. I'm trying not to think about the worst case."

Ryan shuddered. The oven went off.

"Hang on a sec," she said.

She went back around the counter and grabbed a mitt and took out the tray. The quiche looked delicious—a bright combination of cheese and eggs and tomatoes and onions.

"Just needs to cool a minute," she said. "You've been up all night, I assume. You need to eat something."

"I've got to change clothes and go looking for her," I said.

"How? Shout her name at every street corner?"

"I don't know."

"I want to help. I told the office I need to take a few days off. Family emergency."

"You watch Callie," I said. "I'll watch out for Friday."

"Fine."

"Nice socks, by the way."

"Shut up."

"Been a while since we've had a quiet breakfast, hasn't it?"

Ryan shook her head. She gave one of those despondent smiles where her eyes became little thunderclouds and tears might fall next.

"The last couple days I started to wonder," she said, "what if we never saw each other again?"

I walked behind the counter and, with my thumb, wiped away a tear on her cheek.

"Hey," I said. "I'm here."

"Maybe this whole thing has made us crazy. Is that possible?"

"Nah. At worst it's temporary insanity."

"I'm a strong, independent career woman," Ryan said, "but sometimes a girl just needs her husband."

"I know. I'm glad to hear it."

She nodded and hugged me again, her cheek pressed against my chest, her hip pressed against my waist. She felt something and pulled back and raised up my shirt.

"Where'd you get a gun?"

"It's one of Powell's. He's letting me borrow it till this blows over."

I took out the Beretta and set it on the counter. Ryan stared at it.

"I've been saying all this time you needed a gun," she said. "Now I don't like looking at it."

"Because you know its purpose."

"Probably so. You know how to use it?"

"Yep."

"Because you're from Texas?"

"Why does everyone say that?"

She smiled. "I made a mental list on the way over here. This week you have been threatened, punched, arrested, followed, and kidnapped. You've had a gun pointed in your face. You've suffered a concussion. You've witnessed a shooting in self-defense. You've seen the body of a murdered woman. You've had to hide your family at a safe house because a pair of fugitives were at large."

"You forgot one of them also bit me."

"Oh, right. Is that better?"

"Much better. Oh, and Friday broke his leg with a baseball bat."

"That's my girl."

Ryan looked at the empty couch. "I didn't expect to say this a few days ago, but I miss her."

"Me too."

"Will you guys find her, please?"

I put my arm around Ryan and kissed her forehead.

"With a little luck," I said, "we will."

# CHAPTER 52

I'd never been inside Saints Peter and Paul Church. I'd only driven past it on diaper runs or Uber rides. The address always creeped me out: *666 Filbert*. The church got destroyed by a massive earthquake in 1906 and rebuilt over embers and ashes. They did a nice job. The Gothic cathedral was an elegant blend of stone and brick with matching gold crosses atop slender twin spires.

An hour ago my phone buzzed. The call was from a 510 number I didn't recognize.

"Be inside the church on Filbert in one hour," the man said, "if you want new information about Ross and Colin Dunne. I'm a friend."

I didn't recognize the man's voice. It was deep and distinguished. I finished breakfast with Ryan and walked the three and a half blocks from the house to the church. Morning mass was over. Across the street, Washington Square was sparsely dotted with people.

Ten yards from the church entrance a homeless man sat on the sidewalk. He looked like someone had unearthed him from a shallow grave. His face and arms were caked in dirt. His khaki-colored shirt and pants blended with wet, stringy dark hair and a matted beard hanging three inches past his chin.

The man pointed skyward.

"He's watching," the man said to me.

"Sure," I said.

"He's watching all of us," the man said.

I walked up the steps and into the cathedral. A silver-haired man in tan slacks and a dark blue jacket sat alone on a wooden pew in the back. I sat next to him.

"Charlie Shaw."

"Name is Jonah," the man said.

We shook hands. Jonah stared at the altar many yards in front of us. The cathedral was more beautiful than I'd seen in pictures, with wooden coffered ceilings, brilliant lighting, and a red-carpeted nave that matched the robe of Jesus in a fresco reminiscent of the Sistine Chapel.

"Why are we here?"

"This is a safe place," Jonah said. "A discreet place."

"Except in *Dirty Harry*."

Jonah smiled. "I read that you and Inspector Dwayne Powell were attacked outside your home last weekend. And that the police have arrested Ross and Colin Dunne in connection with a series of crimes. I'm pleased to see that."

"Me too."

"Did you and Inspector Powell help the police investigate?"

"Yes."

Jonah continued looking at the altar. He had tired blue eyes, weathered by life and age.

"Who are you?" I asked.

"Now or then?"

"Let's start with now."

"Now I'm just an old man with a bad hip and a bad knee."

"Who were you then?"

"I used to be a police officer," Jonah said. "In Derryville."

"When?"

"Going on thirty years ago."

"Why did you stop being a cop?"

"I was arrested."

"For what?"

"Something I didn't do."

A man and a woman entered the church behind us. They paid us no attention. They walked past us down the aisle, taking in the beauty of the cathedral. They sat in the front pew and began to pray.

"I was a new detective," Jonah said. "I was young and idealistic, just like you, hopeful that a little effort and commitment and a wet rag with some soap could clean the spotty perspective of my city."

"I'm not so idealistic," I said.

"It's okay to be idealistic. To be hopeful. As long as you don't get lost and wander into naivete."

"Why were you arrested?"

"I was investigating Derryville's most notorious criminal."

"Jimmy O'Rourke?"

"Yes."

"Powell told me about him. San Francisco cops finally got him on attempted murder charges in the late nineties."

"June 12th, 1998. Sadly, I wasn't there. Two years earlier, on Christmas morning, I was arrested for possession of a large amount of cocaine in my home."

"It wasn't yours?"

Jonah shook his head.

"Jimmy O'Rourke ran his operation in the back room of a sporting goods store. For years no one could touch him. I began to build a case. Precisely. Meticulously. I was getting close. But I was naive enough to believe all of my colleagues had my back."

"You were betrayed."

"One of them planted the coke in the cabinet below my bathroom sink. My own department took me away in handcuffs on Christmas morning in front of my wife, my two children. I can still hear their cries in my nightmares."

"Tragedies like that happen more often than people know."

"Yes. I did six years before an attorney reviewed my case and got my conviction overturned."

"Did you reunite with your family?"

"I did."

"Away from Derryville, I assume."

"Yes. There are good people in Derryville. What the community has lacked, then and apparently now, is good leadership."

"We're still searching for the missing girl on the news," I said. "Her name is Friday Finley."

"I don't have information on her, unfortunately."

"You told me on the phone you had information about the Dunnes."

"I do."

Jonah reached into his pocket and handed me a closed envelope.

"My wife saved it for me while I was inside," he said. "I didn't make the connection until I saw the Dunnes' pictures on the news. Perhaps it might in some way help you find her."

"Why give this to me?"

Jonah smiled. Wrinkles formed around his mouth and forehead.

"You're about the same age I was when I got hauled away," he said.

He offered his hand. I shook it. I tucked the envelope in my back pocket and left the church. The homeless man was sleeping on the sidewalk. A wind gust blew three of his newspaper blankets down the street. He remained motionless on his back, facing the sky.

# CHAPTER 53

"Callie and I literally just got home," Ryan said. "Now you're driving to Nevada?"

"Reno," I said. "Actually, thirty miles north of Reno. Little town called Conquer."

"What's in it?"

"Maybe a clue."

"To find Friday?"

"Maybe."

"Is Mr. Powell going?"

"No, he thinks I'm wasting my time."

"Tex?"

"He agrees with Powell."

"Can't you just fly?"

"The next available flight to Reno isn't for three hours, and the first flight home isn't till tomorrow morning. I won't need to stay that long."

"That's assuming the Bronco . . . what did you name it?"

"Mango."

"That's assuming 'Mango' doesn't crap out in the desert," Ryan said.

"We'll stay hydrated," I said.

Callie had just finished her breakfast in Ryan's lap. Her little mouth and bib were caked with applesauce. So far, Callie approved of applesauce and sweet potatoes in her new solids diet. She also liked to chew on anything that would hold still: toys, clothes, and fingers.

"I don't feel entirely safe at home yet," Ryan said.

"Powell and Tex will keep an eye on the house," I said. "SFPD is still rolling through the neighborhood periodically."

Callie had begun to gnaw on her knuckles. Saliva dripped onto her bib. Ryan gently pulled her hand away. Callie disapproved.

*"Aboo lele hua!"*

"She's been waking up at five thirty, six in the morning," Ryan said. "Teething something fierce."

"We could turn that into her first chore. She could chew open the mail."

"Is this trip gonna be dangerous?"

"Only the chance of sunburn."

"You swear?"

"Scout's honor. I'll bring you back something."

"Let's start with all your limbs."

"Funny."

"When this is all over," Ryan said, "you and I are going on vacation."

"With or without Callie?"

"Without, God love her."

"Where do you wanna go?"

"Not Conquer, Nevada."

Ryan held up Callie's fist and waved it back and forth. Callie approved of this one. She giggled slightly.

*"Shamala pla."*

"I'll be back before morning. I'll miss you guys very much."

"We'll miss you too. Callie, say, 'Bye, Daddy.'"

*"Ahbooah."*

"Close enough," I said.

I packed a few travel items in the event that Mango did, in fact, expire in the desert. I tested my new portable charger. Then I put on a polo and pressed jeans and hit the road with a box of Friday's Raisinets in my hand and Jonah's envelope in my pocket.

It was a 230-mile drive into Nevada, a straight shot on I-80. If traffic cooperated, I could get there in four hours. Traffic did not cooperate. Cars jammed up leaving San Francisco and approaching Sacramento. During idle stretches, I called Ryan to check on the house and called Tex for updates on Friday's location. The police had made no progress. They'd gotten in touch with Friday's aunt in New Jersey, who simply asked them to keep her informed. Some loving family.

When the gridlock eased up, I watched cars fly past me. Mango was uncomfortable with high speeds. She cheeped like a scared sparrow at anything above seventy. Her odometer read 112,000 miles. I didn't push her.

The scenery evolved as we moved east. Brown surrounding hills reminded me of rural Texas. Flatter urban stretches reminded me of Dallas or Houston. Lush, dense pine trees greeted me past Sacramento as the winding highway entered the Sierra Nevada foothills. I thought about my sister, Sophie, who never saw the ocean or the mountains in her entire life. I thought about Callie, who didn't yet understand the concept of oceans or mountains. I thought of Friday and wondered if she'd ever see something beautiful again. I pressed harder on the accelerator, and Mango grumbled forward.

I arrived in Conquer, Nevada, just before dusk and bought a convenience store turkey wrap of questionable quality.

"Travel far?" the clerk asked.

"A ways," I said.

"What brings you to town?"

"Visiting an old friend."

Conquer looked like Desert Derryville: small and plain and forgettable, but hotter and drier and bleaker. It had started as a mining town that boomed and busted and narrowly avoided ghost status. It looked like a place someone might go to bury their head from life's curses.

I'd found two families in town with the last name "Crawford." Marsha and Audrey Crawford lived closest to Hope High School, where Dalton Crawford had attended. I drove there first.

At Tumble Street, I parked on the narrow tree-lined road three houses down from a modest, blue-shingled home. A blue Subaru Outback was parked in the driveway adjacent to the house. The windows and blinds in the front were drawn. I put on a plain baseball cap, fixed my collar in the rearview mirror, and grabbed the clipboard sitting on the passenger seat. I got out and walked up the front steps and rang the doorbell. It was a traditional doorbell, with no built-in camera.

A slender, grim-faced woman in her sixties opened the door. She did not seem pleased to have a visitor.

"Yes?"

"Hi, I'm Lanny Poffo with, uh, Blue Jay Roofing. Sorry I'm late. I got a little backed up with appointments in your neighborhood."

"Blue Jay Roofing?"

"Yes, ma'am."

"I don't have an appointment with you."

I glanced at my blank clipboard.

"Audrey Crawford? At 117 Tumble Street? I have you down for a consultation about hail damage repair to your roof."

The woman had on a navy tie neck blouse and white chino shorts. She had graying hair side-swept with blond highlights. Her face remained unfriendly.

"This is the Crawford residence, but my name is Marsha. And I most certainly did not call about hail damage. We haven't had a storm here since May."

"Your name is Marsha Crawford? Not Audrey Crawford?"

The woman's face tightened. She frowned. Wrinkle lines formed below her mouth toward her chin.

"Audrey was my sister. She passed away three years ago."

"I'm so sorry, ma'am. I deeply apologize. We installed a new appointment scheduling system and it's been acting up something awful. My mistake."

She shut the door on me, hard, before I could say "mistake."

I crossed the street and hopped inside Mango. The sky had

turned purple-gold. My phone said the outside temperature was holding steady at 101. I wished I'd worn shorts to my roofing job.

I found a tolerable alternative rock radio station and stretched my shoulder and sat in the car for forty-five minutes. I tried two bites of the turkey wrap and threw it in the back seat. I texted Ryan that I'd made it alive. I checked Callie's crib app. Sleeping. I found a local all-sports station on the AM dial. A guy was bitching about the Las Vegas Raiders' draft class. Sports fans are the same no matter where you go.

The sky turned dark. Nothing moved inside the house. I might've arrived too late in the evening. I searched online for nearby motels in case this became a two-day trip.

Finally, Marsha Crawford came out of her blue house and locked her front door and got in her Subaru and drove past me out of the neighborhood. I jumped out again and crossed the street toward the house and walked around back. No lights shone through the side windows. The tiny backyard was empty. I pulled two latex gloves from my pocket, put them on, and tried the back door. It creaked open. I was in a dark laundry room. Light creeped out from the open dryer door.

"Hello?"

No one answered.

I found a lamp in the kitchen and flipped the switch. I had illegally entered a clean, modest house with a fifties vibe: wood floors and wood cabinets and wood fan blades hanging from popcorn ceilings. Next to the kitchen was a small wooden breakfast table with antique wood chairs. A single place mat was set. No sign of a dog bowl on the floor.

"Hello?"

No one answered.

A framed print of *Christina's World* hung in the living room. Various antiques adorned the house: a lighthouse in the living room, an old ship in the hallway, a pair of roosters by the stove.

There were three bedrooms. All three beds were made. Only one room had enough decoration to seem occupied.

On Marsha Crawford's dresser, next to her jewelry, sat a group of framed photographs.

One showed Marsha in her twenties with another woman in her twenties. The sibling resemblance was clear. The woman next to Marsha was stunningly beautiful, with long, dark, wavy hair and almond-colored eyes. The next photo was Marsha and the other woman in their thirties standing next to a young boy in front of the blue house. Both women wore forced smiles. The boy was frowning. Beside them were more framed pictures of the boy as an adolescent, as a teenager, as a student. He was frowning in those too.

I took out Jonah's envelope and compared its contents with the photos on the dresser. I took pictures of the photos with my phone.

I went to the boy's bedroom. It appeared mostly empty except for a Manny Ramirez poster hanging above the made bed. I went to the dresser and tried the drawers. The top two were empty. The bottom drawer had some old papers and various pictures of the boy: at school plays, at baseball practice, at birthday parties. I snapped more pictures of the pictures.

I hadn't found everything I was looking for, but I didn't have all night. Marsha Crawford might've gone to dinner, or the movies, or on a quick trip to the gas station before work in the morning.

I went into the boy's closet and rifled through crates of old toys, old sports magazines, old schoolbooks. I opened a book of Irish poetry. Wedged inside the binding on page thirty-seven, there it was.

I turned off the lights, exited the house through the back door, took off my gloves, briskly walked back to Mango, and left. I pulled into the convenience store parking lot and called Tex.

"We haven't found Friday," he said. "Just a bunch of crackpot tips."

"Go find Dalton Crawford," I said. "He's not really Dalton Crawford."

# CHAPTER 54

I had Tex and Powell on speakerphone as Mango rumbled down I-80 at well over seventy miles an hour. The desert night had cooled the temperature by several degrees. I'd asked Mango if her engine could hang in there for a few hours. She cheeped at me dubiously.

"Both of us got the pictures you sent," Tex said. "Please repeat to Inspector Powell what you said to me."

I had to shout over the roar of the tires and the wind hissing against Mango's black vinyl top.

"Dalton Crawford is not Dalton Crawford from small-town Nevada," I said. "Dalton Crawford is Declan O'Rourke from Derryville, California."

"Great," Tex said. "Who the hell is Declan O'Rourke?"

I let Powell do the honors.

"The son of Jimmy O'Rourke," Powell said.

"The notorious Jimmy O'Rourke?"

"Yes," Powell said. "Son of a gun."

"I just met a woman who lives at 117 Tumble Street in Conquer, Nevada. Said her name is Marsha Crawford. Look at the first picture I sent. She's the woman on the left. The woman on the right is her sister Audrey. Marsha said Audrey died three years ago."

"The woman on the right, Audrey, looks familiar," Powell said.

"Now look at the screenshot of the newspaper clip. The story is from the *Chronicle*, December 17th, 1998, the day Jimmy O'Rourke was convicted of RICO and attempted murder charges and ultimately deported to Ireland to serve a fifty-year sentence. There's Jimmy in the courtroom. Look behind him in the gallery."

"Same woman," Powell said. "Jimmy's wife. I remember her from the case. Her name was Abbie. Abbie O'Rourke."

"Somewhere along the way, after Jimmy got convicted, I'm guessing Abbie changed her name to Audrey and started going by her maiden name," I said. "Crawford."

Tex read aloud the caption on the newspaper clip.

"'Wife Abbie O'Rourke and son Declan look on as Jimmy O'Rourke, convicted Derryville crime boss, is sentenced in San Francisco.'"

"Now," I said, "compare the courtroom picture with the picture of the young boy frowning in the backyard of the Nevada house."

"I'll be damned," Powell said.

"Audrey Crawford is Abbie O'Rourke," Tex said. "Dalton Crawford is Declan O'Rourke. Mother and son."

"They must've moved to Nevada and lived with Abbie's sister Marsha after O'Rourke got deported," I said.

"Inspector Powell," Tex said, "did the department keep tabs on Abbie O'Rourke after Jimmy got pinched in ninety-eight?"

"Not that I'm aware of," Powell said. "I was just a patrol officer back then."

"Finally," I said, "look closely at who else was sitting next to little Declan and his mother Abbie in the courtroom that day."

"This picture's almost thirty years old," Tex said, "but if I had to guess, I'd say that's what Ross and Colin Dunne might've looked like at seven or eight years old."

"I'll be damned twice," Powell said.

"Where'd you find this?" Tex asked.

"A source."

"And the family pictures are from inside the house?"

"Yes."

"Tell me Aunt Marsha invited you to look around and collect evidence incriminating her nephew."

"Let's not get into details. Point is, if you go back to the same house, you'll find the pictures. And probably more evidence."

"Let's focus up here," Tex said. "You're telling me that Dalton Crawford, CEO of Rivet Security, a multimillion-dollar cybersecurity company, is actually Declan O'Rourke, the son of twentieth-century Derryville crime boss Jimmy O'Rourke?"

"Yes."

"And that Ross and Colin Dunne, twenty-first-century Derryville wannabe crime bosses, are Declan O'Rourke's childhood buddies?"

"Buddies," I said. "Maybe even half brothers. I also took the liberty of digging through little Declan's things. Inside a book, I found a gold signet ring with a green emerald in the center."

"Same as the two rings the Dunnes wanted back so bad?"

"Yep. Even has the same engraving on the inside. Declan's real initials. 'D.O.R.' Next to the initials, it also says 'Poppa.' Seventh paragraph of the courtroom article says, 'At sentencing, O'Rourke turned to his family in the gallery and whispered, 'Poppa loves you.'"

"I think we should go talk to Dalton-Declan Crawford-O'Rourke," Tex said.

"Let's," Powell said.

# CHAPTER 55

I was back home watching Callie try raspberries, as Grace Chen had suggested. Ryan had cut them into little furry red pieces and set them on a *Bluey* plate.

"I think she likes them," Ryan said.

"She hasn't eaten one yet," I said.

As with most new solid foods, a piece would make it onto Callie's tongue, Callie would make an uncomfortable scrunchy face, and the piece would roll off her tongue and onto her bib like a rock down a hill.

"This is harder than I thought," Ryan said.

"Maybe she's realizing she has choices."

"And trolling us?"

"Yeah."

"She's much too young for that. She's getting stronger, though. Sitting up on her own to eat regularly now."

"Still teething?"

"Yeah. Was chewing her toes on the changing table this morning."

"They do sorta look like a ten-pack of Chick-fil-A nuggets."

"*Mmmm. Mmmm. MMMMM*," Callie said.

"She's trying so hard to talk," Ryan said. "To express herself."

"Soon she'll be talking so much, we can't get a word in."

"I'm not ready for that."

"At least she'll be able to tell us her needs, her opinions. Like, 'Mom, these raspberries suck.'"

She yawned. I yawned.

"Why don't you get some rest," she said. "You're running yourself ragged."

"Couldn't sleep," I said. "I keep thinking about her."

"Friday or Sophie?"

"Both."

I told her about the Dalton-Declan discovery in Nevada.

"Except so far it's a bust," I said. "Tex and Powell couldn't find him in his office or at home."

"Maybe he split just like his buddies did," Ryan said.

"Maybe. Tex said the Dunnes still won't say what they did with Friday. Won't confess to anything. Won't admit they've known Dalton, or Declan, all their lives. Now he's apparently disappeared too."

Lips pursed, eyes closed, Callie swished a tiny raspberry piece around her mouth. She smacked her lips again and again and again. Finally, the piece went down the hatch. Ryan and I burst into applause as if she'd just been accepted to college.

"Grace was right," Ryan said. "I'm adding raspberries to the list of things she likes."

"Wasn't the most delightful dining experience of our lives, but we'll take it."

Ryan laughed. "She did look like an old man gumming his food, didn't she?"

Something clicked in my mind. I stared at the floor for a moment. Ryan shook me out of it.

"Charlie?"

"Yeah. Sorry."

"You all right?"

"Yeah," I said. "I think our daughter just cracked the case."

# CHAPTER 56

"Good afternoon," said the woman behind the front desk. "How may I help you?"

"Hi there. I'm here to visit Mr. Crawford."

"Great. And you are?"

"Charlie Shaw. I'm a close family friend. We're all going out to lunch today, get some fresh air. Guess I'm a little early."

The senior living home next to La Rousse casino had a nice reception area. I'd circled the parking lot and hadn't seen Dalton Crawford's black Ferrari.

"That's just fine," the woman said. "You can wait here in the lobby if you like, or you can go on through."

"Terrific. Do you know the apartment number? It's my first time visiting."

"Welcome, Mr. Shaw. Mr. Crawford's apartment is on the second floor, room 214. You may take the elevator down the hall on your right or the staircase on your left."

"Thank you very much. Have a wonderful day."

"You too, sir."

I took the stairs. Room 214 was halfway down the hall on the left. The door was unlocked. I pushed it open softly and went in. The apartment was nearly equal to the size of my house and generically furnished with an open kitchen connected to a living room and a bedroom down the hall.

"Mr. Crawford?"

A man sat facing the window in a Victorian high-back chair

next to a chenille-covered couch. The window blinds were open, inviting a view of the courtyard. The air-conditioned room felt cool. Sunshine provided the only light in the room. It peeked through the blinds in bright little rectangles.

The man didn't answer.

I walked through the kitchen and living room. There were no pictures, no keepsakes, nothing personal in the bare space. I stood beside the man.

"Mr. O'Rourke?"

He wore gray pajamas covered by a black satin robe and black slippers. His head tilted to the left. His mouth hung open. His eyes were closed. His chest expanded and compressed with each breath, just below a snore. His hands lay limp at his sides. I checked his fingers. No jewelry. A silver necklace hung around his neck.

Carefully, I began to open one side of his robe, partially exposing his thin, sagging chest. His nose made a snuffle, and I froze. His eyes stayed shut. The slumber persisted.

I pulled enough of the robe back to get a glimpse of his necklace. Another signet ring with an emerald in the center.

I searched the apartment: the hall closet, the pantry door, both bathrooms, under the bed, anywhere that could fit a human being.

In the bedroom closet, I found her.

Friday Finley sat in an office chair among scattered pairs of shoes and clothes hangers, her hands bound with rope at the wrists, a piece of gray duct tape over her mouth. Her black eye had healed nicely, but her left cheek had a fresh bruise and some swelling. Her eyes were peacefully closed. She looked as if she might've been smiling if her mouth weren't taped shut.

I held my breath and checked for a pulse. Faint, but alive, just like her father the night I found him unconscious. Gently, I removed the tape from her mouth. Somehow that didn't wake her.

I went back into the living room where Jimmy O'Rourke dozed.

The detached malevolence of a gun muzzle greeted me. The man who called himself Dalton Crawford stood just inside the doorway.

"I heard footsteps," he said. "Didn't know my father was expecting company."

# CHAPTER 57

"Hi, Declan," I said.

Declan had on casual CEO dress: a navy blue blazer over a white T-shirt and jeans with brown loafers, no socks. His almond-colored eyes were unfriendly. He took a step forward and closed the door behind him. The CEO smile was gone. The gun in his right hand pointed at my stomach. He looked down at his incapacitated father.

"Eight milligrams of galantamine after each meal makes him drowsy," he said. "He also has a mild painkiller prescription for his back. The combination puts him out cold."

"Twenty-six years on an Irish prison cot must be hell on your lumbar spine," I said. "Is that the dose you gave Miss Finley?"

Declan took a step forward. The gun remained steady on me.

"Miss Finley," he said, "is a feisty young woman. She has a tendency to raise her voice."

"You slapped her around too?"

"No. Ross struck her, once, before he and Colin were arrested. Ross has always had a temper. I warned them that you and your inspector friends would be persistent and creative in your attempt to get Miss Finley back. They insisted on executing their plan. It didn't work."

"Let her go," I said. "I don't care about O'Rourke family history. I just want her."

"Too late for that," Declan said. "You've already meddled in my family's business. Ross and Colin Dunne are my brothers. By blood, no. But they are my family."

"Family," I said. "Is that what the rings mean? The rings they tried to kill me for? The ring around your father's neck right now? The ring you kept at your aunt's house?"

Declan's almond eyes narrowed. He took another step forward.

"You have my ring?"

"The cops do."

He aimed the gun at my head.

"Turn around. Lift your shirt up."

I did. I wasn't armed. I'd left Powell's gun in the car.

"You were correct in assuming my father is not a physical threat. He is seventy-seven years old. He suffers from Alzheimer's. It's progressing."

"Hence, assisted living?"

"Yes, and memory care."

I glanced at Jimmy O'Rourke asleep in his chair. His features barely resembled the pictures of the imposing figure I'd seen in old newspapers. His hair had gone gray. His face was gaunt and chalky white, with no hint of outdoor exposure. His arms looked almost skeletal, covered only by a sleeve of unhealthy skin.

"It's over, Declan. Your father's sick. Your 'brothers' are in jail. The cops know you're involved. You're not a killer, or Friday would be dead by now. Let me take her home. Let her and my family go on with our lives."

Declan laughed.

"You want your happy little existence on Stockton Street back? You have no idea what it's like seeing family ripped away from you. Not for a couple of days. Try almost a lifetime."

He pulled another chair toward him and sat down, the gun still balanced in his hand, his almond eyes still on me.

"Step away from my father," he said. "Sit on the couch."

I did.

"You want to know about family, Charlie? Family is securing passage for your ailing father five thousand miles across the Atlantic. Family is your ailing father hiding in a container ship for three weeks just to reach this country again, to see his son again. That's family. That's loyalty. That's love."

"How'd he get out of prison?"

"My father began showing signs of cognitive decline. The Irish government granted him a compassionate release."

"And once he got out and got in touch, you arranged a way home."

"To Boston, where I was working at the time. The price was enormous, but I'd done well financially."

"You're doing even better now."

"Yes."

"Why go back to San Francisco?"

"At my father's request. He wanted to go home, or, at least, as close to home as possible."

"So you found the best memory care facility in the Bay Area. Which just so happens to be just up the 101 from a new casino, where you have weekly catch-up time with the Dunne brothers."

Declan's CEO smile was now more of a sneer.

"You've got it all figured out, don't you, Mr. Private Eye? Mr. Roving Reporter?"

"Most of it is educated guesswork," I said. "A thorough investigation will confirm it, uncover the rest."

"And what does your educated guesswork tell you?"

Declan shifted in his chair. The gun stayed level. It was the third time in a week I'd stared down a barrel. I placed my palms on my knees to keep my hands from shaking.

"I knew somebody was pulling the strings behind the Dunnes' little Derryville operation—the operation Friday's father, Shawn, left abruptly a couple weeks ago. I didn't know who was backing the Dunnes. I just knew they couldn't possibly be smart or shrewd enough to start a front business and a side business and keep them afloat for any length of time. They must've had a benefactor. But it had to be someone wealthy, someone they knew well, someone they trusted. Now I know you check all those boxes."

Declan sat back and crossed his left leg in the chair. His left foot dangled so casually I thought his loafer might slip off. I had to keep talking, buy some time, the way I had with Bosh.

"Let's start at the beginning," I said. "Your father was an Irish immigrant. He came over with your grandparents in the late forties when he was a small child. I've heard the stories. Your grandfather played it straight, lived an honest life, died in a work accident. Your father, out of grief or personal preference, chose a faster life. By the time he reached his late thirties, almost the age you are now, the city of Derryville ran through him. It was quite lucrative until he got arrested in San Francisco, convicted, and sent back to Ireland in 1998 when you were eight years old. Your mother moved the family—just you and her—to a tiny little desert town where her sister lived. Your mother changed her name from Abbie O'Rourke to Audrey Crawford, her maiden name. She had your name changed—from Declan O'Rourke to Dalton Crawford—so you could start a new life. And to shield you from your father's disreputable reputation."

Declan glanced at his father, still asleep in the chair.

"You grew up just outside Reno with your mom and your aunt. Maybe that's where you learned to play cards. You also got terrific grades. You got into MIT. You applied yourself, graduated with honors. You got a computer engineering job at a Boston start-up right out of school. You were doing very well for yourself, building a legitimately successful life, dreaming of starting your own business. You developed proprietary software for a cybersecurity platform. Three years ago your mother died. That must've been very difficult. A year later you learned that your father was a free man in Ireland. He was in poor health. He wanted to see you. He wanted to go back to California. This was a chance, after twenty-six years of estrangement, for father and son to not only reconnect, but to reverse roles. Now you could be the protector. Now you could show your father the man you became while he was gone."

"That sounds a little dramatic, Charlie."

"May I finish? I'm almost to the good part."

"Please, continue."

"Two of your MIT classmates, Eric Maniet and Ram Khatri, had already moved to San Francisco for the tech gold rush. Two years ago you decided to do the same. You came back to the Bay Area a grown man with a new identity. You brought your father with you, but he needed an alias too. You got back in touch with Ross and Colin Dunne. They were still in Derryville doing small-time crook stuff. They helped you secure fake identification for your father. You moved him into this care facility here, a short drive from San Francisco. You started Rivet Security. And you decided to help the Dunnes graduate to a new class of criminality. What was the line in the poem? 'Mere anarchy is loosed upon the world . . . The ceremony of innocence is drowned.'"

Declan's eyebrows arched.

"You know the poem," I said. "'The Second Coming' by William Butler Yeats. There's a reference to it hanging inside Cashel Rock. There's a Yeats collection in your old bedroom. I found the ring inside the book."

"You broke into my childhood home."

"And you're holding a child hostage in the next room. May I finish the rest of my theory?"

"Go on."

"The Dunnes were going nowhere in life. You got your friends on their feet. You gave them some seed money to buy a nicer house, buy the bar, start their little enterprise. But to do that, they needed cover like your father once had. They wanted the Derryville cops in their pocket. So they pulled a trick that Jimmy O'Rourke probably used years ago. They blackmailed Chief Mike Gramble with pictures of his extramarital exploits. Chief Gramble wants to run for public office someday. So he gives the Dunnes a long leash to set up shop, which includes some illegal gambling activities and God knows what else.

"Meanwhile, Rivet Security had a great first year. You and your MIT guys were doing very well with your various ventures. Away from the office y'all liked to play a little poker. Maybe y'all played cards together in school. The Dunnes' new bar was up and running, but they wanted some more cash flow. So, last summer, you told your MIT guys about this private poker game at a Derryville dive bar called Cashel Rock—a little sketchy, but cool, just like the movie *Rounders*. Big weekly buy-in, big stakes, and a big rake for your childhood pals Ross and Colin. Cashel Rock became a Thursday night poker spot. On Fridays you and the Dunnes came up here to the casino to gamble, and probably to clean some of their illegal money, though that would be very difficult to prove. While you were up here, you'd make discreet visits to check on your sick father. If anyone ever asked why you frequent the casino or Cashel Rock, you'd simply say you're training for the World Series of Poker. Why wouldn't anyone believe you? You're an MIT grad, a smart guy, an altruistic guy, the founder of a multimillion-dollar business that protects fellow companies from financial ruin. You're Dalton Crawford, an all-around good egg."

"MIT," he snorted. "I never liked those stuck-up brats. Rich kids from Boston. I grew up in the middle of nowhere with damn near nothing. All the money we had was either confiscated or spent on lawyer fees during my father's trial."

"So you and the Dunnes scammed poor Eric and Ram every Thursday night at Cashel Rock?"

"Not every week. We had to keep them coming back."

Declan stared at me awhile longer. Then he smiled ruefully.

"I would've been valedictorian at MIT," he said, "but I tanked a couple classes my last semester to lower my GPA. I didn't want extra attention on my mother. I was afraid someone might recognize her. We'd lived all those years in Nevada without any hassle. It's a small town like Derryville. People mostly keep to themselves.

She appreciated that. But she never found happiness after my father left. Then she got sick."

"And when she passed, you reunited with your other family."

"I've never cared much for my aunt, even though she took us in. She's a cold woman. No children, never married. After my mother died, Ross and Colin were the closest thing to family I had left. I had no biological siblings. They were brothers to me before I left Derryville. They came from a broken home. They saw my mother as their mother. They saw my father as their father."

"In all those years he was in prison," I said, "didn't you have any communication with him?"

"None. My mother wouldn't allow it. I understood why. She was only protecting me. She knew I had a future in front of me. For a long time I resented my father for leaving us. And for a long time I resented her for moving us away. Imagine being eight years old, Charlie, and you're suddenly told you must be someone else, you must cut off all communication with the people in your life, the only life you know. I lost myself during that transition. I tried to focus on my schoolwork and then my career."

"Then your father came back into your life."

"He reached out to me when his sentence ended. We reconciled. My father might have done illegal things, but I see now that he had the right perspective about life. You must take what you can in this world. My grandfather came here from Ireland with almost nothing. He died here with almost nothing. Irish immigrants flooded here during the Gold Rush with almost nothing. They broke their backs building the railroads, positioning California for prosperity. They were treated like garbage. They died with almost nothing. And by the time cancer had devoured my mother, she died with almost nothing too. But I no longer blame my father for our financial struggles. He did what he could to provide for us while he was here. He gave me a good life."

"So you came back here to continue his legacy."

"And help my friends. My brothers."

"Why didn't you just teach the Dunnes how to hack into somebody's bank account and steal money that way? You must know all the tricks."

"Call me sentimental," Declan said. "Ross and Colin dreamed of having a business like my father's. The old-fashioned rackets."

"You could've let them sponge off you. You're rolling in dough."

"I wanted to give them a life," he said. "I wanted to empower them. My father isn't very lucid these days, but I believe he'd be proud of what we've built."

"'The Second Coming,'" I said.

"Yes."

"And the rings?"

"My father had them made and engraved during his trial. They were a gift to Ross, Colin, and me, something we could grow into. He knew we'd have to split apart, that my mother would take me away from Derryville after his trial. He said as long as we had the rings, we'd be together."

"You're a smart guy," I said. "But you made a couple mistakes. First, you spread yourself too thin. You had your legitimate business to run in San Francisco. You let the Dunnes run wild in Derryville without any oversight. They were way too sloppy. They hired some ex-army lunatic called Bosh who tried, and failed, to kill Shawn Finley for stealing their money and their rings. When I spoiled that, they panicked and killed Colin's girlfriend, Tate Wilson, for snitching. Then they tried, and failed, to kill me. They left way too many tracks that the police are finding—the real police, not Chief Gramble. Tracks that ultimately lead back to you."

Declan remained quiet.

"But before all that," I said, "you were the sloppy one."

"Oh?"

"A couple weeks ago, you asked Bosh and the Dunnes to assault your ex-employee, Scottie Coburn, outside his houseboat in Sausalito. You wanted to send Scottie a message that he better straighten up and stop screwing around with Deborah Wellington.

You were afraid he was gonna tank your company's deal with Arthur Wellington."

Declan shook his head.

"That wasn't my idea," he said. "I'd never met Bosh. He knew nothing of me. One night at poker I told Ross and Colin about one of my executives, a stupid kid, who'd gotten involved with a woman who was married to one of San Francisco's most powerful and influential men. Ross and Colin took it upon themselves to solve my problem for me. They wanted to repay me for my help and support since coming home."

"You shouldn't have told them about Scottie."

"No, I shouldn't have."

"Then you found out Arthur Wellington had already hired me to follow his wife and Scottie around," I said. "So, after the affair got out, and after you fired Scottie, you invited me to your office to find out how much I knew. You probably figured you were in the clear. There was no way to connect you to the Dunnes or Bosh."

Declan stared at me.

"Except you didn't count on a very smart, very resourceful sixteen-year-old girl in the same parking lot outside Scottie's home that night," I said. "She'd followed your buddies from Cashel Rock, looking for her father. She saw the whole thing. And when I found her, she connected the dots for me."

"Well played, Charlie."

"My six-month-old daughter deserves credit. She was gumming her food this morning like a senior citizen. Then I remembered driving past this place on the way to the casino last week and thought, hell, this story's already crazy enough. Could Declan O'Rourke actually be hiding his father in this joint?"

"I read that you were nominated for a Pulitzer for investigative journalism a few years ago," Declan said.

"Yep."

"Now I see why."

"Thanks. You gonna let me take Friday home?"

Declan shook his head. He stood.

"You know why I shared all this with you," he said.

"Because you're gonna kill me."

"I'm not a killer," he said. "But family comes first. Stand up."

I stood. Declan walked over to his father, still unconscious, his chest rising and falling softly in the chair. He kissed his father on the forehead.

"I love you, Poppa," he said. "I'll come back for you."

With tears in his eyes, he turned to me.

"Walk," he said.

# CHAPTER 58

I raised my hands and stood from the couch. Leaving my gun inside Mango had been a mistake, but I'd thought this place might have security checks. I walked a few steps as Declan stepped in behind me, his gun pointed at my back. I glanced at Jimmy O'Rourke asleep in the chair. He hadn't moved during the entire conversation.

"Oh my God," I said. "I think he stopped breathing."

As Declan turned to look at his father, I stepped back and elbowed him in the jaw. He tumbled backward onto the couch. The gun fell from his grip and landed on the carpet. I picked it up just as he steadied himself and got to his feet. He froze.

"I've seen this one before," I said. "Belong to you or your boys?"

Declan stared daggers at me. He rubbed his jaw.

"It's one of Ross's," he said.

"Do you even know how to use it?"

"Not really."

I checked the magazine. It had a full clip.

"You gonna shoot me, Charlie?"

"If I need to, yes."

"I don't believe you."

He stepped to his left, around the coffee table, edging his way toward the door, circling me like a boxer inside a ring.

"You're not gonna shoot me," Declan said. "I bet you've never shot anyone before either."

"First time for everything."

"No," he said. "You won't."

Still facing me, he backed slowly toward the door.

"Leave my father out of this," he said.

"I just want Friday," I said.

Declan shook his head. He reached behind his back for the handle. He cracked the door wide enough to squeeze through and slithered through the opening and disappeared. The door clicked shut behind him. I heard footsteps down the hallway.

He was right. I couldn't shoot.

Jimmy O'Rourke began to move in his chair. I tucked Declan's gun in my waistband and sprinted out the door and down the steps through the lobby and out the front door. The sound of a big engine boomed, and Declan's Ferrari gunned toward the exit. At that moment, in a blur of motion, Dwayne Powell's Dodge Ram slammed into the Ferrari's back right bumper at a ninety-degree angle. The Ferrari fishtailed. Aluminum and steel crunched. Glass broke. Declan's body jerked forward in the driver's seat.

The Ferrari remained still, its right bumper and taillight mangled by the crash. Tex jumped out of the Ram's passenger seat, his pistol gripped in his hand, and ordered me to stay back. Sirens wailed in the near distance.

Tex yelled to the Ferrari, "Dalton Crawford, aka Declan O'Rourke! Open the door and show me your hands!"

Nothing moved inside the Ferrari. Carefully, Tex opened the driver-side door with one hand. He and his pistol peeked inside.

"We're gonna need an ambulance," he shouted.

Declan's head lay limp on the steering wheel. He wasn't wearing a seat belt, and the force of the crash had launched him headfirst into the windshield. Blood stained the cracked glass and his cracked forehead.

I ran to Powell and helped him from his truck.

"Just in time," I said. "You okay?"

Powell grimaced.

"First my back, now whiplash," he said. "Damnit, you were supposed to wait for us, Charlie."

"Sorry," I said. "Come on, let's go get Friday."

# CHAPTER 59

Ambulances arrived for Friday and Declan O'Rourke within five minutes. Powell and I rode in the back beside Friday. Through the window I could see the blinking lights of the casino up the road. Declan O'Rourke and the Dunnes would never play cards there again.

It had taken a few tries to awaken Friday from her drug-induced sleep. She was groggy and disoriented. Thankfully, a bruised cheek appeared to be her only injury. Nevertheless, the medical staff gave her a full workup. It took about two hours before we had some quiet in her room.

"We're going to keep you here a little while longer until I get all the results from your tests," the doctor said. "But I think you'll be able to go home today. I recommend lots of rest. Very little activity for a couple days."

"We're not very good at that," I said.

The doctor smiled. "I'll be back in a bit."

Friday's eyes were still heavy. Her voice was raspy and just above a whisper. She hadn't been permitted to speak for days.

"Thank you," she said to me, and touched my arm.

"No, Miss Finley. Thank you. Seeing you here safe is the best thing that's happened since Callie was born."

Friday smiled. "Where's Mr. Powell?"

"Speaking with the police. They'll want to speak with you too eventually. Much later, when you're feeling better."

"Ryan and Callie are okay?"

"They're doing great."

"The man who brought me to the apartment," Friday said. "Is he dead?"

"I'm not sure. He was alive in the parking lot, but he was in very bad shape."

"Who was he?"

"His name, his real name, is Declan O'Rourke. The son of a mobster."

"Was the old man his father?"

"Yeah. He ran Derryville about thirty years ago. His son came back to San Francisco a couple years ago to restart the family business."

"With the Dunne brothers?"

"Yes. They all grew up together."

"And the police got them too?"

"Yes."

Slowly, she wriggled a little in her bed. I stood and adjusted the pillows for her.

"I don't remember everything," she said. "But after I left Mr. Powell's house, I went by their bar with that bag of money. They grabbed me and took me to some high-rise apartment building first."

"The police found it today," I said. "Actually, Powell and Tex found it when they went to look for Declan at work again. He lived on the top floor of a new high-rise in the 5M district, right by his office. His sales team had an in-house competition going. Bunch of prizes listed. One was the option to move into a brand-new 5M apartment at a reduced rate, including two months' free rent, courtesy of the company. SFPD checked it out. They were hoping to find you."

"A couple days ago, he was arguing with Ross and Colin about what to do with me," Friday said. "He convinced them not to kill me. He warned them not to meet with you guys, about a ransom, I guess. He didn't like their plan. He brought me over here sometime after they got busted."

"He was the only one on the crew with brains and half a conscience," I said. "He's no killer. He's just a screwed-up kid who never had much of a childhood."

"Kind of like me," Friday said.

"No," I said. "Not at all like you."

Friday sat back and stared at the ceiling for a while.

"I'm such an idiot," she said.

"No, you're not. You're the toughest kid on the planet. You're giving Powell a run for his money."

"I was just trying to fix things," she said.

"By giving the Dunnes the money your dad stole?"

"Yeah. Some idea that was."

The hospital room was small and clean and neat. The window view wasn't much—just the parking lot and the senior's home where Jimmy O'Rourke lived anonymously. The nurse hadn't made Friday change clothes. She had on her signature hooded jean jacket and joggers. Today she wore a Bob Dylan shirt underneath the jacket.

"What's your favorite Dylan song?"

"'A Hard Rain's A-Gonna Fall,'" she said.

"It sure feels like we've walked and crawled on six crooked highways."

She smiled again faintly.

"We haven't found your car," I said. "I know your mother's ashes are inside."

"It's okay if we don't find it," she said. "I need to let her go anyway. Gotta grow up sometime."

She stared at the ceiling some more. Slowly she closed her eyes.

"We did find your dad," I said.

Her eyes popped open. She turned to face me, eyes wide with concern.

"He's..."

"Alive," I said. "The police have him. He might be in there awhile. But it might be the best thing for him."

She began to cry. I brought her a Kleenex.

"It probably is for the best," she said. "He needs structure. He needs a caretaker."

"He needs you," I said.

The nurse entered the room.

"Mr. Charlie Shaw?" she said.

"That's me."

"You have a couple visitors outside."

"Don't go running off," I said to Friday.

"Funny," she said.

Tex and Powell were waiting for me in the lobby.

"How is she?" Powell asked.

"Slowly becoming herself again," I said. "Declan drugged her up pretty good. What's his story?"

"Severe head trauma," Tex said. "Still unconscious. That's all we know for now."

"Maybe he'll wake up and never know he became Dalton Crawford."

"Wouldn't that be something."

"What about Poppa O'Rourke?"

"Cuffed him," Tex said. "Not that he understands why. ICE will get involved. It will be a mess."

"I'm just glad you're okay, buddy."

"Ain't that sweet."

"And you too, boss."

Powell had an ice pack around the back of his neck. He, of course, had refused medical treatment.

"I've taken two vacations in twenty-five years," he said. "It's time for another one. After I get my truck fixed."

"I want a vacation too," Tex said. "Not that I'll get one. I've got a stack of cases thicker than a T-bone. That's after we clean up this Dunne/O'Rourke business."

"What'd you find in their hideout?"

"Not much. My guess is Declan cleaned out the place after they got busted. Just got a tip on where some of their contraband might be located, though."

"Where?"

"Would you believe next door to Cashel Rock in Derryville?"

"The cell phone repair shop?"

"Another one of their fronts," Tex said. "We arrested two guys inside. Apparently they're pushers for the Dunnes. Had illegal stuff stored in crates in the back. Matched some of the crates we found in the bar this week."

"Who gave you the tip?"

Two uniformed SFPD cops entered the lobby. Shawn Finley stood between them. He still wore the same ill-fitting clothes I'd given him at my house. He saw Powell and me and looked down at his dirty shoes.

"Mr. Finley has agreed to share testimony on the Dunnes," Tex said. "There's a lot we still don't know about their activities in Derryville. We've agreed to let Mr. Finley visit his daughter before heading back to the station."

Finley's shoulder-length hair still looked stringy and greasy. His face was still unshaven and dotted with gray whiskers. But his eyes looked clear.

The officers stopped him in front of Tex and me. He looked back down and spoke to his shoes.

"I apologize for putting your families in danger," he said. "I didn't want my daughter to see me like this. I'm a mess and I know it."

Then he looked up at me.

"It's time for me to man up," he said. "Thank you for protecting her, Charlie."

The uniformed cops led him down the hall toward Friday's room.

Tex offered his hand to Powell and me.

"I appreciate the help," he said.

"I owe you a double date," I said.

"Remember, Ryan picks the girl."

"Deal."

"Is Miss Finley going home with you?"

"Yep."

"Tell her I'm glad she's okay," Tex said. "I'd like to come by and get a statement from her tomorrow if she's feeling up to it."

Tex went through the automatic sliding glass doors out to the parking lot. He seemed to be favoring his back a little too.

Powell turned to me.

"Well, I must say, this has been some real sloppy detective work, Charlie."

"Oh, really?"

"You should've never gone to Jimmy O'Rourke's place without us. You almost got yourself killed again."

"Hey, I did call you guys. I just had a head start. Every second mattered."

"Sloppy," Powell said. "But effective."

"Well, this is my first *and* final case, so it's nice to finish on a high note."

We stopped by Friday's room to say goodbye. The two officers stood in the doorway. Shawn Finley had bent down over Friday's bed. They were embracing. And sobbing, quietly.

# CHAPTER 60

The house in Modesto was a low-lying one-story at the end of a cul-de-sac with a steep-sloping driveway and front yard. Friday stood beside me at the door. Callie pressed against my chest in one of those dad baby carriers. I felt like a funny-looking kangaroo.

We knocked on the door. A blond woman in maybe her early fifties appeared.

"Mrs. Wilson?"

"Yes."

"Hello, ma'am. My name is Charlie Shaw. This is my daughter, Callie, and our family friend, Friday. We spoke on the phone. We knew your daughter, Tate."

The sound of her daughter's name made the woman blink three times, as if her eyes were holding something back. She forced a polite smile.

"Yes. Please, come inside."

We sat on a powder-blue divan in the living room. A toddler-aged boy in a Spider-Man T-shirt was coloring with crayons at the kitchen table. He had his mother's blue eyes.

"Luke, say hello to our guests," Mrs. Wilson said.

"Hello," he said without looking up. It sounded more like, "*Heh-whoa.*"

Friday had dressed up for this visit. She wore full makeup and black slacks with a gray blouse. A week had passed since our trip to the hospital. Her face was no longer pale and drawn. She looked better, but she seemed nervous.

"Thank you for coming," the woman said. "It's very nice to hear from Tate's friends."

"Yes. We won't be long, ma'am. As I said on the phone, we're from San Francisco. I only knew your daughter briefly, but Friday's father and Tate were good friends."

The woman blinked again at "Tate." I glanced at the mantel behind her. She had arranged several framed pictures of her daughter at various ages in chronological order. The last was of Tate holding baby Luke in her arms. She looked much healthier and happier than when we had spoken at her apartment.

"How old is your daughter?" Mrs. Wilson asked.

"Almost seven months."

She nodded. "A beautiful age. The time passes so quickly. It seems like yesterday Luke was that young."

Callie was pressed so close to my chest, I could hear her little inhales and exhales. I knew I'd have to change into a drool-free shirt when I got home.

I reached into the pocket of my blazer and handed Mrs. Wilson a check.

"Friday would like to make a donation in Tate's memory," I said.

The woman looked at the amount written on the check and blinked at it. She shook her head.

"This is very generous," she said. "Very kind. But I'm afraid I can't accept this much money."

"Please," Friday said. "My father saved it for me, but we both decided that your grandson should have it. For his future."

"Your father and Tate were close?"

"Very. It's my understanding that they both battled addiction. They were each other's supporters. This is his way—our way—of supporting Tate now."

Mrs. Wilson looked at her grandson at the kitchen table and then back at us. She blinked again. A tear dropped from her left eye. I offered her the handkerchief from my jacket.

"Thank you," she said. "My daughter did suffer from addiction.

Since she was about your age, Friday. When she gave birth to Luke, she asked that I take care of him while she tried to stop using. It was a constant battle. I'm not sure if she was winning or losing when she passed."

"It would mean a lot to us," Friday said, "if we could do this for you and Luke."

"It's just so much money," the woman said. "It's too generous."

Friday looked at me.

"My mother recently passed away," she said. "She . . . left me a rather large inheritance. I'd like to share it."

The woman thought about this.

"I'm very sorry to hear about your mother," she said.

Friday nodded.

"Thank you," the woman said. "Thank you so very much."

She stood and hugged Friday and me.

"Luke," she said. "Come thank these nice people for their gift."

The child set down his crayons and hopped off the chair. Friday held out her hand for a high five. He slapped it.

"He's adorable," Friday said to Mrs. Wilson.

"He's my little angel," Mrs. Wilson said. "He's getting me through this."

"If you ever need us," I said, "you have my number."

Back inside Mango, Friday let out a deep breath.

"You okay?"

"I just feel guilty," she said. "If Tate hadn't known my dad, she'd probably be alive."

"I feel guilty too. But she got in with the wrong people, just like your dad did. Don't blame yourself."

"At least the money he stole is going to good use."

My phone buzzed.

"Ryan?" Friday asked.

"No, a woman named Maggie Salvetti. My old editor at the *Chronicle*. It can wait."

We got on 580 West toward San Francisco.

"Hey, that black eye's looking pretty good," I said. "It's pretty much gone."

Friday self-consciously touched the spot that was bruised and swollen when we met.

"You still want to know what happened, don't you?"

"Forgive me," I said. "I'm a reporter. I never let things go."

She rolled her eyes.

"I stopped for gas somewhere on the 5," she said. "On the way down here the first time, before I met you. I was standing at the pump minding my business. This guy was pumping gas on the other side. He looked at me over the little partition. I didn't look back but could feel his eyes on me. It gave me the absolute creeps. He walked over to me. He was middle-aged and balding and had these hairy arms. He asked me if I needed any help. I said, 'No thank you,' without making eye contact. He said, 'I think you do.' He put one of his hairy hands on mine."

"Did you scream for help?"

"No," Friday said. "I pushed him away. He threw a punch. Landed right here."

She pointed to her healed eye. "Knocked me back against my car."

"What'd you do?"

"I kicked him as hard as I could between his legs. He doubled over. I set the pump back on its hook, got in the car, and left. He was still lying on the ground when I turned onto the road."

"He's lucky you didn't grab your bat," I said. "No wonder you didn't trust me when we first met."

"I've been jerked around enough by my own family," she said. "Can you blame me?"

"Nope."

Mango's outmoded AC unit was struggling to keep up with the compressed heat in the Valley. My weather app said Modesto had reached 107 degrees.

"That was a good thing you did back there," I said.

"The cops really didn't need that money as evidence?" Friday asked.

"Nope. They've got plenty to nail the Dunnes with."

"I'm just hoping that kid doesn't grow up like Ross or Colin. Or my dad."

"Your dad's a better man than those two. Addiction got ahold of him too."

"What do you think will happen to him now?"

"He'll have to cooperate with the cops. Tell them everything he knows about the Dunnes. Make a deal."

"You think he's heading back to jail?"

"Maybe. Maybe probation. Depends on the info he gives. He never wanted to get into this mess. He told me that. I imagine that will play in his favor."

Friday looked out the window.

"Jail might be good for him," she said. "Might straighten him out."

"I think his best medicine is being around you again."

"Why?"

"He'll get to see the person you've become without him. It should motivate him to do better."

Friday cracked the window and let in a blast of air from the highway. Then she closed it and we rode quietly together.

Finally, she said, "You really think he can change?"

"Maybe," I said. "All I know is this: The world would be a better place if everyone had a daughter."

# CHAPTER 61

"I thought we were going on vacation," I said.

"After all this crap," Ryan said, "I'd rather not deal with babysitters and Ubers and airports. I'd rather just sit here and look at something pretty."

We were at Mission Dolores Park, sitting on a rich green hill, staring past the palm trees at the San Francisco skyline. We'd laid out a picnic blanket with a delectable spread: beer and peanut butter and jelly sandwiches for us; applesauce and raspberries for Callie. Ryan and I sat on the blanket with two cans of beer. Callie sat in her *Finding Nemo* chair, mad-dogging Sheldon the seahorse. They looked ready to go another round.

"So," I said to Ryan, "is it nice to be back at work?"

"Is it ever nice to be back at work?"

"Fair point."

"Actually, it has been nice," Ryan said. "It's nice to be in the office. To be in my house, my bed, my shower."

"It's nice to have you back."

We sipped our beers.

"And you've been a busy man too, Charlie Shaw. Allow me to read a few headlines in the *Chronicle*. Ahem:

"'Deported Bay Area Mobster Found Living Under Alias.'

"'Derryville Police Chief Indicted for Aiding Dunne Brothers.'

"'Teen Recovers after Mob Kidnapping.'

"'Drugs, Women, Gambling, and Protection Rackets: Derryville's Second Organized Crime Wave.'

"And fresh off the press," Ryan said, "'Disgraced Tech Exec out of Hospital, Revealed as Mobster's Son.'"

"Helps to have direct sources in the SFPD," I said.

"I'm proud of you," Ryan said.

"Thanks."

"Sophie would be proud of her big brother too."

"Yep," I said. "I think so too."

"I'd almost feel sorry for Declan if he wasn't so detestable," Ryan said. "In some backward way, he was trying to reconnect with his father. Just happened to be the most dishonest, contemptible way possible."

"Tex said they officially searched the old house in Nevada," I said. "Sometime as a child, Declan had hidden a batch of pictures, him with his dad. He wedged them in a ceiling tile in his room. If his mother or aunt had ever discovered the pictures, they would've destroyed them."

Ryan shook her head.

"I'm glad Tex is done with all this too," she said. "We need to get him a girl."

"*You* need to get him a girl. He doesn't trust me."

"And we need to do something really nice for the Powells. I think we should pay for their vacation flights."

"Powell would never allow it. I'm not fully convinced he's actually taking a vacation."

"Has he found a replacement for you yet?"

"No, I think his sons have it covered."

"Well, you are a reporter, after all."

"Stringer," I said. "I only told Maggie I'd come back as a stringer. I'm not committing to anything full-time yet. Hell, we might not even stay in San Francisco forever."

"Yeah," Ryan said, "but look at that view. You really wanna leave it?"

"I'd like a little more living space. Maybe a little more peace and quiet. Less crime potential."

We looked at Callie. She was wearing a onesie that read *AB/CD*, mimicking AC/DC's band logo.

"Great gift from Friday," Ryan said.

"The girl knows her classic rock."

"It's really wonderful that they found her car and her mother's ashes. And that she's moving down here to finish school. She needs a support system. She needs to focus on college, all that stuff."

"I just want her to focus on being sixteen," I said. "Admit it, you're a little jealous she's staying with Grace and not us."

"Maybe a little," Ryan said. "But Grace and her husband have more space than we do. And she said she's tired of being an empty nester."

"Sounds like a win-win."

"What do you think happens to Friday's dad?"

"Shawn? I'm not sure. If he does time, I don't think it'll be too long. He's given the police a gold mine of information on the Dunnes. I just found out that among their scams, they were running 'protection' for a Derryville strip joint. That's how they started a little escort service in addition to everything else."

"Gross," Ryan said. "There's one thing I don't understand about this whole Jimmy O'Rourke / Declan O'Rourke thing. Wouldn't Jimmy O'Rourke just be happy that his son became a big success in the corporate world? Wouldn't he be glad his son didn't have to live that nasty life?"

"Tale as old as time," I said. "Men will go to great lengths to please their father, or do things they think will make their father proud. And sometimes, men are irrationally loyal to their friends too."

"Like the Dunnes."

"Yep."

"Some friends."

"Ross and Colin Dunne could barely tie their shoes straight. Declan gave them a comfortable life. At least for a little while."

A blond woman in a yellow summer dress and a Kentucky

Derby-looking straw hat click-clacked her yellow heels on the concrete trail below us. She looked up, appeared to recognize me, and began climbing up the hill toward us with a Prada purse over her shoulder and her right hand protecting her hat from the breeze. Twice she almost tripped before she reached our picnic spot.

"Hope you didn't sprain an ankle in those heels," I said.

"I'm fine, thank you," the woman said. "Charlie Shaw?"

"Yes."

"Dwayne Powell said I might find you here. My name is Deborah Wellington."

"I know who you are."

"I know you know who I am. You're the man who was following me a few weeks ago."

Ryan looked at me and then smirked to herself and drank more of her beer.

"Yes," I said. "Your husband, Arthur Wellington, was a client of Powell and Associates."

"I'm well aware of that now," Deborah Wellington said. "I don't appreciate being followed, Mr. Shaw."

"Just doing my job, ma'am. Where are my manners? This is my wife, Ryan, and our daughter, Callie."

"Pleased to meet you," Ryan said.

They shook hands.

"Your daughter is quite beautiful," Deborah Wellington said.

"I know," I said.

"I'd just like to say," Ryan said, "that I wasn't a huge fan of the investigative work Charlie was doing."

"It is quite sordid," Deborah Wellington said.

"You'll be happy to know that I'm no longer in that line of work," I said.

"Believe it or not, I'm actually disappointed to hear you say that," Deborah Wellington said. "I've read your investigative work on organized crime in Derryville. A nasty story, indeed, but very impressive. As you might know, my husband, Arthur, has filed for divorce."

"I did hear that. I'm sorry."

"Thank you. He has accused me of infidelity, thanks to the evidence you provided through Powell and Associates."

"I'm sorry about that too."

"Thank you."

"Speaking of infidelity," I said, "how's Scottie?"

"He's moving back to Arizona."

"I see."

"My divorce is pending," she said. "It's likely to be a long, lengthy, ugly process. One reason for that is I believe I was not the only unfaithful party in our marriage."

"Oh," I said.

"Mr. Powell said Powell and Associates could not take me as a client, citing a conflict of interest. He said, however, that you might be interested."

"Oh," I said.

"Do you still have your private investigator's license?"

"Yep."

"I would like to hire you," she said, "to find evidence of my husband's own infidelity."

Deborah Wellington held on to her hat with her right hand. With her left, she reached into her purse and pulled out a slip of paper.

"My phone number is listed," she said. "Below it is my offer for a retainer."

"I see."

"Please think it over and contact me," she said. "I'd like an answer by tomorrow. Good day."

"Nice meeting you," Ryan said, and drank more of her beer.

Hand over her straw hat, Deborah Wellington stumbled down the hill to safety on the concrete path. She click-clacked her way out of sight.

I reached over and held Callie's hand. It felt just like Play-Doh.

"Baby girl," I said, "your daddy's on a roll."

"How much did that woman offer to pay you?" Ryan asked.

I looked at the slip of paper. I looked at Ryan. I raised my eyebrows.

Ryan smiled.

"Don't even think about it," she said.

# ACKNOWLEDGMENTS

Writing is hard. At times it's like taking a road trip down a long, unfamiliar highway in the dark—you don't know exactly where you're going, and at times it's a bit unsettling, but you have this urge to keep the pedal down through the darkness. Supporting a writer is even harder, because it requires blind faith in their talent and their dreams without assurance that the light lies somewhere ahead.

To my parents, Robert and Cathy, thank you for your indomitable belief in my writing since 1988, when my first-grade short story about our backyard birdbath (riveting stuff!) made the elementary school morning announcements. Mom, you're the best writer I've ever met. Thank you for your English-professor wisdom, your interminable grammar lessons, and your lifelong love for mysteries. I may never have found Chandler or Christie or Stout without you. Dad, thank you for teaching me the value of discipline and persistence at an early age. Without those two principles, a writer has nothing.

To my wife, Katie, thank you for your endless support down this wonderful life detour. How many people wake up and get to do what they truly love? I'm so proud of what you've accomplished over these many years, and I'm so thankful that you understand what storytelling means to me—it's a *have-to*, not a *want-to*. I love you.

To my father-in-law, Steve, another mystery aficionado—thank you for your kindness, encouragement, and advice throughout this process. Let's crack open a Vernors to celebrate.

To my "Aunt" Brenda and the Kruses, thank you for loaning your word processor long ago to a kid who had to get his story ideas down on something other than pencil-smudged paper. You understand what this book means to me as much as my own family does.

To Minotaur Books, thank you for believing in my talent and introducing me to a world of immensely talented and gracious writers and professionals. The support has been overwhelming, and I'm so honored to be part of such a prominent, accomplished team. To my wonderfully talented editor, Hannah Pierdolla, what are the odds that two Texans (and Aggies!) would get matched together on this project? Your belief in the story, and my quirky dialogue, have meant so much. Thank you for pushing me to take this book to another level.

And to my daughter, Emmy, thank you for giving me a purpose and joy I didn't know were possible. This book, above all else, is about fathers and daughters and the space a little girl takes in her daddy's heart. Hopefully many years from now, when I'm gone, you can always pick this book up and know how much I loved you.

## ABOUT THE AUTHOR

Andrew Hancock

**Rob Phillips** grew up in the Dallas area, where he became an Emmy-winning sportswriter covering the Dallas Cowboys for print, radio, and television. Rob and his wife are proud parents to a spunky senior King Charles Spaniel and a lively young daughter, who's still waiting for her first stakeout. His debut novel, *Stakeouts and Strollers,* won the Minotaur Books/Malice Domestic Best First Traditional Mystery Novel Award.